THE MURDER TEAM

A Martello Family Thriller

DAVID L PRESTON

ISBN:
Paperback 978-1-966890-18-8
eBook 978-1-966890-16-4
Audiobook 978-1-966890-17-1

Azalea City Publishing, LLC
Mobile, AL 36693
www.azaleacitypublishing.com
Cover design: Artillery Design Company Ltd
https://www.artillerydesign.co

DEDICATION

To Aunt Kathy

ACKNOWLEDGEMENTS

Thank you to Brian Lambrecht and Deza' Rae Collins for proofreading this book and making it better

Chapter 1

The Triumphant Return of Óscar

The midday heat clung thick over Matamoros Airport, the kind of oppressive warmth that made the horizon waver and turned the tarmac into a shimmering sheet of glass. A single federal transport shuttle rolled across it, slow and deliberate, until it hissed to a stop near a cluster of private hangars.

For a moment, nothing moved.

Then the door folded open with a metallic groan.

Óscar Alvarez Vasquez stepped out.

He was leaner than the man who had entered U.S. custody years ago. His face was drawn and hair thinner with his posture etched with the rigid discipline of confinement. But the weight of his presence hadn't diminished. If anything, the silence around him deepened, as if the desert heat itself held its breath.

Two Gulf Cartel lieutenants waited several yards away, standing still, not daring to approach until he acknowledged them.

The older of the two, Saúl "El Tigre" Morales, cleared his throat and stepped forward. "Jefe," he said, voice low, reverent. "Welcome home."

Óscar descended the steps without replying. His boots struck the pavement with the quiet certainty of a man reclaiming territory that had been his for decades.

The second lieutenant, younger and visibly nervous, lowered his eyes as Óscar approached. The man's hands fidgeted at his sides until he forced them still.

Saúl extended a hand. Óscar took it with one firm shake, nothing more. His gaze flicked to the younger lieutenant.

"¿Nombre?" Óscar asked.

"Ramón, señor," the man answered quickly. "It is an honor…"

Óscar moved past him before he finished, the dismissal quiet but absolute. He surveyed the airport perimeter that had guards stationed at corners, plainclothes watchers near the hangars, a line of black armored SUVs idling with engines rumbling.

Finally, in a voice low and steady, he said:

"Llévenme a casa." Take me home.

No small talk. No greetings for cameras or family. No acknowledgment that years had passed.

Only the mission.

Saúl nodded sharply. "Sí, Jefe. Everything is prepared."

They escorted him toward the convoy. The younger lieutenant hurried ahead to open the rear door of the lead SUV. Óscar paused at the threshold, eyes sweeping once more across the open tarmac with its heat and emptiness a quiet welcome to a man whose legend towered over the area.

A kingdom waiting for its king to reassert control.

He ducked into the SUV without another word.

The door shut behind him with a heavy, final thud, echoing across the bright expanse as the engines revved and the convoy began to move.

The convoy rolled out from the airport in a tight formation with three armored SUVs in front, three behind. Escorts flanking them like a silent procession. The road shimmered beneath the heat, stretching out toward the scrubland that fringed the city.

Inside the lead vehicle, the temperature dropped immediately. The air conditioning hummed softly. The interior smelled faintly of leather and gun oil.

Óscar sat in the back seat, posture straight, hands resting on his knees.

No chains. No guards. No warden's eyes.

Just freedom…and the storm simmering behind his own.

Saúl rode in the passenger seat. Ramón, eager to prove himself, sat beside Óscar with a tablet clutched in his hands but hadn't yet spoken. His foot tapped against the floor until he caught himself and forced it still.

Minutes stretched.

Finally, the tablet's screen lit with a flick of Saúl's hand from the front.

Ramón swallowed. "Señor… we gathered everything from the New Orleans police servers. Reports. Photos. Surveillance logs." He hesitated. "Some of it is…difficult."

Óscar didn't look at him. "Muéstrame." Show me.

Ramón tapped the screen.

First appeared a headline from a New Orleans news outlet. *TURF WAR SUSPECTED IN NIGHT OF FIRE* Óscar's expression didn't change.

Another headline. *BODY OF CARTEL HEIR RECOVERED FROM BURNT VEHICLE…*

A faint tremor moved through the tablet in Ramón's hands.

He swiped again.

Coroner photos. Angles of charred metal and scorched flesh. A watch… Carlos's watch… half melted, warped beyond recognition.

The SUV hit a small bump in the road. The photos jolted. Óscar's hand shot out. Not with violence, not with abruptness, but with the controlled precision of a leader to steady the screen.

"Detente," he said quietly. Stop.

Ramón froze.

Óscar studied the photo of the watch. His son's watch. A gift he himself had given Carlos on his twenty-first birthday. The only thing the fire hadn't completely erased.

Saúl glanced back from the front seat, voice soft. "We did everything to confirm the chain of events,

Jefe. The bodies of Michaela and the little girl… they were burned beyond…"

Óscar cut him off with a small motion of his fingers. Not now.

He closed his eyes for a single breath and then opened them with a cold steadiness.

"Continúa," he said. Continue.

Ramón swiped again, forcing himself to look at the images even as his stomach churned. Police transcripts, statements from witnesses, blurry screenshots of traffic cameras. A New Orleans detective's notes full of half-formed theories and redactions.

The temperature inside the SUV felt like it had dropped another few degrees.

Ramón hesitated. "Señor… with your permission… I want to say, on behalf of all of us, that we're sorry about Carlos and his family. They were good people. We…"

Óscar turned his head slowly toward him.

Not angry nor emotional. Just a stare carved from stone.

"Grief," Óscar said, voice quiet enough that Saúl leaned back slightly to hear him, "is for later."

Ramón's throat bobbed. "Sí, señor."

"Ahora," Óscar continued, "solo hay trabajo." Now, there is only work.

He reached out and tapped the tablet himself, swiping to the next photo of the burnt remains of the SUV where Carlos and his family died.

His jaw tightened, the muscle along it twitching once.

"Todo," he said. Everything.

Ramón resumed, hands trembling slightly. More photos. More reports. More fragments of the truth.

Óscar's knuckles whitened against his knee, but he made no sound.

Outside the window, the dry Tamaulipas landscape blurred past with a sun-bleached, hard, unforgiving frenzy. This was a place forged in heat and violence.

A place perfectly suited for the kind of man Óscar had become.

The convoy turned off the highway onto a long, unmarked dirt road bordered by tall brush and rustling mesquite trees. Dust trailed behind the vehicles as they wound deeper into the countryside, far from the noise and eyes of the city.

Ahead, beyond a final bend, the compound came into view.

A sprawling ranch estate surrounded by high adobe walls. Guard towers at each corner. Sentries with rifles slung across their chests. Surveillance cameras sweeping arcs over the entrance. A steel gate rolled open at the convoy's approach as though the land itself recognized its owner.

Óscar watched it all through the tinted glass. There was no awe nor nostalgia. There was just a quiet evaluation.
A leader returning to the territory he had built with blood, loyalty, and fear.

When the SUV rolled to a stop in front of the main house, the door opened immediately. Saúl stepped out first, giving a sharp nod for the other vehicles to settle into position.

Óscar emerged second.

Heat hit him with a sharp, but familiar slap across the face. A dry wind tugged at the edges of his shirt as he stepped onto the stone courtyard.

A small group waited there.

Senior lieutenants, old guard men who'd served under him for decades. They stood in a rigid line, heads bowed in respect. Beyond them, lower-ranking soldiers lingered at a distance, watching with the tense reverence reserved for myth rather than man.

At the front of the line, Isabel, his wife, stood perfectly still.

Time had etched new lines into her face, softened some things and hardened others. Her eyes, however, held the same dark fire he remembered. The ones that had always seen more of him than anyone else.

She approached without hesitation and wrapped her arms around him.

For a moment, the courtyard seemed to fall silent. Even the wind paused.

Óscar didn't lift his arms, not right away. His body stayed rigid beneath her embrace, as though he hadn't yet decided whether he was allowed to feel anything at all.

Finally, one of his hands rose and rested against her back, briefly, gently, before falling away.

Isabel stepped back, searching his face. "Mi amor," she whispered. "You've lost too much."

He didn't answer. His eyes drifted past her to the men waiting in line.

Saúl cleared his throat softly. "Todo está listo, Jefe. The reports, the intel. We prepared your office."

Óscar didn't move toward the house.

Instead, he began walking toward the left side of the courtyard, where a small stone arch led to a secluded garden. The path wound between agave plants and flowering shrubs, ending at a quiet corner shaded by a large ceiba tree.

There, beneath the tree's heavy branches, stood a memorial shrine.

Candles. A cross. Photos framed in wood. A few personal items were carefully arranged.

Carlos. Michaela. Little Violetta.

A soft breath escaped Isabel as she followed a few steps behind him. The lieutenants remained at the courtyard entrance, giving space without being told.

Óscar stepped into the shrine's circle of flickering candlelight.

He reached out, fingertips touching Carlos's photo. His boy's arm around his daughter, smiles bright and unguarded. The edges of the frame were warm from the sun.

For the first time since stepping off the plane, Óscar's shoulders lowered.

He dropped to one knee.

The wind rustled through the ceiba leaves overhead, whispering through the branches like voices reaching across the years.

Óscar traced the outline of Carlos's face with the back of his knuckle. His voice, when it came, was barely audible.

"Lo siento, hijo." I'm sorry, son.

He stayed there for a long moment, still as stone.

Then he stood.

Grief folded neatly back into the armor of purpose.

He turned toward the courtyard, toward Saúl and the others who waited like soldiers before a king.

His voice was quiet, but it carried with the weight of a decree:

"Tráiganme a todos." Bring me everyone.

The lieutenants dispersed instantly, hurrying inside the house to summon leadership, analysts, and the unexpected visitor waiting to test the boundaries of Óscar's patience.

The storm he had brought home was beginning to gather.

The interior of the main house was cool, dim, and quiet with thick adobe walls swallowing the afternoon heat. The hallway opened into Óscar's private office, a large room with a heavy carved desk and a long conference table that could seat a dozen men.

Tonight, it needed all twelve.

One by one, lieutenants, regional commanders, and intelligence officers filled the room. Some whispered among themselves; others stayed silent, eyes lowered. The tension was taut and electric.

Óscar was already at the far end of the table.

He didn't sit. He stood with both hands resting on a stack of folders, each marked with police insignia, American agencies, and internal cartel codes. Surveillance images were spread across the table like a mosaic.

When the last man entered, the room fell silent.

Saúl locked the door.

Óscar lifted the photo of Carlos's burnt SUV and held it up, turning it slowly so every man around the table had to see it.

"Esto," he said quietly, "es lo que hicieron." This is what they did.

No one dared to speak.

He set the photo down with deliberate care.

A middle-aged analyst stepped forward, voice steady but cautious. "Jefe… based on all gathered intelligence, we believe the initial attack in New Orleans was directed by Vincent Castenllo Jr. The Martellos had…"

The door opened.

Everyone turned.

A man in a gray suit entered without invitation, flanked by two escorts wearing the insignia of Zetas Vieja Escuela. The intruder's presence was a blade cutting through the room's composure.

Óscar didn't look at him.

Not at first.

The Zetas representative, Comandante Barrera, gave a thin, polite smile. "Señor Alvarez. Bienvenido de regreso."

Saúl stiffened. "You were not invited."

Barrera shrugged lightly. "Your jefe returns from America after years away. You think we would ignore such an event? Our organizations share history… and enemies."

The lieutenants bristled. Hands hovered near weapons. But Barrera didn't flinch. He stepped closer to the table, eyes flicking to the photos.

"The Martellos," he murmured. "They have overstepped."

Óscar still hadn't acknowledged him. He flipped open another folder instead.

Inside was a printed timeline: Carlos's arrival in New Orleans. His disappearance. The fire. Police delays. Evidence gaps. A meticulously documented chain of events shaded with the corruption and incompetence of foreign law enforcement.

One of his senior lieutenants, a thick-set man named Alvarado, cleared his throat. "Our sources confirm the order came from the Martello boss. Vinny Castenllo Jr."

Still, silence from Óscar.

Barrera took another step forward. "This is an opportunity, señor. For both of our organizations. The Gulf Cartel and the Zetas…"

Óscar lifted his eyes.

The room froze.

Barrera's words faltered, swallowed by the cold, precise stare leveled at him.

Óscar rested two fingers on Carlos's coroner photo and spoke in a voice calm enough to turn bone to ice.

"¿Quién hizo esto?" Who did this?

The analyst swallowed. "La orden vino de Vincent Castenllo Jr., jefe."

A single beat of silence.

Then Óscar closed the folder gently, almost tenderly. His hand smoothed the edges, an old ritual for a man who rarely reacted without intention.

When he finally spoke, the words were soft. So soft that everyone in the room leaned in to hear them.

"Entonces… responderemos en la misma moneda." Then we will answer in kind.

The lieutenants exchanged looks of fear, resolve, and anticipation.

Barrera let out a slow exhale, a faint smile forming. "If war is what you want, señor Alvarez, we are…"

Óscar spoke over him, not raising his voice, but slicing through his words like a blade.

"I was not finished speaking."

Barrera's smile evaporated.

Óscar stepped closer to the table, placing both hands flat on the wood.

"The Martellos believe distance protects them. That American laws, American borders, and American police can shelter them." His eyes swept the room. "They are wrong."

He straightened.

"War," he said simply.

The room remained utterly still.

No cheers. No threats. Just the heavy, collective understanding that something irreversible had begun.

The briefing dissolved slowly, men filing out in tense silence. Orders would be carried out. Calls made. Networks activated. But none of them lingered when Óscar's expression made it clear he wanted the room emptied.

Saúl was the last to leave. "Jefe… if you need anything…"

Óscar gave a small nod of permission to go, and nothing more.

The door shut with a soft click.

The office fell silent.

For a long moment, Óscar remained where he stood, his hands resting on the table's edge. The sound of distant engines and muffled radio chatter drifted through the adobe walls, but the room itself was still.

When he finally moved, it was the slow and deliberate movement of a man carrying far more weight than his frame suggested.

He made his way down the narrow hallway that branched from the office, past photographs of his early days in the organization, past old maps and framed articles that chronicled the empire he had built. He walked until he reached a simple wooden door at the end.

His quarters.

He stepped inside.

The room was sparse with no luxury and no indulgence. Just a bed with a plain blanket, a small dresser, a crucifix above the headboard, and a single window overlooking the compound. Dust motes drifted lazily in a bar of sunlight cutting across the floor.

Óscar closed the door behind him.

The click sounded louder than it should have.

He sat on the edge of the bed, elbows on his knees, palms pressed together. His breath came out slow and steady, but the tension running through him was unmistakable.

On the nightstand sat a small wooden box, unchanged since the day he left for the States. He reached for it, fingertips brushing the lid before lifting it open.

Inside lay a handful of trinkets:

A set of marbles Carlos had played with as a child. A tiny matchbox car with blue paint chipped at the corners. A frayed friendship bracelet that little Violetta had made for him during a visit. And a folded drawing.

Óscar hesitated before picking it up. Children's drawings were fragile things that were not meant to survive fire, violence, or the weight of vengeance. But this one had been kept safe. Protected.

He unfolded it carefully.

Crayon lines. A stick-figure family and a taller figure standing beside them.

Papá.

Óscar's throat tightened, a silent pulse of pain hitting hard enough that he closed his eyes against it.

One breath… Another… Then, as though a dam cracked inside him, tears slipped free.

Not sobbing. Not broken.

Just quiet, controlled lines of grief tracking down his face.

He pressed the drawing gently to his forehead. For a moment, he allowed himself to feel the hollow ache that had defined every second since the note he got in prison, the absence that shadowed him even in dreams.

In the privacy of his quarters, where no lieutenant, wife, or soldier could witness the moment, Óscar Alvarez Vasquez allowed himself to be a father mourning his son.

Only for a moment.

He wiped his face with the back of his hand, slow and deliberate. He folded the drawing again, placed it back in the box, and closed the lid.

Grief returned to its cage.

He rose to his feet.

At the window, he stood looking out over the compound of men moving with urgency, vehicles repositioning, radios crackling with orders. A machine stirring to life under his command.

His voice, when he spoke, was almost a whisper.

"Les haré sentir todo lo que yo he sentido." I will make them feel everything I have felt.

He turned toward the door.

The storm inside him had hardened into resolve.

Evening settled over the compound in a wash of deep gold and rising shadows. The sun dipped low behind the distant hills, casting the courtyard and the surrounding walls in a final burst of light before surrendering to dusk.

Torches were lit along the walkways like an old signal, a tradition from years before the organization adopted modern systems. Their flames flickered in the warm wind, illuminating the movement of soldiers preparing vehicles, checking radios, and gathering equipment.

A machine waking. A network tightening. A war is being born in real time.

Óscar stepped out onto the balcony overlooking it all.

He had changed into a clean shirt, sleeves rolled neatly to the elbows. No jewelry, no insignias. There was nothing that suggested vanity. Only purpose. The kind carved into every line of his face.

Below, several lieutenants waited, assembled in a half-circle. Saúl at the center. Barrera from the Zetas stood slightly apart, hands clasped behind his back in a display that was equal parts respect and quiet self-importance.

The men straightened the instant they saw Óscar.

He leaned both hands on the balcony railing, taking in the sight of the compound, which was the lifeblood of his empire.

The torchlight painted flames across his expression.

When he spoke, his voice carried with a calm, deadly clarity.

"Prepárenlo todo." Prepare everything.

No one moved. They waited for specifics. For direction. For the decree that would set the next chapter of blood and violence into motion.

Óscar's gaze shifted from face to face, lingering on none of them for long.

"Quiero una reunión esta noche," he said. "Zetas. Gulf leadership. Todos." I want a meeting tonight. Zetas. Gulf leadership. Everyone.

A few men exchanged glances. There hadn't been a full summit in years. Not one led by Óscar himself.

Saúl cleared his throat. "¿Para discutir los siguientes pasos, Jefe?" To discuss the next steps?

Óscar shook his head once.

"No." He straightened. "The meeting is to declare what comes next."

Barrera stepped closer, unable to hide the slight upward curl of intrigue at the corner of his mouth. "And what is that, señor?"

Óscar's eyes locked onto his with the unblinking steadiness of a predator that had already chosen its path.

"Guerra." War.

The single word fell heavy, final, and unshakeable.

Around the courtyard, the atmosphere changed subtly but unmistakably. Muscles tensed. Expressions hardened. Radios crackled louder. Soldiers checked their weapons with renewed urgency.

The world outside the compound had no idea what had just been set in motion.

But inside, every man present understood:

By sunrise, nothing about New Orleans or the Martello Family would ever be the same.

Óscar turned from the balcony without waiting for acknowledgement or applause. His command had been given. The fuse had been lit.

Behind him, the compound roared quietly to life with vehicles starting, men moving with purpose, and torches blazing brighter against the darkening sky.

A storm was gathering.

And Óscar Alvarez Vasquez had just called it down upon his enemies.

Chapter 2

The Cartel Summit

Security cameras blinked red along the outer wall of the compound, their lenses sweeping in steady arcs. On the rooftops, men with rifles moved about, settling into prone positions with their scopes aligned toward the access roads that bled in from the highway and the scrubland beyond. Snipers checked their lines of sight once, then again. Radios murmured. An armored truck rumbled as it reversed into a new position, blocking one of the less-traveled entrances. Another vehicle rolled forward to cover the main gate at an angle that offered overlapping fields of fire. From the courtyard below, the compound no longer looked like a ranch. It looked like a forward operating base.

Inside the main house, servants moved quickly and quietly, setting a long table in the war room. The polished wood disappeared under layers of maps, tablets, folders, and encrypted radios. New Orleans at night glowed on one of the large screens with a satellite image divided into color-coded sectors, each zone tagged with notes. The details meant little to the servants, but they could read tone in the men who passed by. Tonight was not about business. Tonight was about vengeance.

Saúl stood near the head of the table, hands on his hips, scanning every inch of it. "Move that," he said, nodding at a stack of folders near the end. "I want the Martello intel front and center." A younger lieutenant shifted the files. "Like this, jefe?" "Higher. If the Zetas sit on that side, they see exactly what we know about New Orleans before they open their mouths."

At the far wall, an intel tech tapped through a menu on a laptop, bringing up traffic patterns, heat maps of police response times, and ports-of-entry data. "You sure the encryption's solid?" another lieutenant asked. The tech didn't look up. "Better than what the federales use." "That," Saúl said, "is a low bar, cabrón. Triple-check it anyway."

He glanced toward the doorway, half expecting Óscar to appear and demand some adjustment, some correction. Instead, when the man finally entered, he said nothing at all. He wore the same clean, rolled-sleeve shirt from earlier, the same unadorned watch. No rings. No visible weapon. The only thing that had changed was the temperature in the room.

The lieutenants straightened at once. "Jefe", Saúl said. "We're almost ready. If you want anything moved, we can…" Óscar's gaze traveled slowly across the table. His eyes paused on the New Orleans satellite image, on the glowing pocket of the Garden District. He walked the perimeter of the war room, scanning the corners, the windows, the cameras in the ceiling. His eyes lingered briefly on the far wall, where a framed map of Tamaulipas hung next to a crucifix. He returned to the head of the table, stood there, and simply nodded once. "It's ready," he said.

Saúl exhaled, a breath he hadn't realized he'd been holding. "We've doubled the perimeter security. Snipers on all four towers, plus two roving teams outside the walls." "One at the east drainage channel?" Óscar asked. "Sí, Jefe. And we're monitoring comms from the highway. If the Zetas bring extra cars, we'll know before they hit the gate."

A younger lieutenant named Ramos, lean and perpetually on edge, hovered nearby, arms folded. "They don't like coming here without flexing," he muttered. "They'll show off the moment they step out of their trucks." Saúl shot him a look. "You'll keep that thought to yourself when they arrive." Ramos rolled a shoulder but nodded. "Sí."

Óscar's attention remained on the maps. New Orleans looked small from up here. Contained. Manageable. The illusion comforted some men. It did not comfort him. "This meeting," he said, "does not leave this room. No one outside the leadership core needs details." "Yes, Jefe," came the chorus. "If any of our men disrespect the Zetas delegation," he continued, "they will answer to me, not to them." Ramos hesitated. "Even if they disrespect us first?" Óscar finally looked at him. "Their arrogance is their weakness," he said. "Not ours." Ramos swallowed. "Entendido."

A chime sounded from a radio near the table. One of the guards lifted it to his ear, listened, then turned toward Saúl. "Convoy approaching from the south road," he reported. "Three SUVs, insignias removed. ETA five minutes." Zetas Vieja Escuela. Old enemies. Old allies. A relationship written in gunpowder and opportunism. "Positions," Saúl said. "Everyone knows their role." The lieutenants filed out, each man peeling away to his assignment. Some men were to greet, some to watch, and some to hover like ghosts along the walls once the summit began.

Only Óscar remained. For a moment, he was alone with the maps and the screens and the quiet hum of electronics. The satellite image of New Orleans glowed in the dim light, a foreign city that had already taken everything from him. He stared at it, his face unreadable.

Carlos. Michaela. Violetta. The names passed through his mind like beads on a rosary, each one a wound, each one a promise. He tapped one finger against the Garden District sector, a small, precise motion. "Tonight," he said softly, "we start taking it back."

From the open balcony doors down the hall, a gust of warm night air drifted in, carrying the distant sounds of the rumble of approaching engines, the shifting of men on the walls, and the low murmur of radios. He turned from the table and walked out toward the main entrance, alone. He didn't need an escort. His presence at the gate would do more to keep the peace than any rifle. Behind him, the war room waited, prepared down to the last cable and folder.

In front of him, far down the dirt road, three sets of headlights cut through the darkness, drawing closer with each passing second. The Night settled over the compound like a held breath. Torchlight flickered along the walls, casting jagged shadows across the courtyard as the Gulf soldiers took their position.

The low rumble of engines grew louder. At the main gate, two guards stepped forward and slid the steel doors open. Dust rose as three black SUVs rolled inside, each stripped of insignias, plates swapped for clean numbers. The vehicles moved in tight formation with the disciplined coordination of military precision.

Saúl stood just behind the threshold, jaw set tight. Ramos hovered near him, shoulders tense, fingers drumming impatiently on the grip of his holstered weapon. "They always drive like they're rolling into hostile territory," Ramos muttered. Saúl didn't take his eyes off the vehicles. "They *are* rolling into hostile territory. Don't let your mouth make it worse." Ramos gave a humorless snort but said no more.

The SUVs slowed, then stopped in a neat line. For a moment, the compound was silent except for the ticking of engines cooling in the night air. The doors opened simultaneously. Out stepped the Zetas delegation. The first man was unmistakably

Comandante Barrera; with his sharp suit, neatly trimmed beard, and the confidence of someone who'd spilled blood in at least two countries and never apologized for any of it. His eyes scanned the courtyard lazily, like a predator assessing weaker animals. Behind him emerged five operators, each armed and alert despite the diplomatic nature of their visit.

The tension in the courtyard thickened instantly. Gulf soldiers shifted subtly, hands brushing rifle stocks, weight shifting to the balls of their feet. One wrong look could turn the air into gunfire.

Then Óscar stepped forward. He came alone, walking through the center of his men with a steady, unhurried pace. The effect was immediate on every soldier, Gulf or Zetas. They stiffened as if gravity itself bent differently around him.

Barrera smiled thinly. "Señor Alvarez," he said, spreading his hands in a gesture of greeting. "It seems the rumors of your iron spine were true. You summoned us, and here we are." Óscar stopped a few feet from him. His expression didn't change. "You came quickly." "Vengeance tends to inspire efficiency," Barrera said lightly. "Besides… we respect you enough not to delay."

Saúl watched from behind, noting the choice of words. *Respect*, from a Zetas commander, was never simple. It was seldom genuine. But it was always a negotiation. Óscar extended his hand. Barrera took it. The handshake was firm, formal, and entirely devoid of warmth.

Behind Barrera, one of the Zetas operators shifted, eyes scanning the Gulf soldiers. Ramos stiffened. Saúl stepped subtly between them, a silent barrier. Óscar released Barrera's hand and gestured toward the interior of the compound. "You came for a purpose," he said. "Let's not waste time." Barrera's smile sharpened. "Straight to business. I prefer that." Óscar turned toward the main house, and the delegation fell in behind him.

As the group walked through the courtyard, Gulf soldiers followed their movements with cold, suspicious eyes. The Zetas operators did the same, hands never straying far from their weapons. To an outsider, it would look like two armies walking inches from war. Ramos leaned slightly toward Saúl, murmuring under his breath. "You feel that? Like lightning waiting to hit something metal." Saúl kept his gaze ahead. "Then don't be the lightning rod."

Óscar led the combined group into the hall, the heavy door swinging shut behind them with a deep, echoing thud. Óscar didn't look back to see if the Zetas followed. He knew they would. And the moment they crossed that threshold, every man present understood that tonight was no alliance of trust. It was an alliance of vengeance.

The war room was already lit when Óscar entered. Maps littered the table in structured rows, each one annotated with red ink and digital markers. A large monitor showed the charred remains of the SUV from New Orleans, paused on a still frame before the flames swallowed everything. The room quieted as Gulf lieutenants rose.

Behind Óscar, the Zetas delegation filed in. Barrera took his seat as though he'd been invited into a cathedral he planned to admire before eventually burning down. Óscar didn't sit. He remained standing at the head of the table, eyes tracing the silhouettes of the images arranged before him. Saúl took his place to the right. Ramos stood further back, near the wall, doing a poor job of hiding the tension tightening his jaw.

Óscar nodded once. A Gulf Tech tapped a tablet. The screen flickered, and the first image appeared. Carlos. Alive. Laughing. A photo taken months before New Orleans. His arm around Michaela, Violetta perched on his shoulders. A second tap. The same SUV before and after the fire. Tap. Coroner photos. Tap. Burn patterns. Trajectory analysis. A grainy surveillance shot of the Martello street corner. Tap. The final photo was what remained of the family after the flames.

Silence settled over the room like a thick blanket. Even the Zetas operators, hardened as they were, shifted slightly. Barrera's eyes narrowed with calculation. Revenge was a language he understood, and what lay on the screen was a script he'd read many times. Finally, Barrera broke the silence with a low exhale. "Blood demands blood," he said. His voice carried through the room, cold and flat.

Saúl looked down at the table, jaw working. Ramos stared at the screen, eyes burning with anger he didn't dare voice. Óscar lifted his gaze from the image and looked slowly around the table, taking in every face. Men who had fought in border wars, survived prison massacres, and dispatched rivals in broad daylight. When he spoke, his voice was calm and deadly. "They died in a foreign city because the Martellos believed distance would protect them. They believed they could touch my blood…" His gaze returned to the screen. "…and live." He let the moment linger, tension tightening like piano wire. "We are here," Óscar continued, "because they were wrong." The lieutenants murmured quiet agreement. Even the Zetas operators seemed to nod, just barely, acknowledging the gravity of the room.

Barrera leaned back in his chair, watching Óscar closely. "We came because you called. But understand, señor Alvarez, what you propose is no simple reprisal. It is an operation with… consequences." Óscar didn't blink. "Consequences are for men who hesitate." Saúl glanced toward the Zetas side of the table. The Gulf lieutenants did the same. A current of anticipation rippled through the room, with every man waiting to see whether Barrera would push back, provoke, or defer. Barrera's lips curled into a faint, calculated smile. "You want justice," he said. "We want the same. The Martellos lit a fire they cannot control." He gestured toward the screen. "This is not just your loss. It is a message. And if we do not respond together, the Americans will think we are weak."

Ramos muttered, almost too quietly, "Let them think we're monsters instead." Saúl shot him a warning look. Barrera pretended not to hear the comment, but his eyes flicked briefly toward Ramos with mild amusement.

Óscar stepped forward, placing a hand flat on the table beside the photos. "Tonight," he said, voice low but sharp as a blade, "we decide how that message is returned."

Another tap from the tech changed the screen. This time to a satellite overlay of New Orleans. Neighborhood sectors glowed faintly, tagged with coordinates. The next tap on the tablet changed the screen again, this time to a map of New Orleans, glowing faintly against the dimmed lights. Streets crisscrossed in white lines; districts were shaded in blue or red, each color representing cartel influence, police response zones, or Martello-controlled neighborhoods.

The Gulf intel officer, Delgado, stepped to the edge of the table and cleared his throat. He wasn't a soldier.

He was thin with a bespectacled look, with the posture of a man who lived more among data than gunfire, but even he felt the weight of Óscar's gaze. "Señores," Delgado began, tapping the screen. "This is our complete breakdown of the Martellos' known infrastructure." The map zoomed in. The lines of the Garden District sharpened around a cluster of blocks. Labels began to pop up. *Martello residence. Martello-owned legitimate businesses. Front companies. Suspected stash houses. Security contractor ties.*

Delgado continued, voice steady. "Vincent Castenllo Jr. maintains a primary residence here. Surveillance suggests..." "Suggests?" Barrera interrupted with a raised brow. "Or confirms?" Delgado swallowed. "Confirms. He rotates between his home and two business locations, but the Garden District remains his stronghold." Barrera leaned back in his chair. "Of course it is. The American mafia loves its little mansions. All image, no discipline."

Saúl shot him a warning glance, but Delgado pressed on. "We also mapped out NOPD response times." He tapped the screen again. A series of colored bars appeared, each one marking minutes to respond in each district. "These areas show significant delays. Particularly in the early morning hours." Ramos snorted from his post near the wall. "Which means nobody's watching their backs." Delgado nodded. "Precisely. Most response times worsen around two specific neighborhoods..." He tapped the map. "Various street crews control the Lower Garden

District and Warehouse District. None directly tied to the Martellos, but many owe them favors."

Barrera smiled faintly. "Useful chaos." "Chaos we can use," Delgado said carefully. "But it also means unpredictable variables during an operation."

Delgado shifted to another slide of photos showing Martello enforcers, vehicles, storefronts, and meeting spots. "These are the men most likely to be armed around-the-clock," he said. "Russo, Mancini, and a rotating security team. If we strike, they'll either need to be neutralized first or avoided entirely." Saúl nodded. "Russo won't run. If he's on-site, he'll fight." "He's dangerous?" Barrera asked with mild curiosity. Saúl smirked. "He's suicidal when angry." Barrera's eyes gleamed. "My favorite kind of enemy."

The next slide flashed up with a click, showing a chart of Martello police connections. Delgado's voice grew careful. "There are… individuals in NOPD known to look the other way. Some for the Martellos. Some for other groups." "Name them," Barrera said. "No," Óscar answered, the first break in his stillness. Delgado's breath caught. Óscar stepped closer to the table. "Naming them puts them at risk before we know who is useful. If they're corrupt, we may need them. If they're clean, we gain nothing by exposing them." Barrera tilted his head, amused. "Pragmatic." "Efficient," Óscar corrected.

Delgado resumed. "We have also identified several potential *entry routes* into the city that minimize detection." He tapped through images of highways, waterways, and industrial areas. *I-10 freight corridors. Abandoned marinas. Commercial fishing routes from the Gulf. Private landing strips with minimal FAA oversight.* Barrera nodded slowly, impressed despite himself. "You've done your homework," he said.

Delgado exhaled gently, relieved. But Óscar wasn't looking at Delgado. His eyes were fixed on the map, specifically, on the glowing outline of the Garden District. "That's where he sleeps?" he asked quietly. Delgado nodded. "Nearly every night." Óscar's jaw tightened. "Good."

The Gulf officer turned to the final slide which displayed a timeline. "Based on travel routes, predictable patterns, and police activity, a strike team could infiltrate here," he pointed to a small alley near Coliseum Street, "just before dawn. Police shift change. Lowest traffic. Highest vulnerability." Barrera sat forward, steepling his fingers. "And you believe this can be done cleanly?"

Delgado glanced nervously at Óscar before answering. "With… the right team? Yes." Barrera's smile returned, sharper this time. "The right team," he repeated. "That's what we're here to discuss." The room tensed. Everyone knew what that meant.

Óscar finally stepped back from the table, hands clasped behind him. "All this information is worthless without one answer." He turned his gaze onto Barrera. "Can it be done," he asked, "without sparking a border war?" Barrera's smirk was slow, controlled, and dark. "Oh, señor Alvarez," he said, "that's the beauty of what we propose."

He leaned forward, eyes sharp. "Send ghosts. No flags. No witnesses..." A chill passed through the room. And Óscar's silence this time was not doubt... it was interest.

For a moment, Barrera's words hung over the table like drifting smoke. The kind that warned of fire. Ramos shifted near the wall, unable to contain his reaction. "Ghosts," he muttered. "Always with the dramatic bullshit." Several Zeta operators turned their heads sharply toward him. Saúl stepped forward before anything escalated. "Cálmate," he hissed. "Now isn't the moment." Ramos looked away, jaw tight.

Alvarado, the oldest Gulf lieutenant, pushed back from the table. The legs of his chair scrapped against the floor, cutting across the tension like a blade. "No," he said. "This is madness." Alvarado pointed to the satellite map still glowing above the table. "Crossing into another country with elite gunmen? Storming a mafia boss's home in a residential neighborhood? You think the Americans won't respond? The FBI will be crawling across the border.

The DEA will…" Barrera chuckled softly. "Señor, the Americans couldn't stop El Chapo from escaping a mile-long tunnel. They will not stop trained men slipping through their own backyard." Alvarado's eyes hardened. "Your arrogance will get us all killed." "And your fear," Barrera replied coolly, "will keep you from avenging your own." Saúl exhaled sharply. "Enough."

Ramos stepped forward, arms crossed. "We lost Carlos. His wife. A little girl. And you," he shot a glare at Alvarado, "want to talk about caution?" "My job is caution," Alvarado snapped. "My job is to keep our people alive. Not feed them into an American meat grinder." A Zeta operator barked a laugh. "What people? You barely keep your streets alive." Saúl raised a hand. "Watch it."

The Zeta man shrugged coldly. "If they're afraid, let them say it." "Afraid?" Ramos shot back. "We're not the ones hiding behind ex-military contractors…" Barrera's chair scraped as he stood. "Say that again, niño." The insult lingered in the air.

Óscar lifted one hand. The room went silent instantly, as if someone had cut the sound from the world. Barrera remained standing, though his expression shifted. It was no longer amused; now it was measuring. Óscar's voice came low, even. "This bickering dishonors the dead."

He walked toward the table, stopping at the image of Carlos smiling in that final family photo. "You speak as though we have a choice," he said. "We do not. The Martellos chose for us when they crossed the line." Alvarado inhaled slowly. "Jefe… I am not refusing justice. But this operation is not what we normally do." "No," Óscar agreed. "It is not."

Delgado, still standing near the screens, swallowed hard. He had seen Óscar angry before, but never carrying grief like a quiet bomb under his skin. Óscar placed both hands on the table. "When they killed my son," he said softly, "they did not just strike at blood. They struck at my future. They struck at everything I built, everything I protected." The emotion in his voice was barely there, but every man felt it. "They killed a child," he continued. "My granddaughter. They killed innocence without hesitation, without mercy." Silence thickened until the weight of it felt physical. Óscar lifted his gaze, eyes sharp enough to cut through steel. "And you ask me to worry about the FBI?"

Alvarado lowered his eyes. "No," Óscar said. "There will be no hesitation. There will be no negotiation. The Martellos will learn what it is to lose everything." He turned to Barrera. "And we will need specialists to do it."

Barrera sank back into his chair, satisfaction flickering across his face. He had won, not through manipulation, but through inevitability. Óscar straightened. "So speak plainly, Comandante. Show us what you brought."

The Zetas commander reached into the leather briefcase beside him and withdrew a thick black folder. Its cover bore a single white phrase: EQUIPO FANTASMA The Ghost Team. Barrera placed the file on the table with a quiet thud. "This," he said, "is how you strike a foreign city… and leave no trace behind." Barrera slid the black folder toward the center of the table. Even before a single page was turned, the room felt different, like something radioactive that every man sensed but couldn't see.

Óscar remained standing, unmoving. Saúl took a slow step closer, gaze fixed on the white lettering across the cover. Ramos muttered under his breath, "Ghost Team… sounds like cartel folklore."

Inside were dossiers, each with a photo clipped to the front and lines of encrypted data beneath. The faces staring up from the pages were hard-eyed men, some with military haircuts, others with blank expressions that hinted at the things they'd done and forgotten. "These," Barrera began, tapping the first photo, "are not cartel soldiers." Ramos leaned in. "I can see that." "They are not street killers," Barrera continued. "Not gunmen. Not hitmen." He looked up, letting the silence thicken. "They are professionals. Former military; special forces, Kaibiles, GAFE, ex-federal tactical units. Men trained to take buildings, not corners."

Even Alvarado found himself staring at the faces with reluctant interest. Barrera flipped to the first dossier. A man with a shaved head, expression flat as stone. "Gabriel 'Sombra' Reyes. Ex-GAFE. Urban breaching specialist. Disappeared from the official roster after a… disagreement with his commanding officer."

He flipped to the next. A man with a thick beard, eyes cold, scars tracing his jawline. "Raúl Ortega. Counter-surveillance. Former Mexican intelligence contractor. No official record of his dismissal."

Next. A lean man with the expression of a starving wolf. "Mateo Cárdenas. Kaibil. Expert in night raids and close quarters."

He paused. "This one," Barrera added, "prefers not to leave survivors." Some of the Gulf lieutenants exchanged glances. Not fear, but respect. Or something close enough to it. Óscar still hadn't spoken.

Barrera tapped the final page and slid a photo across the table toward him. Unlike the others, this man was not posing. His picture was taken mid-motion, weapon slung, expression unreadable. "And this," Barrera said, "is their leader." The Gulf lieutenants leaned forward. "He has many names. We call him El Silencioso."` Ramos frowned. "He doesn't talk?" "He talks," Barrera said with a thin smile. "He just doesn't talk much."

Saúl picked up the photo carefully. The man's face was calm. Almost gentle. Which somehow made him more dangerous. Barrera folded his hands. "These men have executed operations hundreds of miles outside their own territory. They work in teams of three. Always three. Small. Surgical."

He closed the folder. "They do not carry insignia. They do not use traceable weapons. They do not use radios unless necessary. They do not leave fingerprints. They do not leave bodies unless instructed." Alvarado exhaled slowly. "So this… this is not a hit squad." "No," Barrera replied. "This is a death squad."

Ramos lifted his chin. "Can they handle a target like Castenllo Jr.? Protected, paranoid, armed to the teeth?" Barrera leaned back. "They have taken fortified compounds. They have taken politicians in their own homes. They have taken men surrounded by armies." He paused. "A mafia boss in a city full of corrupt cops? That is not a challenge."

Ramos whistled softly. "Shit." Saúl elbowed him. "Quiet."

Barrera turned to Óscar directly. "You asked us to bring you something worthy of the blood you lost." He tapped the folder once. "This is the most effective tool we have ever created."

Finally, Óscar moved. He reached out and placed his hand on the folder, fingers resting on its dark surface. He didn't open it. He didn't flip through the pages. He simply absorbed the weight of it. The room watched him like the air was holding its breath.

Óscar lifted his eyes. "Will they follow orders?" he asked. "Yes," Barrera said. "Will they finish what they start?" "Always." Óscar's gaze sharpened. "And will they honor… limits?" Barrera frowned slightly. "Limits?" Óscar's jaw tensed. "I want the wife and children left alive." A flicker of surprise crossed a few faces around the table. Barrera studied him, reading the lines of grief beneath the steel. "Alive?" he repeated. Óscar nodded. "Alive." "For leverage?" Barrera asked. "For justice," Óscar replied. "My son did not kill innocents. Neither will I." Barrera slowly nodded. "Then yes. They will honor your parameters." Óscar straightened. "Good."

He tapped the folder once, lightly. "Then these are the men who will go north."

The war room felt alive with something sharp and dangerous. The Gulf commanders stood straighter. The Zetas delegation leaned forward, their eyes glinting in the dim light. Even the air itself seemed tighter, charged with the realization that this was no longer theoretical.

Óscar placed both hands on the table, steady and deliberate. "Now," he said, "we define the mission."

Delgado switched the screen again, pulling up a multi-phase infiltration map. Colored lines traced routes into New Orleans from the Gulf, from the interstate corridors, and from the river. Each path had been studied. "Phase One: Entry," Delgado began. "Primary option is maritime. Small craft leaving from Mexico and landing near Port Sulphur or Venice. Limited radar coverage. Minimal Coast Guard presence."

Ramos crossed his arms. "And if the Coast Guard does show up?" Delgado didn't flinch. "Then the operators sink the boat, swim to shore, and proceed on foot. They've done it before." Barrera nodded with pride. "More than once."

The map zoomed. "Phase Two: Safehouse placement," Delgado continued. "We've identified three potential properties owned by shell corporations tied to our network. Each one can be stocked with weapons, comms, and vehicles." Saúl stepped closer. "Are they clean?" "Clean," Delgado confirmed. "No ties to the Gulf. No ties to Mexico." Ramos let out a low whistle. "Ghosts with ghost houses." The Zetas commander smirked. "We prepare well."

Delgado tapped again. "Phase Three: Surveillance. The team will infiltrate New Orleans and conduct shadow-step observation of Castenllo Jr.'s routines." He brought up a timeline of Vinny Jr.'s daily movements. Barrera leaned back. "They will watch him. Follow him. Study him. They will know his habits better than his own men."

Óscar watched silently, expression unreadable.

Delgado continued. "Phase Four: Breach and execute. This occurs at the weakest point in the daily pattern, pre-dawn." A red icon blinked over the Martello mansion. Alvarado narrowed his eyes. "And if they have guards posted?" Barrera answered without hesitation. "They will be eliminated quietly. Quickly. No alarms. No screams."

"Phase Five," Delgado said, "extraction. Routes return south via air or water, depending on circumstances." He dimmed the screen.

Óscar finally spoke. "I want precision," he stepped closer to the table. "I want Vincent Castenllo Jr. dead." Delgado nodded. "I want his home breached without warning." Barrera tapped the folder. "They can do that." "I want his wife and children left alive." This time, every man in the room listened more closely. This was not a tactical detail; it was a decree. "They are innocent," Óscar said. "No one touches them." Barrera inclined his head. "Understood."

"And one more requirement," Óscar added, voice turning to steel. "His death must be recorded. I want to see it." Several lieutenants shifted. Ramos straightened. Barrera's eyes sharpened. "You want proof," the Zetas commander said softly. "I want closure," Óscar corrected. He turned to the Zetas' tactical advisor. "Your team can do this?" The man nodded once. "Sí, señor. We can." Óscar considered him for a moment, weighing the certainty in his tone.

"Then," Óscar said, "we agree on the timeline." Delgado stepped forward again. "Three weeks would be optimal for prep…" "No," Óscar shot. Delgado blinked. "Jefe… multi-national coordination requires…" "No," Óscar repeated, louder this time. "Too long." Barrera raised an eyebrow. "What timeline do you propose?" Óscar looked at the map of New Orleans again, eyes narrowing. "Seven days."

A ripple of shock moved through the room. Even the Zetas delegation exchanged glances. "Seven days?" Alvarado said, stunned. "Jefe, that is…" "It is enough," Óscar cut in. "Barely," Barrera murmured. "Even for them." Óscar faced him directly. "Then they will prove their worth." Barrera studied him for a long second and nodded. "They will be ready."

Delgado hesitated. "And… communications, Jefe? If things go wrong, they'll need backup." "No communications," Óscar said. "No signals linking us. If they fail, they fail alone." Ramos let out a low breath. "Damn." Saúl murmured, "This is war." "No," Óscar said quietly. "War has rules." He rested a hand on the folder again. "This is vengeance."

Silence swallowed the rest of the room.

The room emptied slowly after the tactical decisions were set. However, Barrera did not move. Neither did Óscar. Saúl noticed the stillness and motioned for the others to clear the space completely. When the last soldier stepped out, and the heavy door thudded shut, an anticipatory quiet fell over the room.

Barrera stepped forward, removing a slim black case from the inner lining of his jacket. Without a word, he placed it on the table and opened it. Inside lay a ceremonial knife. Its handle was carved bone, darkened with age. The blade gleamed under the dim overhead lights.

Ramos muttered, "What the hell is that?" Saúl shot him a sharp look. "Show respect." Barrera smiled faintly. "Your lieutenant is young. He doesn't understand tradition." He lifted the knife with both hands, holding it out for Óscar.

"This belonged to one of our founders," Barrera said. "Used only for blood oaths that tie organizations together. When we make a pact... this seals it."

Óscar didn't immediately take the blade. Instead, he studied it, as though weighing the symbolic weight more than the physical object. The bone handle bore shallow cuts. Marks from years of use, each one representing an oath made and, presumably, executed.

Saúl stepped closer. "Jefe… you don't have to do this. A deal is a deal. No need for…" "This is not a deal," Óscar said softly. "This is vengeance." Saúl fell silent.

Barrera extended the knife again. This time, Óscar took it. His hand didn't tremble. He walked to the far side of the table, where a small wooden frame lay. A photo of Carlos, Michaela, and Violetta smiling at a family dinner. The kind of moment that looked fragile now, like glass that had already shattered. Óscar set the frame in the center of the table. Barrera nodded approvingly. "This is how we honor blood lost," he said. "By binding ourselves to its justice." Óscar raised the knife. No hesitation. Not even a breath of doubt. He sliced across his palm. The cut was clean. A thin line of blood welled immediately, dark and vivid against his skin.

Saúl closed his eyes briefly, as if absorbing the gravity of the moment. One by one, the Gulf lieutenants approached. Alvarado first. He took the blade, turned his hand, and cut deep. He smeared the blood across the side of the frame. "For Carlos," he said quietly. Ramos was next, jaw set tight. He took the knife with something like reverence, something like fury. "For the little girl," he whispered, and cut. He pressed his blood to the wood, jaw trembling not with fear but rage. Saúl came last among the Gulf. He cut hard, letting the blood rise full and heavy before pressing his palm over the corner of the frame. "Para la familia," he said. "Always."

Then Barrera stepped forward. His demeanor changed subtly; less arrogant, more solemn. He sliced his palm without flinching, letting the bead of blood rise and fall onto the table beside the frame. "For alliance," he said. "For vengeance."

His Zetas operators followed suit, each cutting and marking the table as a sign of commitment. No theatrics. No hesitation. These were men who had made oaths before, and would again, but this one had weight.

When the last man stepped back, the blade returned to Óscar. Blood from multiple men stained its edge, glistening under the war room lights. Óscar set the knife on the table beside the frame, then placed his bloodied palm over Carlos's smiling face. His voice was barely a murmur. "Por mi hijo." For my son. Silence roared in the room.

He lifted his hand and turned to the assembled men. "The ghosts will be unleashed," he said. A current rippled through the room. Just the cold, focused acknowledgment of men who understood the gravity of what had been set in motion. Barrera nodded once. "Then the pact is sealed."

Óscar stared at the bloodied frame, the crimson smudges forming something like a shield. And when he finally looked up, his eyes burned with purpose. "We begin," he said.

The night air outside the war room felt cooler than before. The compound had transformed in the span of an hour. Engines rumbled. Radios crackled. Men moved with purpose instead of routine. The entire estate pulsed like a living organism preparing for violence.

Óscar stepped out first. The torches lining the courtyard cast warm, wavering light across his face, catching the streak of drying blood still visible along the crease of his palm. Behind him, Saúl, Alvarado, Ramos, and the Zetas delegation followed in a loose formation, unified now, bound by oath and necessity.

Guards standing watch stiffened the moment they saw their leader emerge. Conversations died. Weapons were lowered respectfully. Even the dogs near the perimeter quieted, sensing the energy shift. A cluster of Gulf soldiers stood waiting at the base of the stairway. Among them was Martín, Óscar's top logistics lieutenant. He was a wiry man with sharp eyes and perpetually ink-stained fingers from years of handling manifests and coded ledgers.

He stepped forward. "Jefe. The perimeter is secure. Snipers are doubled on the east wall. All communications channels are silent unless you authorize otherwise." Óscar nodded once, acknowledging the report. Then he descended the steps, slow and deliberate.

The men hushed. Every pair of eyes in the courtyard fixed on him. The Zetas watched too, aware this was a moment that defined more than a mission. It defined a movement.

Óscar stopped before Martín. "Contact the man in New Orleans," he said. His voice was low. Controlled. But it carried across the courtyard with force. Martín's jaw tightened. He understood the gravity instantly. "The new one?" "Yes," Óscar said. "Tell him: it begins now." No fanfare. Just the simple command that would ripple across borders and set the first gears of vengeance in motion.

Martín bowed his head, already reaching for the encrypted phone at his belt. "En seguida." At once. He moved quickly, disappearing into one of the side rooms where radio interference was lowest. González and two others followed to secure the channel.

Óscar stood alone now at the center of the courtyard. Alone, but not lonely. The silence around him was the silence of respect and the silence before a storm.

Behind him, Barrera approached. "Your men move fast," he said lightly. Óscar didn't look at him. "Speed is survival." The Zetas commander smirked. "And what comes next?"

Óscar watched two soldiers load crates of armaments into a waiting vehicle. The weapons clattered with the sound of men preparing for war. "What comes next," he said, "is consequence."

Saúl stepped beside him. "We'll begin stocking the safehouse pipeline. Martín will coordinate with the handler in New Orleans." "Good," Óscar said.

From a distance, Martín reemerged from the shadows, radio in hand. He approached quickly, but with visible composure. "Jefe," he said. "The message was received." "And?" Martín's eyes reflected the torchlight. "The contact said one thing." Óscar waited. Martín swallowed lightly. "'Entendido." Understood. Óscar nodded.

That was all he needed. The compound seemed to breathe then. The machine was in motion. Irreversible. Precise.

Barrera and his operators turned toward their convoy. "My men will begin preparations," he said. Óscar gave him a single nod. Barrera paused, watching him for a moment longer. "Señor Alvarez," he said, "I have seen men lose sons. I have seen them lose worlds. None of them carried their grief as you do." Óscar turned slightly. "And how is that?" "Quietly," Barrera said. "Like a man sharpening a knife." Óscar didn't respond. He didn't need to.

The Zetas delegation departed toward their vehicles.

Saúl remained at Óscar's side, waiting for further instruction. But Óscar gave none. He simply looked out across the courtyard. The same courtyard where he had once watched his son run barefoot as a child.

His voice when it came, was a murmur, intended only for himself. "Venganza sale al norte al amanecer." Vengeance goes north at dawn. Saúl heard it, so did the night. A storm was gathering, and the first winds were already rising.

Chapter 3

Whom Shall We Send

The compound did not sleep. Not after a night like this. Engines rumbled in the dark as vehicles repositioned. Radios crackled. Boots thudded across concrete and dirt. Men moved with the kind of urgency that only came when a decision had been made that could not be undone.

The faint smoke from the torches curled through the air, mixing with diesel exhaust and the tang of weapons being loaded and checked. The summit was over. The war was beginning. Óscar walked through it all like a shadow with purpose.

Saúl followed a few steps behind him, clipboard in hand, glancing occasionally at the men scrambling across the courtyard and perimeter. Operators from both sides clustered in smaller groups near the trucks and tool sheds, speaking in low, tense voices. "They're waiting," Saúl murmured. "They should be," Óscar replied without stopping.

He pushed open the door to a small operations room tucked behind the main house. It was a location typically used for smuggling routes, shipments, and border intelligence. Tonight, it had transformed into a war forge. A long steel table stood at the center, littered with files, maps, tablets, and radios. Two portable fluorescent lamps cast harsh white light over the piles of dossiers. On the far wall, a corkboard held pinned photographs of men; some mugshots, others blurry field images, others military portraits.

The room buzzed with quiet intensity. Saúl set his clipboard down. "The preliminary rosters are here." Óscar didn't answer. He went straight to the table.

Saúl opened a metal case and laid out stacks of personnel files, one side marked ZV for Zetas Vieja Escuela, the other GC for Gulf Cartel. "These are all vetted candidates," Saúl said. "Ex-military. Former Kaibiles. GAFE deserters. Rogue federales. A few… established Sicarios." He hesitated before finishing. "This is close to a battalion, Jefe." Óscar flipped open the first file.

He didn't read the biography. Didn't examine the medals. Didn't care about the decorated past or criminal accolades. He looked only at the face. Into the eyes. After three seconds, he set the file aside. "No." He opened another. "No." The third. "No."

Saúl blinked. "Jefe… you're eliminating people who could run an entire region alone." Óscar didn't look at him. "I'm not running a region. I'm ending a war."

He opened the next file. The candidate's face stared back with a hard, stone-eyed expression. However, something in the expression wavered. Fear? Ego? Uncertainty? "No." He moved faster now. File after file. Soldier. Hitman. Specialist. Tracker. Ex-federal commander. All rejected.

"Nahual?" Saúl protested, picking up a discarded file. "This man killed an entire police convoy outside Reynosa on his own. He's a legend…" "Legends get sloppy," Óscar said. He opened a new file. A young Kaibil with a commendation for jungle warfare. "No."

"How are you choosing?" Saúl asked. "By what matters." "And what is that?" Óscar paused only long enough to answer: "Who can walk into a man's home, kill him, and walk out without leaving a shadow?"

He continued. Twenty-seven files in. Twenty-seven rejections. Saúl rubbed the back of his neck. "At this rate, we won't have a team…" "We don't need a team," Óscar corrected. "We need *ghosts*." He picked up the twenty-eighth file. One glance. One heartbeat. "No." He closed it hard.

Saúl exhaled slowly, watching the piles grow higher in the rejection stack. "This," he muttered, "this is a battalion, Jefe." Óscar looked up finally, eyes sharp. "It's justice." The word cut through the room like a blade. Saúl said nothing else.

Óscar reached for the next file. The night outside continued moving around them, but in this room, the world had narrowed to a single question: Whom shall they send to kill a king? The answer waited further down the table. And Óscar Alvarez Vasquez intended to find it tonight.

He left the operations room for the compound's guard house. The fortified guard house sat on the far side of the compound with thick adobe walls, barred windows, and reinforced doors. It had once housed cartel accountants who needed protection. Tonight, it housed something far more dangerous: the men who might be chosen to kill a king.

Óscar entered without knocking. Inside, the lights were bright but harsh, casting stark shadows across the briefing table where two metal cases lay open. One of them belonged to the Zetas commander, the other to the Gulf Cartel. Barrera stood waiting, sleeves rolled, posture crisp. He looked energized, almost invigorated by the night's momentum. "Señor Alvarez," he said. "We've prepared the next phase." Saúl took up his place beside Óscar, clipboard ready but expression tight. Ramos lingered near the back wall, quietly watching but trying to look like he wasn't.

Barrera snapped open the first metal case. Inside lay dossiers arranged with military precision, each file thicker and more detailed than the ones in the operations room. These weren't names pulled from a broad pool. These were the finalists. Men who had already survived more than most soldiers ever would.

"These," Barrera began, "are my top recommendations." He tapped the first file.

#1 Hugo 'El Tejón' Valverde
— Ex-GAFE reconnaissance
— Survived four ambushes in Michoacán
— Known for disappearing into urban terrain.

Ramos muttered, "Looks like he eats concrete for breakfast." Barrera grinned. "Sometimes lunch too." Óscar ignored the comment. He flipped open the file. The man's eyes were sharp, predatory. Too expressive. "No," he said, closing it. Barrera hid his annoyance well. "As you wish. Next."

#2 Iván Castañón
— Trained sniper
— Former federal tactical
— Dismissed for brutality during interrogations.

Saúl skimmed the notes. "He'd be useful for perimeter overwatch." Óscar lifted the photo. The man smiled in it. "No." He dropped it to the side.

Barrera exhaled slowly through his nose. "Smiles offend you tonight?" "Confidence does," Óscar answered. He opened the next file.

#3 Santiago Reyes
— Close-quarters specialist
— Decorated Kaibil
— Rumored to have executed entire safehouses alone.

Óscar studied the face for several seconds. Then: "Maybe." Saúl's eyebrows rose. "A maybe?" "Put him aside," Óscar ordered.

Barrera's expression flickered with satisfaction. One potential down. He opened the other case that belonged to the Gulf. Alvarado stepped in from the hallway, carrying additional folders. "Our men are ready too, Jefe." Óscar nodded for him to proceed. Alvarado opened a file and slid it toward Óscar.

#4 Mateo 'Lince' Serrano
– Tunnel rat during the Reynosa siege
– Expert in silent entry
– Survived a cartel betrayal with a single knife.

Saúl whistled softly. "He's a ghost." Óscar nodded once. "A possibility." Another file.

#5 Ernesto 'Carbón' Godoy
– Veteran of the Matamoros conflicts
– Surveillance specialist
– Operates drones, trackers, jammers.

Ramos leaned forward. "We'll need someone like him for recon." Óscar didn't look up. "Useful. Not essential." But he didn't reject him.

Then Barrera opened the final Zetas file in the first stack. He eased the photo forward. "This one," Barrera said, "is the standout." The room seemed to pause, a slight shift in posture among the men present.

In the photo: A man with a square jaw, haunted eyes, and a deep scar running from temple to jawline. His expression was blank. Not cruel. Not angry. Just… empty. "Name?" Óscar asked. "Federico Alemán," Barrera said. "Ex-military scout. Deserted after an incident involving an entire convoy disappearing." He tapped the page. "Not destroyed. Not bombed. *Disappeared.* No bodies." Saúl frowned. "You're saying he killed them alone?" "No," Barrera replied. "I'm saying they vanished under his watch. The truth is… unknown."

Óscar stared at the photo longer than any of the others. A long silence stretched. Then he closed the folder and placed it gently into the "possible" pile.

Alvarado stepped forward with the final Gulf file in his stack. "Jefe…you should see this one." He slid the dossier forward. A thick folder. No photo, just a red stamp: CLASSIFIED. Óscar opened it. A single image was tucked inside at the back, a grainy surveillance still showing a man's silhouette mid-strike with a blade in hand, motion blurring his features.

Saúl squinted. "Who is he?" Alvarado swallowed. "A legend," he said. "We don't say his name out loud unless he's in front of us." Ramos stared. "Does he have one?" Alvarado nodded. "One that people whisper."

Óscar turned the folder, reading the name. A single word. CUCHILLO. *Knife.* Óscar narrowed his eyes.

"Is he loyal?" Alvarado hesitated. "He is loyal to death." Barrera scoffed lightly. "Loyalty means nothing if a man can't follow orders." Alvarado bristled. "He follows orders. He just… interprets them."

Óscar closed the folder sharply. "No." Saúl blinked. "Just like that?" "He is unpredictable," Óscar said. "We cannot send unpredictable men into a foreign city." Alvarado accepted the decision with a stiff nod.

Barrera smirked. "At least your Jefe understands." Óscar ignored him. He organized the "possibles" pile. Three files. "From dozens," Ramos said quietly. Óscar answered without looking at him, "This mission cannot afford weakness."

Saúl studied the three candidates. "Jefe… these men together could topple a government." Óscar's voice was cold and final. "They're not toppling a government." He tapped the folders. "They're killing one man." The table fell silent.

Outside, engines revved as teams prepared equipment and loaded cases. The compound moved like a living beast gearing up for something monstrous. Óscar stepped back from the table, his eyes drifting toward the hallway that led to the armory. "Bring me the Team Leader," he said quietly.

A low hum pulsed through the armory as lights flickered against steel walls, shadows stretching long across racks of weapons. The room smelled of gun oil, dust, and old battles. Men came here to prepare for war. Tonight, they came to meet the man who had already lived through too many.

The armory guards stiffened instantly, stepping aside without a word. Saúl had a clipboard tucked under his arm, though for once, he didn't look at it. His attention stayed fixed on the figure standing at the center of the room. The Zetas commander, Barrera, waited near a workbench. He gave a small nod as Óscar approached.

"He's ready," Barrera said. Óscar did not reply. He simply said, "Bring him." Barrera gestured toward the far doorway. Two Zetas operators stepped aside, revealing a man who had been standing just out of sight with an unmoving silence that carved from the dim light itself.

He walked forward. Not with swagger. Not with menace. With precision. His footsteps made no sound despite the concrete floor. He stopped in front of Óscar.

He was tall, lean but muscled, the kind of build meant for endurance more than brute force. His face carried a map of scars, one thick line that cut from the edge of his brow to the corner of his mouth, pale against sun-worn skin. His eyes were something else entirely. They were cold, still, deep as a well with no bottom.

Óscar studied him openly. "You," Óscar said, voice quiet, "are the one they call *El Silencioso*." The man nodded once.

Up close, Saúl noticed something odd. There was no tension in the man's jaw, no anxiety in his shoulders. He existed in a calm that felt… inhuman.

Óscar stepped closer. "You have led forces before." "Yes," the man answered, his voice was low and controlled. His accent was faint, almost unplaceable. "You've crossed borders?" Óscar asked. "Many." "You've killed targets under protection." "Yes." "Failed?" A pause. "Once."

Ramos stiffened among the other men, surprised that the leader admitted it. Óscar's expression barely changed. "Explain." The Team Leader looked at him without blinking. "I misjudged timing. My team extracted. I remained behind." Another pause. "It will not happen again."

Saúl shifted. There was no bravado in the man's voice. No defensiveness. The words were simply facts that were delivered with uncaring precision.

Barrera stepped in. "He has executed operations alone that normally require entire squads. His discipline is absolute. His methods…" Óscar lifted a hand. He looked back at the man. "What motivates you?" Óscar asked. He tilted his head slightly.

"Mission." "Nothing else?" "Not anymore." "And loyalty?" "To the operation."

Óscar considered the answer, weighing every syllable. "Fear?" he asked. The man blinked once, as though the concept were foreign. "Unnecessary." Óscar nodded slowly.

He turned, resting his hand on the nearby workbench where a series of weapons lay disassembled. One knife in particular stood out. It was a heavy steel, well-worn blade engraved with a single set of initials: E.R. The man stepped forward instinctively. Óscar picked up the knife and held it out. "Is this yours?"

The man took it with careful reverence. Something flickering in his eyes, a memory perhaps, or an oath long buried.

Saúl caught the moment, quiet as it was. "The initials… someone he lost?" Barrera answered. "He never said. And we do not ask."

Óscar watched the man sheathe the blade. "You are disciplined," Óscar said. "Efficient and Detached." He held his gaze. "You will lead them," Óscar continued. "Through water, land, and shadows. Through the edge of two nations. Into the home of a man who believes he is untouchable." The leader remained motionless. "You will kill Vincent Castenllo Jr.," Óscar said. "And you will leave his wife and children alive."

A brief flicker crossed the man's eyes, not of reluctance, but understanding. A rule was added to the mission. A new line etched into his internal map. "Yes," he said. Óscar stepped closer until their faces were only inches apart. "This mission," Óscar said softly, "does not forgive mistakes." "It will not see any," the Team Leader answered. Óscar nodded. "Then you are the man I will send."

The Team Leader dipped his head once in acceptance, a vow, and a warning all at once. And with that, the shadow who would one day stand in the Martello home stepped back into silence. Óscar turned toward the door. "Bring him to the war room," he ordered.

The war room hummed with a low static tension as Óscar, Saúl, Barrera, Alvarado, Ramos, and the Team Leader stepped inside. The overhead lights glared off the maps, casting reflections across the table like slashes of white steel. The screen at the far wall displayed the rotating tactical layout of New Orleans. It looked less like a city now and more like a target schematic. The Team Leader stood at the far end of the table, expression unreadable, posture erect. Not a soldier waiting for orders, but more like a weapon waiting to be aimed.

Barrera pulled out a folder thick with operational drafts. "Based on the intel," he began, flipping the folder open, "I propose overwhelming force. Two squads. Twelve men total. One breaching team, one perimeter control. Quick, loud, and efficient."

Ramos snorted. "Quick and loud gets you shot on the Mississippi Bridge by a rookie state trooper." Barrera's eyes narrowed. "Your negativity is exhausting." "It's realism," Ramos fired back. Saúl stepped between them before it escalated. "Focus. We aren't here to bicker." Óscar didn't even have to say anything yet. His presence alone was enough to drag silence back into the room.

Barrera tapped the map again. "Twelve men. Full kit. One push through the weakest point of the estate. With the right distraction…" "No," Óscar said. Barrera blinked. "No?" Óscar stepped forward, palms resting lightly on the table. "Too many men. Too much noise." "Noise is how we control a street," Barrera countered. "We are not controlling a street," Óscar said. "We are infiltrating a nation." A hard silence followed.

Alvarado, arms crossed, nodded in agreement. "Our men stick out in America. Tattoos. accents. backgrounds. Twelve men will draw eyes." Ramos chimed in. "Hell, even five will. But three?" He gestured toward the silent leader. "Three disappear." Barrera scoffed. "Three men can't take a fortified mansion."

The Team Leader spoke for the first time since entering the room. "They can," he said. The simplicity of the statement froze everyone. Barrera turned. "Care to elaborate?" "No," he replied. "The mission needs quiet. Stealth and precision are our allies."

He pointed at the map with a single finger. "Three groups. Three ingress points. Each with selective tasks."

Barrera frowned. "Three groups? That's even more reckless." The Team Leader continued, ignoring him. "Group One breaks perimeter. Group Two infiltrates the interior. Group Three intercepts escape or reinforcement." He lowered his hand. "Only survivors continue."

Ramos murmured, "Jesus." Even Saúl stiffened slightly. Not in fear, just recognition of what kind of man they were dealing with.

Barrera folded his arms. "And what if Group One dies? Or Group Two is compromised?" The Team Leader's eyes didn't flicker. "Then Group Three adapts."

"This is madness," Alvarado said under his breath. "No," Óscar corrected, voice low with deadly calm. "This is a necessity." He looked around the table, meeting each man's eyes one by one. "Numbers attract attention. Vehicles attract cameras. Noise attracts police."

He tapped the map at three separate entry points: the river, the street, and the industrial zone. "We avoid all three with a single principle: fragmentation." Saúl nodded slowly. "Multiple approaches. Minimal footprint. Scatter their detection capabilities."

"Exactly," Óscar said. "Three teams make one strike."

Barrera let out a slow, reluctant exhale. "This is… very unorthodox." "Unorthodox is how we honor the mission," Óscar replied. "And how we survive it." The Zetas commander glanced toward the Team Leader. "And you support this?" The man nodded once. "Only the strong and careful deserve the mission." Something cold rolled through the room with his words.

Óscar straightened. "Roles." Delgado, who had just slipped in with an armful of documents, began laying out sheets across the table. "Breacher," he said. "Comms tech. Recon specialist. Medical support. Spotter. Each group needs its function."

The Team Leader scanned the assignments, finger gliding across the names. Reyes, Serrano, Castañón, Godoy, those who had survived Óscar's earlier scrutiny. "They will do," he said. It was neither approval nor praise. Just certainty.

Barrera rested his palms on the table. "So it's decided then. Three groups. Fragmented entry. Multiple approaches. And a single objective." Óscar looked at the glowing schematic of the Garden District. "Kill Vincent Castenllo Jr.," he said. Everyone nodded.

Barrera exhaled. "And the timeline?" Óscar's voice was absolute. "A week." The room reacted; some with surprise, others with acceptance. But the Team Leader didn't blink. "Understood," he said.

Óscar turned, heading for the door. "Prepare the courtyard," he ordered. "We choose the final soldiers tonight."

The courtyard burned with firelight. Torches flickered along the walls. Engines idled in low, steady hums. The compound felt like a beast pacing in the dark. A line of men stood in formation beneath the open sky… men that even cartel soldiers avoided making eye contact with. Men who had lived through things others could not survive. Men who had done things others could not imagine. These were the final candidates.

Óscar stepped from the archway into the courtyard. The atmosphere shifted immediately. El Silencioso, the newly appointed team leader, emerged at his flank, expression unreadable, posture rigid as iron. Saúl joined on the other side, clipboard in hand, though he didn't bother looking at it. He knew Óscar no longer needed it. At this point, the mission wasn't being recorded on paper; it was being carved directly into the night.

They walked to a smaller table set up beneath the torches. The final list lay there with a single sheet, edges weighed down by a stone. Saúl cleared his throat softly. "These are the men who passed every filter." Óscar didn't sit. He leaned over the table, scanning the list, not reading the names, but confirming their existence.

Santiago Reyes. Mateo Serrano. Ernesto Godoy. Federico Alemán. And beneath them, at the bottom, a single name with no title or accolades: El Silencioso. *Team Leader*

Saúl spoke quietly, almost uneasily. "I don't trust them." "I don't need to trust them," Óscar said. "I trust the mission." His hand hovered over the list, fingers brushing lightly over each name… until they stopped on the Silencioso's. Óscar tapped the photo with a single finger. "He," he said, "will be the last thing that Castenllo sees." Saúl didn't respond. There was nothing to say.

Óscar turned. "Bring them forward." The order carried across the courtyard like a crack of thunder. The line of operatives stepped to attention in perfect unison. These weren't men preparing for a job. They were weapons awaiting deployment.

Óscar walked the line slowly, boots echoing against the tile. He passed Mateo Serrano first with his silent, eyes forward. Then Reyes' expression blank, Kaibil discipline radiating from every muscle. Then Godoy was already calculating, scanning, and analyzing the perimeter even though he knew it by heart.

And finally… He stopped before the Team Leader,. The courtyard seemed to contract around them. El

Silencioso didn't speak. He didn't blink. His hands rested behind his back, shoulders squared, chin lifted with quiet precision. Óscar studied him as if memorizing a tool he was about to unleash into the world.

Then he spoke with such clarity that every man in the courtyard held their breath. "You will travel far," Óscar said. "Across rivers, borders, shadows. You will enter a city that does not know you." He paced, voice tightening. "You will kill the king of New Orleans. A man who believes he cannot be touched." He stopped, turning slightly so the entire formation could hear. "You will leave his family alive. You will leave no trace. You will move like smoke… and vanish like ghosts. And you will return as legends…" A long pause. "…or not at all."

The men didn't react. They didn't have to. Their discipline was the response. Óscar faced them all. "You leave in forty-eight hours." A hum rippled through the courtyard. But the operatives did not move. They stood still and silent. Until Silencioso stepped forward, reached down, and lifted the list.

He folded it once, tucked it into his jacket, and turned toward the darkness at the far end of the courtyard. No one stopped him. He needed no escort. He disappeared between two buildings without a sound… slipping into the night like something the world had never intended to see.

Óscar watched him go. The torches flickered. The engines hummed. The night deepened. The ghosts were now fully assembled and moving toward New Orleans.

Chapter 4

Looping In the New Guy

The house was too quiet. Isaías Velasco, known on the streets and in whispers as El Contador, the Accountant, sat alone at a kitchen table in a fortified rental property deep in New Orleans East. The blinds were drawn tight. The hum of the refrigerator was the loudest sound in the room. In front of him were two burner phones, a ledger filled with coded entries, a laptop running on a VPN, and a muted news broadcast replaying footage from the Garden District.

A reporter stood in front of one of Vinny Castenllo Jr.'s businesses, talking about *economic expansion, charitable donations, and community partnerships*. Isaías snorted under his breath. "*Míralo…* shining like a saint," he muttered. "If they only knew."

He'd been in the city for two months now, supposedly as a low-level investor, quietly laundering money into small trucking fronts and convenience stores. In reality, he was the Gulf Cartel's quiet foothold in Louisiana. The man who kept the network invisible. The man who cleaned up after others. And the man who'd watched, with growing frustration, as the Martellos thrived despite everything.

He flipped a burner open and scanned the last text thread. Nothing. Same for the other phone. The stillness was suffocating. Then… *BZZT*. A vibration rattled across the table. It wasn't the burner. Nor the backup phone.

His encrypted Q-link device pulsed with a single flashing command: *SECURE LINE. MIDNIGHT.* Isaías froze. His hands didn't jerk, nor did his breath stutter, but something inside him locked up like a tightening noose. Only one man sent that signal, Óscar.

He closed the ledger with trembling fingers and killed the news stream. The silence in the room thickened, like walls closing in. Isaías stood, moving with sudden urgency.

He crossed the small house quickly, flipping switches, pulling blinds tighter, checking peepholes. His mind sharpened. His heart slowed into a steady, combat-like pulse. Whatever this was, it wasn't routine.

Óscar didn't send "Secure Line" for small requests. He didn't send it for smuggling updates, wire transfers, or petty conflicts. He sent it when death was coming.

Isaías locked the last window and returned to the kitchen. He opened a drawer and took out a compact pistol, racking the slide quietly before placing it beside the Q-link on the table.

His eyes didn't move from the device. Midnight was fourteen minutes away. He sat with his back straight and his hands folded. He stared at the flashing message like it was a countdown. The quiet paranoia tightened around him like a second skin. Something BIG was coming.

The fortified house fell into complete stillness as Isaías moved down the narrow hallway toward the back room. The faint floor creak under his steps was the only sound, swallowed by the dense humidity of the New Orleans night. He pushed open a door disguised as a linen closet. Inside were no towels. It was his improvised comms room. A patchwork of cartel-level paranoia and ex-military precision.

Isaías flicked on the desk lamp. It gave off a low-watt warm angle that was just enough to illuminate the equipment without casting shadows against the blinds. He took a breath, rolled his shoulders once, and began the ritual.

He always followed *the order*, never deviating. Protocol was the only thing that kept men like him alive. He reached for the wall panel and flipped a switch. A static hiss filled the room as white-noise jammers came online, vibrating through the drywall like an angry swarm. Phones within twenty feet were now useless. More importantly, they were undetectable. Isaías checked the sound frequency. Stable and safe. "Good," he muttered.

Next, he opened the rugged laptop that had no ports except for two which were sealed with tamper-proof tape. Booting took longer than it should. That was the point. The security included layers of firewalls and spoofed MAC addresses. Scrambled DNS routes bouncing between Belize, Denmark, and an offshore shell in Azerbaijan offered an extra layer of security. He waited while it constructed its digital maze… He always waited.

Then he unlatched a metal box and pulled out the Q-link, a palm-sized, military-grade satellite communicator. He connected it to the laptop via a single shielded cable. A blue light came on. Then a red one flashed. Finally, a steady green pulse appeared. He was connected. Isaías exhaled one shallow breath.

Finally, he removed a small plastic stick from a foil sleeve. It was a single-use, untraceable dongle. It was preloaded with cartel cipher keys. Once it was used, it self-corrupted. Once it self-corrupted, it melted the data. He slid it into the port. The laptop screen dimmed and flickered, recognizing the encryption handshake. A small prompt appeared: *AUTHENTICATION?* Isaías typed the passphrase without hesitation, each keystroke deliberate.

He never said the phrase out loud. He never even thought it fully in his head. Muscle memory took care of it. The screen flashed once. *SECURE.*

Isaías reached into a drawer, pulled out his last burner SIM card, and snapped it cleanly in half. He dropped the pieces into a steel ashtray, lit a match, and watched them curl and blacken. He didn't take his eyes off the flame until it died. "Clean slate," he whispered.

He sat… with his back straight, hands still, and breathing controlled. The jammers hummed. The laptop connected to satellites that no civilian could access. The encryption dongle pulsed like a heartbeat.

Midnight approached. The last minute dragged like a long, stretched, thin tension wire about to snap. He thought of Óscar Alvarez Vasquez. He had only spoken to the man once before. Never by video, only voice. Even then, Isaías had felt something crawl up his spine. A cold precision. A predator's patience.

If Óscar was reaching out tonight… something monumental was coming. Something violent… Something inevitable.

The laptop pinged softly. *INCOMING CONNECTION*. Isaías straightened. The green light on the Q-link turned solid. Then the screen blinked and flickered. It resolved into the encrypted interface. A voice filter clicked on. Then… "Prepare yourself," came a deep, stern voice through the scrambled channel. "Mexico is calling." It wasn't Óscar. It was his lieutenant.

Isaías swallowed. The encrypted feed stabilized, the scrambled pixels aligning themselves into a grainy silhouette. The figure on-screen was a man Isaías recognized instantly, not from personal contact, but from reputation alone. It was Dominic "El Sargento" Valdez, Óscar's senior lieutenant. A man feared even in the Gulf. A man who did not waste words.

"Isaías Velasco," Valdez said, his voice filtered but unmistakably sharp. "Confirm your channel." Isaías adjusted the mic. "Q-link active, satellite tunnel stable, white-noise jammers at ninety percent. This line is clean." Valdez nodded. "Good. Then listen carefully. Do not interrupt." Isaías straightened in his chair. "Sí, señor."

Valdez lifted a stack of papers: mission manifests, procedural codes, faces partially visible through the distortion. "Three teams are being sent north," Valdez said. "Not together. They will arrive separately, depending on weather, transport, and… survivability." Isaías felt his pulse hitch. "Survivability?" Valdez looked directly into the camera. "Men this good are often hunted by those who fear them." The implication settled heavily into the room. Isaías said nothing.

"You will prepare two safehouses," Valdez continued. "Stock them with what they need but leave no fingerprints. No personal items. Clean walls, clean floors, and clean history." "Understood."

"You will procure vehicles. Disposable ones with low profiles. No luxury brands. No aftermarket parts. If the police impound one, it should be indistinguishable from a thousand others." Isaías nodded again. "Sí, señor."

"You will arrange a weapons pipeline," Valdez said. "Not flashy, but reliable. NATO calibers only with no serial numbers. Don't ask me where to get them. *You already know.*" Isaías did… and he hated that he did.

Valdez leaned closer to the camera. "And you will provide cash. Enough for emergencies. Enough for disappearances." Isaías wet his lips, throat suddenly dry. "How much?" "Enough," Valdez said, "that you'll feel the weight even before you carry it." Isaías swallowed hard.

Valdez continued. "No direct involvement. No showing your face. You will not meet them unless they demand it. Support the operation invisibly." The warning sharpened. "If you fail to remain invisible, Óscar will take it as betrayal." Isaías nodded. "I understand." "No," Valdez said softly, "you don't."

He tapped something off-screen. A new feed window opened beside him. It flickered for a second… then solidified into the face of Óscar. Isaías's breath locked in his chest.

Óscar looked older than the last photo Isaías had seen. His skin was drawn tighter, his hair silvered at the edges, and the weight of grief etched deep into the lines around his eyes. But the power? The command? Unchanged. "Isaías," Óscar said. His voice was calm. Steady. Terrifying in its control. "Señor…" Isaías managed. "You know what the Martellos did to my family," Óscar said. It wasn't a question. Isaías nodded. "I do, Jefe. I saw it myself. I…"

Óscar cut him off. Not sharply. Just enough to remind him who held the power in the conversation. "Do not tell me what you saw," Óscar said. "Tell me what you understood." Isaías's throat tightened. "I understood," he said carefully, "that they destroyed something sacred. Something irreplaceable."

Óscar's eyes softened by a fraction. "Good," he said. "Then you also understand why the men I am sending are…different." Isaías nodded. "Sí, Jefe."

Óscar leaned closer, his voice dropping to something quieter and colder. "There will be three teams. There may be casualties before they reach you. You will not ask questions." "No, Jefe." "They will move like smoke. You will treat them like shadows." "Sí, Jefe."

"And Isaías…" Óscar paused, letting his grief and fury bleed through just enough to make the warning real. "If they fail, you fail." The words hit like a knife to the chest. "And you," Óscar finished softly, "do not want to fail me." Isaías swallowed hard. "No, Jefe. I will not."

Óscar studied him for another moment. Then he nodded once. The screen flickered, disconnecting Óscar, leaving Valdez alone.

Valdez leaned forward one last time. "You have what you need," he said. "Prepare your city." The feed cut. The room fell silent except for the hum of the jammers. Isaías sat motionless, staring at the darkened screen, his pulse a thunder in his ears. He took a slow breath. Then another. He knew what Óscar had just handed him.

Not an order. It was a death sentence… if mishandled by even a fraction. He stood. The safehouses wouldn't prepare themselves. And the ghosts were on their way.

The secure feed went dark, leaving the comms room in a low amber glow. Velasco didn't move for several seconds. He just stared at the blank laptop screen, breathing slowly, as if any sudden movement might trigger something unstable inside the machine or inside himself.

Then the laptop chimed a faint, metallic tone. A message appeared: MISSION PACKET RECEIVED DECRYPTING… DO NOT INTERRUPT. Isaías leaned forward.

Lines of code scrolled down the screen, decrypting in layered segments. The first files unlocked themselves with soft pops, like pressure valves releasing.

ARRIVAL WINDOWS
INGRESS ROUTES
GPS WAYPOINTS
SAFEHOUSE CANDIDATES
TARGET PHOTOGRAPHS
OPERATIONAL PRIORITY: VINCENT
CASTENLLO JR.

The last file hovered at the bottom: TEAM LEADER
PROFILE (Protected — additional key required).
Isaías didn't touch it. He didn't want to know what
kind of monster Óscar was sending north.

He clicked the first file. Arrival Windows A timetable
filled the screen; precise, staggered times covering a
forty-eight-hour span. No names. No faces. Just
symbols marking each team:

ALFA
BRAVO
SOMBRA

Isaías shivered. "Sombra" meant shadow. Whatever
team carried that call sign… they were the dangerous
ones.

GPS Waypoints Green dots flickered across a map of
South Louisiana. Wetlands, industrial piers, and rural
highways are lost between sugarcane and swamp. One
note caught his eye: "If compromised, burn materials
and move to Waypoint Delta." He exhaled. "This is
beyond a hit…"

He clicked the next file. Aerial Photos of the Target Vinny Castenllo Jr.'s Garden District mansion appeared in high resolution. Bird's-eye angles with thermal overlays. Roof access points. Entry lanes for two-man breaching teams. Blind spots in the street cameras. Isaías muttered under his breath: *"Dios mío… esto es militar.* God… this is military."

The blueprints were marked with red annotations that were handwritten. Not from Mexico. From someone else. Someone who had already studied this house. The realization made Isaías' stomach knot. Óscar hadn't just chosen the teams. He had chosen a killer who knew exactly what he was walking into.

Surveillance Data From Mexico Dozens of still frames: Vinny Jr. outside a restaurant. Vinny Jr. entering a union hall. Vinny Jr. leaving a private meeting with a politician. His wife with grocery bags. His daughter stepping into a car. A security guard scratching his crotch near the front gate. Isaías felt sweat bead at the back of his neck. This wasn't reconnaissance. This was an execution pipeline.

As the files continued to decrypt, he exhaled shakily. He needed help. But not *trusted* help, that didn't exist. He needed *useful* help. He switched off the laptop display, grabbed his jacket, and stepped out into the hallway. He checked the peephole, counted to three, then unlocked the door and slipped into the night.

Mid-City Bar 1:27 A.M. The bar was one of those New Orleans places that didn't have a sign, just a red light above the door and a bartender who didn't ask questions. Two gang lieutenants sat in a booth, one from a local street crew tied loosely to the Gulf, the other a fixer who handled illegal imports on the river. Both men stiffened as Isaías slid into the booth.

"You called late," the first said. "You always call late," the second corrected. Isaías ignored the comments. He placed a small envelope on the table. It thumped heavily as cash spilled out. "I need vehicles," he said. "Four. Different types. No plates if possible." The river fixer nodded. "I can get you three by morning." "Four," Isaías repeated. The man swallowed. "Okay."

Isaías pushed the envelope closer. "And garages. Places nobody will look." "We got a few," the other lieutenant said. "Old spots the cops don't care about. Why? You expecting heat?" "No questions," Isaías said. "Just do it." They exchanged glances. No one argued when the cash was that thick.

Isaías leaned in slightly, lowering his voice. "And cameras," he said. "City feeds. If you know anyone who can loop or scrub them…" "We do," the river man said cautiously. "But it costs extra." Isaías slid another envelope across the table. "No problem." They didn't open it. They didn't need to.

Back on the streets Isaías walked briskly toward his car, head low, eyes scanning the shadows. The city breathed around him with humid air, distant sirens, and laughter from a late-night restaurant, music muffled behind walls. None of it comforted him. Not after what he saw tonight. The ghosts were coming. And he was preparing their hunting ground.

Back in the Comms Room 2:44 A.M. Isaías returned home, locked the door behind him, and moved straight to the comms desk. He tapped a command into the secure channel. NOLA PREPARED. ROUTES CONFIRMED. AWAITING GHOSTS. He hesitated only a second before hitting send. The reply came almost instantly. UNDERSTOOD.

The final message flashed beneath it: SOMBRA IN TRANSIT. Isaías stared at the screen. The air in the room seemed colder suddenly. He rubbed a hand over his jaw. "Let them come," he whispered. It wasn't bravado, nor anticipation. It was resignation.

Because once these men entered New Orleans… nothing would ever be the same again.

Chapter 5

Making Preparations

Dawn broke over Matamoros in a thin red line, staining the horizon like a fresh wound. Inside the walled training facility, the morning heat was already rising off the concrete in shimmering waves. The compound was alive with the crack of rifle fire, the clatter of gear, and the steady cadence of boots on hardened dirt long before the sun ever showed its face.

The Murder Team assembled in formation with three rows of twelve men. There was no talking and no wasted movements.

Only breath, discipline, and the quiet certainty of killers who had already accepted the outcome of their mission was life or death. There was nothing in between.

At the front of the formation stood El Silencioso motionless and perfectly balanced. He did not bark orders. Nor did he did t pace. His presence alone was enough to force the men into rigid stillness.

Behind him, the firing ranges echoed with controlled bursts of operators rehearsing muscle memory on steel targets that shattered into sparks.

The men waiting for inspection carried duffels brimming with tools of war. There were matte-black battle clothing, med kits packed with advanced trauma gear, comms earpieces and untraceable weapons wrapped in oil cloth, and maps and hand-drawn notations of infiltration routes.

Each duffel was laid neatly at their feet, the zippers aligned in identical orientation. Not by instruction, but by instinct.

On the sidelines, the Zetas commander watched with unmistakable pride, arms crossed, expression taut with satisfaction. These were his finest soldiers. This was his legacy as much as Óscar's revenge.

But beside him stood Dominic Valdez, Óscar's lieutenant. The man Isaías had spoken to over a satellite link. Valdez's expression was different.

It wasn't pride nor satisfaction. It was a cold and unforgiving judgment that was measured in its intensity. He tracked each man with the quiet awareness of someone counting survivors before the battle even began.

El Silencioso finally stepped forward. His inspection was terrifyingly silent.

He walked the line with slow, precise steps, stopping at each operative long enough to take in their stance, breathing, and finally their eyes. The invisible tension behind the muscles was palpable.

He lifted one man's duffel, testing the weight, set it down, and moved on.

He nudged a scarf on another's rifle, which barely shifted out of alignment and then looked at the man until his posture was corrected by instinct alone.

When a newer operator inhaled too sharply, betraying his nerves, the Team Leader paused, stared, and moved on.

The message was clear: Weakness would never be tolerated. Not here or in New Orleans.

The Zetas commander smirked. Valdez, however, watched the Team Leader's movements with quiet interest, calculating how many of these men would still be alive in a week.

When the inspection ended, the El Silencioso stepped back to the front of the formation. The sun crept over the wall, casting long shadows across the ground. He spoke without raising his voice. *"Hoy nos preparamos."* Today, we prepare. He lifted his chin slightly with his eyes hardening. *"Mañana, nos movemos."* Tomorrow, we move. No cheer followed, and there was no acknowledgment. These men didn't react to speeches; they only reacted to orders.

Valdez stepped forward then, his face stone hard. He scanned the group, then said with chilling calm, "Óscar expects perfection." The men held still. "Not effort. Not bravery," Valdez continued. "Perfection." His gaze swept the line like a blade. "Fail, and you will not die in New Orleans." A beat. "You will die here." Still no reaction. These were men who had accepted long ago that death would follow them until it caught up.

Finally, El Silencioso raised one hand. "Armory," he said. The men lifted their duffels in one synchronized motion and turned toward the facility's steel doors. They marched as one, their boots pounding a steady, ominous rhythm against the concrete.

The steel doors of the armory slid open with a heavy, hydraulic groan, releasing a blast of chilled air that washed over the men like a breath from another world. Inside, fluorescent lights hummed above long metal tables lined with weapons, tools, and gear; each item arranged with ritualistic precision.

There were no banners or insignias. There were no personal touches. This gave off the vibe of a cartel armory. This was a factory for ghosts. A thick-set armorer with balding hair and faded tattooed eyes like burnt gunpowder stood behind a reinforced counter with a clipboard in hand.

"Step forward," he said. "One at a time." No one rushed, nor did they hesitate. They moved with the discipline of a silent machine. The first operative approached and signed the ledger. Not with a real name but with an alias. ALFA-1. The armorer handed him a sealed case. Inside the case was a suppressed AR-15 with adjustable stock, a Glock 19 with three magazines, a standard-issue Ka-Bar knife, already sharpened, a compact med kit, a set of night-vision optics, a breaching charge wrapped in plastic, and a burner phone with no SIM installed.

"Next," the armorer said. BRAVO-2 signed his alias and received his kit. Sane thing with SOMBRA-3. The pattern repeated with mechanical consistency. Each operative stepping aside afterward, silently checking the chamber of the AR, examining the knife balance, and verifying zeroes on optics.

Two men whispered something under their breath. It was a mild joke, something about who would get the heavier breaching charge. The armorer didn't react, but El Silencioso did. He turned his head a fraction, just enough that his scar caught the overhead light, and locked eyes with the whisperers. No words. Just a stare. The effect was immediate. Both men stiffened, straightened, and looked ahead like statues carved from fear and obedience. The whisper died faster than a spent bullet.

El Silencioso stepped closer to the distribution line, observing each man with the stillness of a predator studying a herd for weakness. His gaze lingered on how they holstered their pistols, how they secured their night-vision gear, and how they loaded their trauma kits. Details mattered. Mistakes killed soldiers. Details killed targets.

The Zetas commander watched him with something that resembled pride. Valdez watched him with something that resembled concern.

When it came time for the Team Leader to collect his own equipment, the room seemed to hold its breath. He approached the armorer and signed nothing. The armorer didn't ask for an alias or hand him a kit. He opened a reinforced container beneath the counter and lifted out a black, unmarked case that was larger and heavier than the others. It bore scars from previous missions. He set it on the table with a heavy thud. El Silencioso unlatched it carefully.

Inside lay his personal tools. A modified AR with a custom suppressor, a Glock with a polished slide, a razor-edged Ka-Bar with initials *E.R.* engraved on the hilt, Extra magazines, an advanced night-vision headset, folded maps, a compact breaching device, a medical pouch meticulously organized, and a single flash drive sealed in black plastic. He ran a slow and deliberate hand over the gear. Every man in the armory watched without meaning to.

The armorer cleared his throat. "You know the rules," he said. "Nothing comes back. Not the guns. Not the clothes. And definitely…" He paused, looking El Silencioso dead in the eyes. "….not the bodies." El Silencioso closed the case with a soft click. "Understood." There was no bravado or posturing. There was only readiness. He stepped back into formation, his presence an anchor around which the others oriented themselves instinctively.

The armorer looked to Valdez. "That's all of them?" Valdez gave a short nod. "They're armed." The armorer exhaled slowly, wiping a hand across his scalp. "Then God help whoever they're sent to kill." Valdez didn't blink. "God won't be involved."

The Team Leader turned toward his men. "Briefing Room," he said. And like a single organism, the Murder Team moved with a silent and lethal inevitability towards the next phase of preparation.

The briefing room felt more like a bunker than a classroom. It was windowless with cement walls painted a dull gray and the stale odor of old gunpowder trapped in the ventilation. A single projector cast a cold blue glow across the Murder Team as they filed in, their shadows stretching long across the floor.

A massive map of Louisiana and the Gulf Coast covered the far wall. Every waterway, pipeline, interstate, swamp corridor, and marsh outlet was marked with handwritten notations. Someone had been preparing for this operation for a long time.

El Silencioso entered last. He stood at the center, not bothering to call attention. His stillness did that on its own. The Zetas commander stepped forward. "Sit." The word wasn't loud, but the operatives obeyed instantly, metal chairs scraping in unison as they took their seats. Their posture was straight-backed and alert, with hands resting on knees.

The commander tapped a laser pointer against the map. "Team A," he said, circling a blue line that cut across the Gulf of Mexico. "You go by boat. You'll leave from an unmarked fishing vessel off the Tamaulipas coast, then slip through the marshlands and come ashore south of Lafitte. Low radar exposure. No Coast Guard interest."

He pointed to the next route. "Team B. Border crossing north, then down the Intracoastal Waterway. You'll pass through Harvey Lock under the guise of a maintenance barge. Slow, but safe." Ramos would've cracked a joke in another life, but there was no humor in the air here.

The red laser shifted to the final route. "Team C. Rural Texas, then straight into Louisiana. Road-only. You'll set up at the Kenner safehouse first."

One man raised a hand. "If Team B is compromised, what's the fallback?" The commander didn't look at him. "Don't get compromised." Several operatives exchanged glances. Then El Silencioso spoke. "Merge with the nearest team." His voice was low, but it cut through the room like a blade. "If one team falls," he continued, "the survivors join the next closest group. Distance doesn't matter. Speed does." The commander nodded. "Correct."

Another man asked, "What about drone surveillance? NOPD runs external eye-sweeps now. And the feds…" "We're ghosts," the Zetas commander said. "They see nothing."

The projector changed slides, now showing structural diagrams of an American-style residence with thin drywall, weak door frames, and narrow hallways. El Silencioso stepped forward. "These houses are not bunkers," he said. "They are paper. You hit hard, you hit fast, and you don't stop moving."

The next slide displayed thermal images of the Martello mansion. "This is your target's home," the Team Leader continued. "Interior patterns. Estimated guards. Entry points. Safe rooms." He tapped a corner room. "This is where he sleeps." There was no emotion in the statement.

The commander raised his chin toward the door. "Training yard. Move." In the training yard, ten minutes later, the heat was brutal. The mock American houses were worse. They were constructed with thin wood and drywall, painted to replicate suburban interiors. One even had fake family photos on the wall, a surreal reminder of the human lives these drills were designed to erase.

Operatives lined up in two teams. "Breacher!" someone called. A man stepped forward with a small, shaped charge. He placed it beside the mock doorframe, tapped twice, and stepped back. BOOM—THUD. The door blew inward. The team surged as one, rifles up, sweeping left-right-center with textbook precision. The smacking of boots against the plywood floor echoed across the yard, blending with the rhythmic pop of suppressed rounds punching through silhouette targets.

Another squad ran through a different house. Drywall dust showered down. Shell casings clinked on the ground. The sun beat down mercilessly.

El Silencioso moved among them like a wraith, silently watching every angle of their clears, every reload, every hesitation. And then hesitation came. One operative paused half a second on a threshold. Enough time to die. Enough time to fail. El Silencioso appeared in front of him before the man even realized he'd hesitated. "Why did you stop?" the leader asked. Serrano swallowed. "Target cross. I thought I saw…" "You thought?" The words struck harder than a slap. "If you hesitate in New Orleans," the Team Leader said, voice quiet, merciless, "you will not come home." Serrano's throat bobbed. "Understood." "Again," the Leader ordered, and the drill reset.

Two hours later, sweat-coated operatives ran knife drills, their blades flashing in the cruel sunlight as they practiced quick, clean, silent kills. No dramatics or flourishes. Just science. The Zetas commander watched proudly. Valdez watched grimly. El Silencioso watched without emotion. And when the last target dummy hit the ground, split open under cold steel, the Leader finally spoke. "Prepare yourselves," he said. "Tomorrow we take the first step north." The men straightened.

By late afternoon, the Matamoros sun had sunk low, casting long shadows across the training facility. The Murder Team had showered, rearmed, and changed into dark fatigues. The crispness of their uniforms contrasted sharply with the dust and sweat of the training yard.

Now they stood assembled in a wide barracks hall that was thirty feet long, concrete floor and fluorescent lights flickering overhead. At the far end of the room, a portable projector hummed softly, casting pale light onto a white-painted wall.

The men formed three perfect rows with their backs straight, eyes forward, and their hands behind their backs. El Silencioso stood at the front, his expression unreadable, a fixed point around which every other man aligned himself.

Valdez entered last. He didn't say a word. He simply tapped the projector remote. The lights dimmed. Static crackled. Then the screen stabilized. Óscar Alvarez Vasquez appeared.. But even though the encrypted video feed was grainy, pixelated, and punctuated by digital noise, his presence swallowed the room whole. The men straightened further, shoulders tightening.

Óscar looked different now than he had days earlier. He looked older and more hollowed out by the rituals of grief and vengeance. His hair was damp, as though he had been pacing or thinking in the heat. His face was still. His voice, however, was razor-sharp. "Operatives," he began, his tone controlled enough to chill the air, "you stand before me because you are the best. Because you do not fear what others fear. Because you do not hesitate when hesitation means death." His eyes scanned the room through the camera, as though he could see each man personally. "You have read the brief. You know the mission. But you do not yet understand the weight of it." There was a slow and measured breath. "Carlos… my son… died inside a burning car in a foreign city." A ripple of tension moved through the men.

"His wife and child," Óscar continued softly, "were murdered beside him. They were innocents. They were family. My blood." His voice did not crack, but the edges of it felt sharpened by something far deeper than rage. "The man responsible lives in luxury. Surrounded by guards. Protected by corrupt officials. Worshipped by criminals who call him *boss*." A faint shadow passed across Óscar's eyes. "Vincent Castenllo Jr. believes distance protects him. He believes borders protect him. He believes *America* protects him." Óscar leaned closer to the camera.

"They do not." Silence flooded the room, thick and heavy.

"You will breach his home," he said. "You will eliminate him. You will leave his wife and children alive." Another beat. "You will record his death. I will see it." The weight of the order pressed down on every man present.

Óscar lowered his head slightly, not in weakness, but in reverence. "Understand this part well, you are not going to war." He raised his eyes again. "You are going to deliver judgment." The word struck the room like a hammer. Óscar straightened with a slow purposefulness. "And if you encounter obstacles," he said, "remove them. If you encounter resistance, silence it. If you are seen..." His voice darkened. "...you were never there."

Behind him, someone spoke faintly, perhaps a lieutenant ensuring the connection was stable. Óscar didn't break eye contact with the camera. When he spoke next, his voice was quiet, almost intimate. "Return with his blood on your hands..." A long pause. "...or don't return at all." No one breathed. Not even Valdez.

Finally, El Silencioso stepped forward, his shadow cutting across the dim glow of the projector. "Señor," he said, voice low and steady, "it will be done." Óscar studied him. Then he nodded once.

The video feed blinked, fuzzed, and cut to black. The projector hummed for a moment before falling silent. The room remained still, the echo of Óscar's words settling like dust over steel.

Then El Silencioso turned. "Prepare for departure." The barracks had never been so quiet. Silence clung to the walls like dust as the Murder Team packed their gear. Each man worked alone at the edge of his bunk; methodical, precise, no wasted motion. The only sounds were the soft clink of metal, the muted rip of Velcro, and the occasional low hum of fluorescent lights overhead.

A few wrote brief notes on scraps of folded paper. One man knelt and buried a tiny medal beneath the wooden floorboard, something religious, worn from years of being held. Another tucked a photo into the lining of his vest, only to remove it seconds later and burn it in a metal dish without a word. Attachments were liabilities. El Silencioso carried nothing sentimental.

He closed his duffel and stood at the far end of the room, watching the others with the stillness of a wolf at the mouth of a cave. When Valdez entered to distribute the final kits, the air tightened. "Line up," Valdez ordered. The men formed a single column with no hesitation. Valdez walked down the row, handing out sealed packets with burner phones, stacks of unmarked US currency, new identities, laminated route markers, coded phrasebooks for emergency communication, and micro SD cards with encrypted contingency files. Each operative accepted the packet with a quiet nod. When he reached El Silencioso, he paused. "You know the stakes," Valdez said. The Team Leader didn't blink. "I do." "Good." Valdez lowered his voice. "Because Óscar expects the impossible." The Team Leader zipped his packet shut. "Then he chose correctly." Valdez said nothing more.

Outside, behind the barracks, a steel barrel burned with a blue-tinted flame. The men gathered around it one by one, tossing in identification documents, personal items, old cell phones, small tokens of past lives. El Silencioso dropped in a single object. It was a strip of cloth soaked with dried blood; someone else's, not his. It curled, blackened, and vanished into flame. When the last item was gone, the Team Leader closed the barrel lid with a metallic clang. Their pasts were ash now, their futures were death.

Isaías Velasco's encrypted channel crackled over the comms station set up in the corner of the yard. A tech toggled switches, aligning frequencies. "Test phrase?" the tech asked. El Silencioso clicked the mic. "Snowfall on Bourbon." Isaías's filtered voice came through instantly. "Then the city waits for winter." The tech nodded. "Channel stable. New Orleans contact is green." The Murder Team moved toward the motor pool and toward their disappearance.

Team A stood by a concealed dock where a tarp-covered fishing boat waited. No lights. No flag. Only shadows and fuel. Team B gathered near two dusty border-bound trucks, each carrying crates labeled as agricultural supplies. The drivers were ex-military and said nothing. Team C assembled beside a third vehicle—an unremarkable freight truck destined for Texas backroads. Its engine already idled with a low, steady rumble. The Zetas commander performed a final walk-around. His expression was tight with pride and fear; pride in the men, fear of what they were truly capable of. "You leave in staggered intervals," he reminded them. "If one team is compromised…" "We merge," El Silencioso said. "We don't fail." The commander nodded once. "Good."

Valdez stepped forward next, hands behind his back, voice cold as steel. "You are not heroes," he said. "You are not martyrs." He looked each man in the eye. "You are ghosts. And ghosts leave nothing behind." A long silence. Then he nodded to the Team Leader. "Move."

Team A boarded the boat and faded into the misty river mouth. Team B's trucks rolled out through a rear service gate, swallowed by the early night. Team C eased onto the main road, its taillights dimmed to near-darkness. Each team vanished in a different direction, three shadows cutting through Mexico with deadly purpose.

The Team Leader boarded his transport last. He climbed into the back of the truck, face blank, movements fluid. He closed the door behind him with a dull thud. Valdez and the Zetas commander watched as the truck rolled forward, disappearing through the open gate and into the dusk. Only silence remained inside the Matamoros compound. A silence heavy with the promise of blood.

The north awaits.

Chapter 6

The Three Teams

Night fell over Matamoros like a cloak with thick, humid, and electric anticipation. The walled training facility, which just hours earlier had echoed with rifle fire and shouted commands, now stood in a state of practiced, suffocating silence.

The floodlights cut out all at once. A blackout protocol had begun with engines hushed and voices lowered. Every man on the compound moved like a shadow.

In the courtyard, three operatives shut off the last exterior generator. Darkness swallowed the facility, broken only by the faint glow of chemical lights taped to stair rails and door frames. The Murder Team moved through the corridors like they'd trained blind for years with no stumbles or noise.

At the compound's southern gate, **El Silencioso** stood with his duffel slung over one shoulder. His face carried no adrenaline or anticipation, just the flat, controlled readiness of a man who had spent his entire life walking into danger with the certainty he would walk out again.

The Zetas commander approached him quietly with no salute or handshake. Just a shared moment between predators. They exchanged a silent nod.

The commander's expression held pride laced with the grief of a man sending soldiers into the unknown.

Silencioso's expression held nothing.

Beyond the gate, the world waited in layered darkness. Behind him, the three teams gathered in their departure formations.

Team Alpha consisted of Six men. Faces painted matte black. Gear waterproofed and strapped tight.

Their panga boat sat concealed under a tarp on a modified trailer, the hull already greased for a silent slip into Gulf waters. The men kept their voices low, adjusting life vests, checking suppressed rifles, and securing night-vision rigs.

A mechanic whispered, "Engines whisper-quiet. Coast Guard won't hear a thing if the weather cooperates."

Alpha's breacher gave a thin, humorless smile. "It never cooperates."

Team Bravo also contained Six more men. They loaded into two convoy trucks painted as agricultural transports.

Under the tarps lay rifles, dry bags, tactical clothing, and a collapsible boat waiting for assembly in Brownsville.

Their driver tested the headlights, one flicker only before shutting them off again.

The tension among the men was sharp and metallic. They were heading into the most law-enforcement-heavy approach. They all knew it. One man crossed himself. Another spat onto the dirt. No one spoke.

Team Charlie had Six men as well. Hidden inside the gutted interior of a produce hauler.

Their route was the longest but least violent, unless luck turned, and luck always turned.

Two sat on crates repurposed as seats, faces blank as they checked each other's civilian disguises with caps, jackets, fake IDs.

One muttered, "I don't like pretending to be alive." Another replied, "Then stay dead." Even in the dark, their grim smiles didn't last more than a heartbeat.

Valdez stepped forward, clipboard in hand, eyes sharp.

"Teams," he said, addressing all three groups at once. "You know your routes. You know your windows.

You know your contingencies." He scanned the men. "No mistakes."

He turned to Silencioso. The two men held each other's gaze. "Updates every six hours," Valdez said.

Silencioso shook his head once. "Only if necessary."

Valdez didn't argue. A man like Silencioso didn't need monitoring. He needed space.

He stepped back. "Move."

Team Alpha peeled off first. Pushing the panga boat into motion under the cover of darkness, boots silent on gravel. Once they hit the rural road, a truck eased forward, headlights still off, towing the boat deeper into the night.

Team Bravo rolled out next with two trucks. Engines grumbling low with tarps fluttering in the breeze.

Team Charlie left last. Its produce truck lumbering forward in a slow, deceptively mundane glide, disappearing behind the southern wall with the sound of an exhale.

Hundreds of miles away, in a dimly lit office covered in maps and coded notes, **Óscar Alvarez Vasquez** sat behind a desk. He did not blink when the first encrypted message arrived on his phone. **ALFA EN RUTA** Alpha on route.

Then another. **BRAVO MOVIMIENTO** Bravo moving.

Then **SOMBRA INICIADO.** Shadow activated.

Óscar leaned back in his chair, jaw tightening as he stared at the glowing screen. His expression did not change from his cold, burning focus. He looked toward the photo shrine in the corner. "Que viajen con mi furia," he murmured. May they travel with my fury.

Another update pinged. Óscar didn't look at it. He already knew that **the storm had begun moving north.**

Moonlight glazed over **Lauro Villar Beach**, turning the surf into a sheet of silver-gray. The world was quiet here, broken only by the soft hiss of waves rolling up the sand and the low murmur of men preparing for a dangerous crossing.

Alpha stood ankle-deep in the water, steadying the **small panga boat** as it rocked against the tide. Their faces were smeared with charcoal, their gear wrapped in waterproof canvas. Every buckle, every strap, every screw had been taped or padded to prevent sound.

They'd been told this route was the "quiet one." Nothing about it felt quiet now. "El motor," one operative whispered.

The breacher crouched at the stern, checking the muffled outboard engine. It purred to life with a thin, whispering hum barely louder than the wind. Good. The Coast Guard wouldn't hear them. Not unless they were unlucky. And luck had already started to run thin.

Alpha leader walked the shoreline, boots sinking into the wet sand with soft thuds. He didn't say anything. He didn't need to. When he lifted two fingers, the men pushed the boat deeper. "Knees in," someone murmured.

The water rose from shins to thighs, cold and biting, until finally the boat floated freely. The men climbed aboard one by one, each movement controlled, rehearsed, and silent.

"Course set," the navigator whispered. The Team Leader nodded. His silhouette was a black statue against the horizon. "Go."

The boat glided off the beach and into the Gulf.

An Hour into the trip while the team was in Open Waters, The night swallowed them whole. Rio Grande lights faded into nothing. The coastline behind them disappeared. Ahead was only the blackness of oily waves, humid wind, and the metallic tang of salt.

The panga cut through the water with surgical smoothness, its engine just above idle to reduce heat signatures. The men sat motionless, rifles across their laps, night-vision goggles clipped to helmets but not yet lowered.

"Radar sweep incoming," the navigator whispered, watching a small detector blink amber.

Raul lifted a hand, and the engine operator immediately eased back to near silence. A hush fell over the boat.

For fifteen seconds, nothing moved but the waves.

Then the detector flashed green again. "Clear."

The engine returned to whisper-throttle, and the panga resumed its ghostlike glide.

Two Hours into the trip, a faint rumble trembled across the surface of the water.

The men looked up as the once-calm sky shifted. Clouds swelled, rolling across the moon like a bruise spreading under skin.

"Storm wasn't on the forecast," the navigator muttered. "Forecasts lie," the breacher replied.

Lightning flashed far off, illuminating a dark wall of churning clouds. Raul, the team leader, didn't react. "Push through," he ordered.

The rain came first like thin needles that pricked skin. Then the wind. Finally, the waves. The boat pitched violently.

One man grabbed the gunwale as the panga lurched sideways. Another cursed under his breath. "Chingado, hold tight!"

A rogue swell slammed the hull, sending spray across their faces. The engine sputtered. "Kill it!" the navigator hissed. "Kill it! NOW!" The operator snapped the switch. The motor died instantly. Silence. Followed by the roar of the storm.

The panga drifted, rising and falling like a cork tossed into the chaos. Lightning cracked again, revealing a shape on the horizon. It was a shadow at first. It appeared as a long, low, metal outline. "Cutter," the navigator whispered. "U.S. Coast Guard, heading perpendicular."

The men froze. No one breathed. The waves slammed harder. The rain became a curtain of needles. The cutter's silhouette passed through the lightning flashes. A massive hull compared to their tiny boat. The storm might hide them. Or drown them.

A violent swell struck the starboard side. One operative went overboard. "¡Hombre al agua!" someone yelled instinctively. Raul whipped around, scanning the dark water. However, the sea was already churning violently. The man was gone. Swallowed by black water and storm.

Raul simply lowered his chin. "Hold," he ordered.

The men gripped the boat with white-knuckled fists as the cutter's engine rumbled nearby, muffled by the wind. Seconds stretched like hours. Another lightning flash and the cutter veered away. It was gone.

However, the storm didn't relent. Water sloshed into the panga, waves battering the hull. The operator grabbed a bucket, scooping frantically. "Pump!" Raul barked. Two men began dumping water over the side with cold efficiency. Another strapped down the remaining gear.

The panga limped onward, battered and reduced. Five men now. One gone to the sea. But the Gulf had not broken them.

When the engine restarted, weak but alive, Raul gave a single nod. They continued north, riding the storm into the black.

The Rio Grande at night looked deceptively calm with dark water sliding between reeds, broken only by the occasional ripple from a drifting branch or distant splash. However, Team Bravo knew better. This river was a border of flesh, blood, and ghosts.

Six men crouched near the bank, hidden beneath mesquite trees and thorn brush. Their faces were streaked with mud, their weapons were wrapped to muffle sound.

A coyote guide, a thin man with jittery eyes, stood waist-deep in the water, motioning frantically.

"¡Rápido! Antes de que venga la patrulla!" *Hurry! Before the patrol comes!*

Bravo moved in silence, filing down the embankment. The first operative slipped into the river, water rising to his chest. The others followed.

Miguel, the Bravo leader, watched from the rear until the last man was in, then slid into the cold current himself, boots sinking into mud.

The moon was hidden behind clouds. Good for infiltration, but terrible for visibility.

Halfway across, a faint hum vibrated through the air. The coyote froze. The operatives froze. One man whispered, "Drone."

Above the tree line, a tiny blinking white light bobbed in a slow and predatory orbit.

The coyote dropped lower in the water until only his eyes were visible. Bravo followed suit. The men sank down, weapons half-submerged, lungs burning as they waited. The drone drifted closer, buzzing like an angry insect. No one breathed.

Rain from the Gulf storm began to sprinkle down, hissing against the water's surface, masking sound, but also distorting sightlines.

The drone hovered… hovered… hovered… Then lurched away, drifting upriver.

The coyote released a shaky breath. "Listo. Síganme." Bravo reached the Texas side within minutes. The coyote scrambled up the muddy embankment and pointed toward a cluster of abandoned storage buildings. "Your truck is waiting there. But…" A gun cocked. The coyote froze.

Miguel stood waist-deep in the river, rifle raised. "You said no patrols," he murmured. "I… I didn't know about the drone, amigo…"

Bravo leader didn't blink. But he lowered his rifle… Barely.

"Go." The coyote vanished into the brush, terrified.

Bravo finished crossing the river and made their way to the hidden structure. A rusted metal door opened into a makeshift garage where a battered white van sat with its engine idling.

The driver, a Gulf-affiliated smuggler, nodded once and said nothing. The men piled into the van without conversation. "Brownsville safehouse?" one operative whispered. Miguel nodded. "Now."

The van pulled into a nondescript warehouse with faded paint and overgrown weeds. Inside, a tarp-covered boat sat waiting: long, low-profile, with a flat hull designed for speed and stealth along the **Intracoastal Waterway**.

The smuggler peeled away the tarp in silence. "She'll get you there," he muttered. "If the Marines aren't running heavy patrol."

Miguel's stare made the man swallow hard. "We launch," the Leader said. "But the Marine Patrol…" "We launch." The man nodded quickly and stepped back.

Bravo loaded their gear into the boat with practiced speed. Engines checked. Fuel levels corrected. Weapons secured.

Within minutes, they pushed off into the narrow canal leading toward the Waterway.

The engine purred beneath them as the boat skimmed along the dark waterway around midnight. Tall marsh grasses swayed on either side, forming black silhouettes against the moonlit sky.

Everything felt too quiet. One operative whispered, "Spotlight sweep usually happens around…" A cone of white light exploded across the water. "DOWN!" someone hissed.

The men crouched instantly, weapons ready. A patrol boat rounded a bend; U.S. Marine Patrol, its spotlight slicing through the darkness like a blade.

Miguel gestured sharply for his team to *hold their fire and hold their position.* The pilot eased off the throttle, letting the boat drift into a patch of thick reeds.

The patrol boat slowed. The spotlight swept closer and closer. A drop of sweat rolled down one operative's cheek. The patrol boat's engine growled, adjusting direction.

The spotlight began to turn directly toward them when, suddenly, a splash echoed behind them.

The youngest operative flinched. His rifle snapped upward. "NO…" the Team Leader hissed, but too late. The operative fired. **CRACK.**

The shot pierced the night, echoing across the water. Silence, then the patrol boat erupted with light and noise. "Gunfire! Gunfire! Port side!" a voice shouted through a megaphone. "Show your hands!"

"Move!" Miguel barked. Bravo's pilot slammed the throttle forward. The boat lurched violently, carving a sharp turn around the reeds as bullets tore into the water.

Two operatives returned fire, short bursts meant to suppress rather than kill. A round struck one of the men in the shoulder.

He staggered and then fell. Another grabbed him by the vest and pulled him down into the hull. The patrol boat's spotlight tracked them relentlessly. "Cut through the tributaries!" Miguel shouted. "Now!"

The pilot veered sharply into a narrow marsh channel, branches scraping the hull as the boat disappeared into the swampy maze. Gunfire echoed behind them. Screams and static on the patrol radios. Then… Silence again.

Broken only by the ragged breathing of the men and the hum of the engine.

Two men were dead and one was wounded. Only four remaining.

Miguel sat in the bow, soaked, unflinching, expression carved from iron. He turned to his wounded man, the bullet had torn through muscle, blood soaking the fabric. "You can still move?" he asked.

The man nodded, jaw clenched in pain. "Then you continue," he said. "We go north."

The boat disappeared deeper into the marsh, swallowed by reeds and darkness. The mission did not pause for casualties.

The produce truck shuddered as it rolled along a desolate stretch of rural Texas highway, headlights dimmed to half-strength. Inside the cargo bay, **Team Charlie** sat in near-total darkness, the only illumination coming from thin slivers of moonlight slipping through the ventilation seams.

The air was hot, stale, and tinged with citrus from discarded crates that had once hidden them better than any forged document.

Six men. Six killers. Packed in silence among crates and duffel bags.

The engine grumbled steadily. The wheels hummed over cracked asphalt. Every bump in the road felt like a warning.

The driver, a Gulf-affiliated smuggler with a nervous twitch. kept one hand on the wheel and the other tapping anxiously against his thigh.

"Checkpoint ahead," he whispered into the cabin mic. "Could be Border Patrol. Could be DPS. Could be nothing."

Inside the cargo box, the men tensed. Silencioso sat near the rear door, his back against the metal wall. He closed his eyes briefly, not to rest, but to listen. He could hear everything. The driver's breathing, the tremor in the road, and the faint hum of fluorescent lights ahead.

"Stay still," he murmured. The command rippled through the men like a current.

Approaching the Checkpoint, the truck slowed. The hum of overhead lamps grew louder. The driver cursed under his breath. "Fuck. It's DPS. They're pulling people over." Inside the truck, no one reacted outwardly. However, tension thickened, turning the hot air nearly suffocating.

Boots crunched on gravel outside. Voices murmured in English, Texan accents, low and authoritative. A flashlight beam swept across the road, bouncing off the truck's rear doors.

The driver forced a casual smile as a state trooper approached the window. "Evening, sir," the trooper drawled. "Evening," the driver replied, voice strained but steady. "Where are you headed?" "Houston. Produce run." "What's in the back?" "Oranges. Some avocado crates. All sealed."

The trooper chewed gum thoughtfully. "Mind if I take a look?" Inside the cargo bay, one operative's grip tightened on his suppressed Glock. Another silently shifted his weight, preparing to spring.

Silencioso didn't move. Didn't open his eyes. He simply whispered, barely audible, "Not unless he opens the door."

Outside, the driver stammered, "Well… uh… it's sealed. And if I break it, the…" The trooper raised a hand. "Relax. Just need the manifest."

The driver handed over a crumpled form, one of the dozens of fake manifests Isaías had funneled through his network.

The trooper scanned it under his flashlight. Seconds dragged like hours. Then… A radio crackled on the trooper's vest. "Unit 5, shift change. Wrap it up." The trooper shrugged. "Lucky night."

He slapped the truck twice. "Get moving." The driver exhaled loudly the moment he pulled away. Inside the truck, Silencioso finally opened his eyes. "We continue," he said.

Hours later, the truck merged onto a busier highway. The atmosphere changed instantly. More cars. More lights. More opportunities for something to go wrong. And something did.

At first, it seemed like a normal slowdown, traffic condensing into a single lane. But then the driver hissed through the mic, "Construction…? No. That's not construction." Up ahead: were orange cones and a long line of cars. Flashlights waved vehicles into separate lanes. And the unmistakable letters on a roadside van, **ICE-** Immigration and Customs Enforcement. The men stiffened.

The driver gripped the wheel hard enough for his knuckles to turn white. "Fuck me…" he whispered. "It's a random pull. They'll want to open the back."

Inside the cargo bay, one operative looked to Silencioso, "What now?"

Silencioso pressed a finger to his lips. "Wait." The truck inched forward. One car pulled off the road. Another waved through. The line crept closer.

The men braced themselves. Hands hovered near weapons. Every breath was measured.

At the front of the line, an ICE officer stepped into view, flagging the truck with a flashlight. "Pull to the left lane!" The driver swallowed. "Left lane. That's… that's inspection." He flicked the indicator. Inside the truck, the men prepared.

But just before the truck reached the checkpoint, A sedan two cars ahead lurched sideways, its bumper skidding into the opposite lane. Tires screamed. The vehicle spun out, clipping an officer's knee.

Chaos erupted. Officers rushed toward the scene. Flashlights scattered. One ICE agent waved the remaining vehicles forward. "GO! GO! CLEAR IT OUT!" The driver didn't hesitate.

He drove straight through the checkpoint with no inspection, no questions, and no eyes on the cargo doors.

Only once they were miles past the scene did he finally whisper into the mic, "I swear to God… someone up there likes you guys." Inside the truck, none of the men smiled. Least of all Silencioso. "Luck isn't real," he said quietly. "Only timing."

He looked at the men around him. "Gear up. We're close."

The truck rumbled on toward Louisiana, cutting through the Texas night like a blade through cloth.

A place of airport motels, strip malls, sleepy neighborhoods, and forgotten industrial streets where no one asked questions so long as the noise stayed low.

It was barely dawn in Kenner, Louisiana when **Team Charlie's produce truck** rolled into the warehouse district, brake lights flaring in the dim gray morning.

The truck eased into a narrow alley, pulling behind a row of dumpsters beside a rust-red warehouse with a single faded number painted above the door, **1132.** The local safehouse.

The engine cut. For a moment, the only sound was the cooling metal ticking in the silence.

Then, the rear latch lifted. Slowly and quietly, the men inside blinked against the humid morning light.

The warehouse beyond them was cavernous and dim. Dust floated in thick beams of sunlight that pierced through high, broken windows. Stacks of empty pallets formed jagged silhouettes.

At the far end, leaning over a metal folding table cluttered with maps, cash bundles, and burner phones, stood **Isaías Velasco**.

He looked worse than before with his eyes hollow from no sleep, shirt damp with sweat, hands trembling slightly as he checked receipts, coded notes, and routes for the hundredth time.

He looked up. When he saw the truck unloading, he froze. Charlie stepped down one by one, moving like specters through the dim warehouse.

Six had left Mexico and all six walked into Kenner. Isaías exhaled with palpable relief.

Until a streak of water dripped from a man's pant leg, pooling beneath him. One of the operatives stepped into the light. He was soaked. Saltwater crusted around his boots. His shirt clung damp to his torso.

He was not from Team Charlie.

Isaías stiffened. He recognized the markings on the fatigues—Team Alpha.

The man's hollow stare confirmed it, **Alpha had made landfall. At least part of it.**

The surviving operative walked past Isaías without a word, leaving wet footprints across the concrete. Isaías swallowed, dread crawling up his spine.

Then a noise echoed through the warehouse. A metallic clank. A heavy door opening. He turned sharply.

The personnel door on the opposite wall creaked open, and inside stepped **Team Bravo, four of them at least**.

One wounded, bloodied through the shoulder bandage. Two grim-faced. One limping.

Their eyes were sunken and wild, like they had dragged death behind them all the way from the Intracoastal Waterway.

Isaías's throat tightened. Six men had left Mexico, and four had arrived. He didn't ask what happened. Their silence told him enough.

The surviving Alpha operative gave a curt nod toward Bravo, an acknowledgment between men who had walked through fire in different ways.

Team Bravo nodded back.

Not in a friendly or emotional way. It was with recognition, respect, and survival.

And then…

The air seemed to thicken.

A presence stepped into the warehouse from behind the wounded Bravo operative.

El Silencioso entered the light. His face was unreadable. He scanned the warehouse, taking stock of the assembled survivors. His eyes flicked over Alpha's lone operative, then over Bravo's wounded man, then to all of Team Charlie.

He nodded once.

"This is who we are now," he said quietly. His voice echoed in the cavernous space. "Three teams began the journey. We continue as one."

The men stood straighter. What remained of them, at least. He stepped forward, placing his duffel on the metal table. "Gear check. Medical check. Eat if you can. Rest for one hour."

His gaze sharpened, cutting through the warehouse like a blade. "Then we move on the city."

Isaías tried to speak some mixture of respect and terror, but his voice stuck in his throat. He simply nodded and stepped aside as the killers moved past him. Something terrible had arrived in Louisiana. A storm made of flesh and silence.

As the Murder Team spread through the warehouse, checking weapons, unpacking gear, treating wounds, and stripping off the grime of their journey, Isaías understood the truth, **New Orleans would never be the same.**

And somewhere far away, in a dark room, Óscar Alvarez Vasquez's phone buzzed. A single message blinked across the screen, **LOS TRES EQUIPOS YA ESTÁN EN LOUISIANA.** *The three teams are now in Louisiana.*

Óscar closed his eyes, and he smiled.

Chapter 7

Arriving in New Orleans

The safehouse on 1132 looked abandoned from the outside, rust eaten into the gutters, weeds choking the narrow walkway, curtains drawn tight over dusty windows. The kind of place people walked past without even realizing it existed.

Inside, it felt like a battlefield dressing station. Rain hammered the warehouse roof. The early morning Louisiana storm rolled across the sky, thunder rattling the metal beams overhead. Every crack of lightning briefly illuminated the interior. Silhouettes moving like ghosts, drying weapons, repacking gear, and checking wounds. They were all survivors. They were all less than what they had been yesterday.

Alpha had one man left. Bravo had four left, one of which was bleeding heavily. Charlie had all six, but they were shaken. Eleven killers remained in total.

Their gear lay spread across the concrete. Wet duffels, taped rifles, medical kits stained with river mud, maps curling at the corners from humidity. A faint metallic smell filled the space. It was the smell of blood mixing with saltwater and gun oil.

On a makeshift table under a hanging bulb, the wounded operative from Team Bravo lay on his stomach. One of his teammates pressed a towel against the wound while another melted the tip of a knife over a small butane torch. The injured man gritted his teeth as they worked. "Hold still," the medic said. "Fuck you," the wounded man growled back, voice hoarse. He didn't mean it. Pain made everyone honest.

The last surviving man from Alpa paced near the far corner, soaked fatigues still dripping on the concrete. His face was hollowed out, eyes red-rimmed from seawater and exhaustion. When a thunderclap shook the roof, he flinched. Not from fear… From memory. The memory of the man swept off the boat.

Team Charlie, meanwhile, moved like an unspoken unit with quiet and discipline. They unloaded ammunition crates, set up a temporary comms station by the wall, and spread a plastic sheet for drying their gear. They didn't say much. This wasn't the time for anything but action.

In the center of it all stood **El Silencioso**, unmoving except for the slow, measured motions of checking his weapons. He fieldstripped his rifle with the smooth familiarity of someone who no longer needed his eyes to do it. Each piece was wiped, inspected, and reassembled.

Every click of metal sounded like inevitability. Isaías Velasco hovered at the edge of the room, out of his depth, feeling the weight of these men like gravity. These weren't cartel soldiers. These weren't hitmen. They were predators that had evolved beyond humanity. He swallowed hard and tried not to show how overwhelmed he was.

Silencioso finally looked up. He counted the men. Not in the frantic way of someone looking for missing numbers, but in the cold, clinical way of someone confirming expected casualties. Eleven men. That was what he had left. He nodded once. There was no emotion. No comment.

Then he turned to the wounded operative. "How deep?" he asked. The medic answered. "Through the shoulder. He'll live." "Mobility?" "Limited." Silencioso held the medic's stare. "He fights?" The medic hesitated only for a breath. "He fights." Silencioso nodded. "Good."

He stepped toward the table where maps were laid out. Rain hammered harder now, leaking through a crack in the ceiling and dripping into a rusted bucket. One Charlie spoke up. "Boss," he said quietly, "we lost half our people crossing." Silencioso didn't turn. "Yes." "That wasn't supposed to happen." Silencioso paused. The storm outside groaned, wind rattling the metal siding. He finally looked at the man who spoke. "What happened," Silencioso said calmly, "is that we survived." The man swallowed and nodded.

Another operative leaned forward, anger simmering. "That rookie fucked us. Fired too early. Got two of our brothers killed." The room shifted. Several heads turned. Blame was dangerous. Blame made men reckless. Silencioso stepped closer. He spoke softly. "Speak his name." The man faltered. "What?" "Speak. His. Name." Silence. Because no one remembered the rookie's real name. And that was the point. Silencioso's voice cut through the storm. "He died on the river. That is all. What matters now is what breathes in this room." His gaze swept across them. "What matters now," he said, "is the mission." Silencioso nodded once, slow and controlled. "Dry your weapons. Change your gear. Eat if you can. One hour." He looked toward the storm-soaked exit. "Then we begin assembling the city routes."

Isaías felt the air shift around them, like the pressure drop before a hurricane makes landfall. Eleven killers were no longer three teams. They were one. And New Orleans would feel Isaías Velasco, who was known locally as *El Contador*, listened to the storm pound against the warehouse roof while Silencioso and the survivors worked. Every roll of thunder made the metal beams tremble. Every flash of lightning revealed something he wished he hadn't seen.

Blood on the floor, mud smeared across the concrete, and weapons drying in organized piles. Men moved with the quiet fatalism of soldiers who knew too well what waited ahead. He had prepared for this moment. He hadn't prepared for these men.

He checked the safehouse door again, for the third time in ten minutes, just in case anyone had followed him. He triple-locked it, slid the deadbolt, pressed his shoulder into the frame. Secure. Then a voice behind him said, "You're jumpy." Isaías spun.

A tall, sharp-faced man leaned against a stack of crates near the comms table. He wore jeans, a windbreaker, and a Saints cap pulled low over his brow. Not a soldier. Not one of the Mexican teams. He was a local. One of *his* locals. "Martín…" Isaías exhaled. "Don't sneak up on me like that, cabrón." Martín didn't smile. Didn't apologize. "Storm's loud," he said. "You should hear them from the parking lot. Sound carries."

Isaías shook off the nerves and stepped closer, lowering his voice. "You brought what I asked for?" Martín nodded and nudged a black duffel with his foot. "Cash, two more burners, and the last set of clean plates. But listen," he leaned in, eyes narrowing, "I need to know what's going on." Isaías stiffened. "You don't." "I do," Martín insisted. "These guys, you didn't tell me they were *military*. You didn't tell me half of them would show up bleeding. You didn't tell me…" "Martín." Isaías raised a hand, tone firmer. "You don't want to know." Martín's jaw tightened. "You think I'm scared?" he asked quietly. "No," Isaías said. "I think you're smart."

Martín flicked his eyes across the room. Team Charlie stripped their rifles. Two of Bravo packed medical gauze into a wounded man's shoulder. The survivor from Alpha sat with his head down, staring at nothing. And then there was Silencioso. He stood at the map table, hunched over a spread of street diagrams and satellite photos, marking routes with a black pen. His calm was unnatural. It was not exhaustion, nor discipline. Something colder. Something carved into him long before this mission.

Martín swallowed. "Who is that?" Isaías didn't look at him. He didn't dare. "The man in charge," he said softly. "That one? Not the older guy from Matamoros? Not the commander?" "No," Isaías said. "*Him.*" Martín watched Silencioso for several seconds. "Something's wrong with him," Martín whispered. Isaías didn't deny it. "He's not like the others." Again, Isaías didn't deny it.

Martín exhaled slowly. "So what do I do?" "You do your job," Isaías said. "You stay quiet. You stay useful. And you don't get close to him." Martín crossed his arms. "I'm your second-in-command. If these men are operating in *my* city, I need to know what we're supporting." "You don't support them," Isaías corrected. "You facilitate them. There's a difference." Martín gave him a long, uneasy look. "You're scared," he said. Isaías didn't respond. Not because it wasn't true, but because it *was*.

The warehouse door rattled in the rising storm winds. A crack of thunder shook dust from the rafters. Silencioso finally turned from the table. His eyes swept across the warehouse, landing on Isaías and Martín like a hunter noticing a rustle in the grass. Martín straightened instinctively. Silencioso approached, boots silent on concrete. His expression didn't change. It never did.

He stopped in front of them. "Name?" Silencioso asked Martín. Martín swallowed. "Martín Reyes, sir." "Role?" "Second-in-command to Isa…" "I didn't ask whose second-in-command," Silencioso said. Martín froze, words caught in his throat.

Isaías stepped in quickly. "Local liaison. Vehicles, safehouses, cash, and logistical…" Silencioso raised a hand. Isaías fell silent immediately. The Team Leader studied Martín with cold, assessing eyes, as if measuring whether he was worth keeping alive. "You follow orders," Silencioso said. A statement, not a question. Martín nodded quickly. "Yes, sir." "You interfere," Silencioso added, "you die." The words were delivered with total neutrality. It wasn't a threat, just *policy*. Martín paled. "Understood." Silencioso nodded once, turned away, and returned to the maps.

Martín let out a shaky breath he didn't realize he'd been holding. "Jesús…" he whispered. "What have you brought into my city?" Isaías rubbed a hand over his face. "Death," he said quietly. "If we're lucky."

Another crash of thunder shook the walls. Silencioso didn't react to the storm. He didn't react to the fear he left behind. He just kept working. Drawing the lines that would cut New Orleans open. And the tension in the room thickened… because everyone understood. **This man wasn't here to survive the mission. He was here to complete it.**

The storm outside had settled into a steady, relentless drumbeat against the warehouse roof, constant and heavy, almost suffocating. Inside, the atmosphere was just as thick. The survivors had gathered around the central table where maps, sketches, burner phones, and weapon parts littered every inch of surface. A single lantern hung from a steel beam above, casting hard shadows across their faces. It felt like a war council, a broken one.

Raul, from Alpha Team, still soaked from the Gulf, leaned over the table and slammed a fist against the plywood. "He panicked," he growled. "On the waterway. Fired before the order. That stupidity cost us two men." A man from Bravo snapped back, "Don't start, cabrón. You weren't there when the patrol drifted on us. The night was killing us already. The kid thought…" "He didn't think," Raul survivor barked. "That's the problem."

The wounded operative, bandage soaked through, glared. "Your squad isn't exactly doing fine either. How many did you bring home? Oh, that's right…just **you**." The insult hit the air like a slap. Several men shifted, hands inching toward weapons not fully drawing, but ready.

Thunder rumbled overhead. The men from Charlie Team watched silently, tension tightening their shoulders. Isaías hovered by the wall, eyes wide, unsure whether to intervene. Martín whispered under his breath, "Stay out of it. They'll eat you alive."

The shouting rose. "You think because you survived the storm…" "You think because you lost men…" "You think the kid deserved…" "He's dead because of you…" "**ENOUGH!**" The word wasn't shouted. It didn't need to be. It came from **El Silencioso**. Everything stopped.

The Team Leader stepped forward, slow and deliberate, like a predator deciding which throat to close its teeth around. He set both hands on the table and looked from one man to the next, expression flat, eyes like dead coals. "Say his name," Silencioso said softly. No one spoke. "Say. His. Name." The men exchanged uneasy glances. Raul looked away. The wounded man from Bravo swallowed. The others went still. No one knew the rookie's name. No one had bothered to memorize it.

Silencioso nodded once, the faintest ghost of contempt in his eyes. "That," he said, "is why you do not argue." He reached for his belt, drew his **Ka-Bar knife**, and without warning… **THUNK.** He drove the blade into the table. The steel was buried deep into plywood, and the maps beneath it. Every nerve in the room tightened. Silencioso leaned in slightly. "You argue," he said quietly, "because you believe the mission cares about your grief." Lightning flashed through the high warehouse windows, illuminating his face in stark white. "It doesn't." There was complete, crushing silence.

He continued, his voice steady as ice. "You believe your dead men died badly." A beat. "They died **doing their job**." His eyes tracked each survivor with surgical precision. "There are eleven of you now who live. Eleven who can still complete what you came here to do." He paused. "And eleven is more than enough."

The men breathed deeper and slower, some in shame, some in anger, all in recognition of the truth they had been avoiding. Silencioso let the silence stretch before he spoke again. "There will be no more arguments," he said. "No more blame. No more voices raised unless I ask for them." He straightened. "These maps," he continued, tapping the knife hilt with his knuckle, "are all that matter. This plan is all that matters. New Orleans is all that matters."

He pulled the knife from the table, wiped the blade on his sleeve, and sheathed it calmly. "In this house," he said, "there is only the mission." He stepped back, giving them space. "Now get ready," Silencioso ordered. "We reorganize." The men nodded slowly at first, then with grim acceptance. Arguments died. Egos as well. Only purpose remained.

Isaías let out a shaky breath. Martín whispered, "Madre de Dios…" Even the thunder outside felt quieter. Because inside the warehouse, something had shifted. Silencioso wasn't just their commander now. He was their gravity. And the mission was about to tighten around all of them.

The storm outside had weakened to a steady patter, but inside the warehouse, the atmosphere had sharpened into something harder. The Murder Team gathered around the table again, but this time no one argued. No one glared, not even breathed louder than necessary. Silencioso stood at the head of the table, maps spread before him, knives and markers laid out like surgical tools. He drew a line across the Garden District. Then another across the Lower Garden District. Then three small X's at several entry points. The men leaned in. "This is the city," Silencioso said. He pointed to the leftmost map of river routes, marinas, and levee access points.

Next, Silencioso tapped a point near Tremé. "Checkpoint mapping, Patrol cycles, and Interdiction grid. Bravo knowledge." The wounded man from Team Bravo lifted his chin, jaw tightening. "I can move," he said. "You will not breach," Silencioso replied. The man stiffened. "I can…" "You will not breach," Silencioso repeated, firmer this time. "Your arm is compromised. But your eyes are not." He slid a small, laminated card across the table. "Spotter duty." The man swallowed hard. It wasn't disappointment, but relief. Survival was a thin thread, and Silencioso had just tied his to it.

Then Silencioso tapped the third map of street routes, side alleys, railroad spurs, and warehouse cut-throughs. "Team Charlie," he said. "You've run this city on paper. Now you run it in reality." One of the men nodded. "We'll lead the ground movement." "No," Silencioso corrected. "You will clear obstacles. You will set secondary exits. You will control the street." He drew a circle around the Garden District mansion. "I will lead." No one questioned it.

He pointed to Martín next, who straightened instinctively. "Vehicles," Silencioso said. "You assemble two. One for extraction and one for emergencies." Martín nodded quickly. "Yes, sir." "You will not enter the Garden District." "I understand." "You will not come within half a mile of the target." Martín swallowed. "Understood."

Silencioso finally looked to Isaías Velasco. "Phones," he said. "Cash. Burn bags. Fallback routes. You provide all of it. Quietly." Isaías nodded. "And you stay alive," Silencioso added. Isaías blinked. "Why… me specifically?" "Because someone must speak for us if things go wrong," Silencioso said. "Someone the Jefe trusts." Isaías felt the weight of that settle on his shoulders. Then Silencioso stepped back, scanning the table. "Eleven men," he said. "No more teams, no more divisions."

He lifted the knife he'd slammed into the table earlier and dragged the tip across the printed maps, joining them in a single line. "One strike force," he said. No one argued.

One of the Charlie operatives spoke softly. "And if one of us falls?" Silencioso didn't hesitate. "The next man steps forward." "And if more fall?" "Then we continue." "And if it is only you?" someone asked. Silencioso looked up. "I will not fall." It was simply the truth spoken aloud. He replaced the knife on the table.

"Gear check in ten," he said. "Route walk-through in twenty. Sleep if you can. Move if you cannot." He paused, eyes sweeping across his killers. "Tomorrow," he said quietly. *"We hunt."*

The storm outside gave a low rumble, as if answering him. The men dispersed, cleaning weapons, repacking ammunition, stitching gear, checking radios, swallowing down whatever fear or hunger or pain remained. They moved like a single creature now.

Isaías watched them, a sense of dread blooming in his chest. Not fear of them, fear of what they would become inside his city. And as Silencioso walked past him, Isaías heard a whisper he wasn't meant to hear… "Judgment comes with the morning." The warehouse lights flickered. As eleven ghosts sharpened their blades.

Chapter 8

Acquiring the Arsenal

The storm had eased overnight, leaving a heavy stillness over the Kenner warehouse. Inside, the air smelled of gun oil, damp concrete, and the faint citrus scent lingering from the discarded produce crates. Pale morning light crept through the high windows, slicing the gloom into long diagonal beams.

El Silencioso stood alone at the folding table in the center of the space, studying the hand-drawn maps and mission diagrams spread before him. His posture was calm and balanced like a predator waiting for its heartbeat to slow before a kill. Around him, the eleven men of the Murder Team moved through the warehouse in near silence, adjusting straps, drying boots, sharpening blades.

Their presence made the building feel too small, like the walls themselves were holding their breath.

Isaías Velasco approached from the side, holding a clipboard and a small black phone. He cleared his throat with the kind of caution reserved for approaching a sleeping wolf.

"Señor… the items you requested." He offered a sheet of paper. Silencioso didn't take it at first. He just looked at Isaías long enough that the younger man felt sweat prick under his collar.

Finally, Silencioso reached out and lifted the page. It wasn't a list for an arsenal. On the list were suppressed pistols, .300 Blackout rifles, Shotguns with breacher muzzles, Thermal scopes, Two disposable burner laptops, Three types of body armor, Seven sets of counterfeit license plates, Ten prepaid phones, A bag of untraceable cash, And a note scribbled at the bottom *Explosives optional. Your call.*

Silencioso read without expression. "Can you get all this?" he asked. Isaías swallowed. "Most. Some require… persuading."

Silencioso raised his eyes. "Persuade them." It was a simple order, but also a dangerous one.

Isaías nodded quickly. "There are people who can move pieces for us. Straw buyers. Street contacts. A warehouse supplier on the riverfront."

Silencioso folded the list. "I will choose the men who accompany you."

Isaías hesitated. "I thought… I assumed I would go alone. Keep things small." Silencioso shook his head once. "You are not alone," he said. "Not in this city. Men die alone."

Isaías looked away, throat tightening. The truth in that was too close and too raw.

Silencioso stepped around the table, scanning the warehouse. Some men were cleaning rifles. Team Brave's wounded man tested his arm movement with quiet grunts. Raul sat on an overturned crate, head down, muttering something to himself in tired Spanish.

Silencioso called out, "Three with me. Two with Velasco." Heads lifted immediately. He pointed, "Toño. Ruiz. Shadow."

Three men stepped forward, one from each team. A cross-section of the survivors. "You go with him," Silencioso said, nodding toward Isaías. The men didn't question it.

Silencioso turned back to the map table and tapped the corner of a route marked in red. "Buy only what we need," he said. "Nothing extra. Nothing flashy."

Isaías nodded. "Understood." "And Velasco…" Isaías paused mid-step.

Silencioso's eyes locked onto his, cold and sharp as glass. "Anyone who touches my men…" A beat. "…or lies about price, quantity, or quality…"

He didn't finish. He didn't need to. Isaías felt the rest in the weight of the silence, *They die.*

Silencioso returned to the maps as though nothing had been said. Thunder rumbled distantly over New Orleans.

Isaías Velasco, clutching the shopping list like it was a death warrant, stepped toward the exit with three killers at his back, knowing he was about to drag New Orleans into its darkest hour.

The Uptown neighborhood was still waking up when Isaías Velasco turned onto a narrow residential street lined with old live oaks. Their branches twisted above the cracked asphalt, forming a canopy that trapped the damp Louisiana air beneath it. Porch lights flickered. A garbage truck rumbled two blocks away. Somewhere, a dog barked halfheartedly.

The four men stepping out of the white SUV did not belong in this world. Isaías walked ahead, trying his best to look like any other early-morning hustler on a quiet street. Behind him came the three operatives. There was **Toño,** scarred knuckles, quiet eyes, deceptively calm. Then **Ruiz,** thick shoulders, Marine-like posture, and hands always near his belt. Finally **Shadow brought up the rear.** He was the quietest of all, a man who moved like air bending around him.

Their presence turned the block into something colder. Something watchful.

The house they approached was a sagging shotgun double painted a sickly shade of green. The porch light buzzed weakly. A cracked Saints flag hung limply from the railing.

Isaías knocked three times. A slit opened behind the peephole. A voice rasped, "Yeah?"

"It's Velasco," Isaías said. There was a pause. Then a lock clicked and the door swung open.

Slim stood in the doorway. He was tall, rail-thin, wearing a tank top and jogging pants, with a cigarette stuck to his bottom lip. His arms were a roadmap of tattoos, and his eyes were sharp despite the early hour.

"Damn," Slim said, exhaling a stream of smoke. "You ain't never call this early unless somebody's dead or you about to ruin my day." He leaned out, peering past Isaías. "That them?"

Isaías nodded. "They're with me."

Slim looked the operatives over with caution, not bravado. He had enough street sense to recognize danger when it stepped onto his porch.

"Fine," Slim said, stepping back. "But no guns out. My neighbors are nosy as hell."

Shadow brushed past him without a word. Toño and Ruiz followed, eyes scanning every corner.

Slim watched them enter and muttered, "Lord have mercy… I knew you were bringing hitters, but these ain't hitters. These some kinda… exorcists or something."

Inside, the shotgun house opened into a cramped living room stacked with crates of shoe boxes, electronics boxes, and gym bags. Not tidy, but not sloppy either.

Slim flicked ash into a beer bottle. "Alright, baby. Whatchu need this time?"

Isaías unfolded the list. Slim read it once. Then again. Then he whistled.

"You ain't askin' for pistols and dope money," he said. "You askin' for real hardware. Thermal scopes? Plates? *Two* sets of clean rides? Velasco, my man… who you about to go to war with?" Isaías kept his face neutral. "The price?"

Slim dragged on his cigarette, thinking. "To get all this? I gotta call three people. Maybe four. Straw buyers I trust. One of 'em owes me anyway. But these boys…" he jerked a thumb toward the operatives "…they better behave. Nobody spooks my network."

Ruiz stepped forward a half pace. "No one will spook your network," he said calmly. "Unless your people make that mistake first."

Slim froze. The temperature in the room seemed to drop two degrees. "…Right," Slim said quietly. "Good to know."

He stubbed out the cigarette and reached for his phone. "Toño," he called over his shoulder, "come check the goods." Slim opened a hall closet. Inside were two duffel bags. Toño knelt, unzipped both, and inspected:

Boxes of .300 BLK ammunition Two suppressor-ready Glocks, Gloves, Balaclavas, A stack of cash envelopes, Vehicle titles

He nodded once. "Quality." "Good," Slim said. "Because I ain't dying for no cheap shit."

Isaías stepped closer. "You can get the rest?" Slim tapped his phone screen. "Two hours. Maybe less. But I need half the cash up front. You know how it works."

Toño handed him a brick of rubber-banded hundreds. Slim blinked. "Goddamn… you came prepared."

He looked again at the three operatives, how still they were, how quietly they breathed.

"You boys cops?" Slim asked. Shadow turned his head slowly. "No," he said.

The way he said it made Slim look at Isaías with wide eyes. "...Right," Slim said. "Didn't think so."

A moment passed. Slim's phone buzzed. He glanced at the screen. "Aight," he said. "Straw buyer on Claiborne is awake. Dude owes me a favor. He says meet him near the gate of the gun store in thirty minutes. Don't go inside, he'll bring it out."

Ruiz lifted an eyebrow. "Trustworthy?" "As trustworthy as somebody who sells guns for cash out his baby mama's car."

Shadow stepped forward, silent as a ghost. "What's his name?" the operative asked softly.

Slim licked his lips. "Kendall." Shadow nodded once. "He lives?" Slim blinked. "Does he... uh... does he need to *not* live?"

Isaías jumped in fast. "Shadow's asking if he's stable. Reliable. Someone who won't panic." Slim let out a relieved laugh. "Damn, y'all gotta say that right. Don't scare me like that."

Shadow didn't blink. He didn't react. He just waited. Slim cleared his throat. "Kendall's jumpy but he ain't stupid. You're good."

Shadow accepted the answer. Isaías pocketed the list and clapped Slim on the shoulder. "Thanks."

Slim gave a thin smile. "Velasco, my man… this feels big. Bigger than anything we done before." Isaías didn't answer. He couldn't.

Slim watched the three operatives file out of the house, moving with predatory calm. He muttered, almost to himself: "What the hell y'all about to start in my city?"

Isaías didn't look back. He didn't have to. The answer was already written in the air like the humidity, **War.**

The gun store sat wedged between a payday loan office and a failing tax prep service on **Claiborne Avenue** in a squat concrete block with peeling paint, a flickering neon sign, and a small parking lot already filling with early-morning customers.

Isaías's SUV pulled into the far corner of the lot, angled so the tinted windows faced the street but not the storefront. Toño sat in the passenger seat, eyes sharp. Ruiz waited in the second row, posture rigid, watching every person who moved.

Shadow, who was silent and unreadable, sat directly behind Isaías. His eyes weren't on people. The SUV idled quietly.

"Remember," Isaías said, voice low, "we don't go inside. Slim said Kendall brings it out." Ruiz grunted. "If he doesn't flake." Toño cracked his knuckles. "If he flakes, he bleeds." Isaías shot him a warning look.

"We don't kill anyone unless necessary." Shadow didn't turn his head. "Necessity is flexible," he murmured.

Isaías swallowed hard and checked his mirrors again.

The ordinary world moved around them with cars passing, a woman jogging, and a teenager unlocking a bike chain. All of them were completely unaware that three killers sat in the shadows, waiting for an arms deal to unfold in broad daylight.

A beater Honda Civic pulled into the lot and parked two rows away. It was Kendall. Young, wiry, jittery. Wearing a hoodie despite the humidity. He scanned the parking lot with the jumpy nervousness of a man who had made too many bad decisions and owed too many people money.

He spotted the SUV. Isaías exhaled. "Okay. Showtime."

Kendall reached into the Civic's back seat and dragged out a black duffel bag with one corner sagging heavily with the weight of packaged metal inside. He kept glancing over his shoulder as he walked toward them.

Shadow sat forward slightly. "Hands," he whispered. Ruiz nodded. "I see it." They watched Kendall's fingers. The kid approached the SUV and tapped the driver's window with one knuckle.

Isaías lowered it halfway. "You Velasco?" Kendall asked, voice cracking with nerves. Isaías nodded. "Got the merchandise?" Kendall lifted the duffel slightly. "Yeah, yeah I got it. But listen, man, Slim didn't tell me I'd be dealing with…" His eyes flicked past Isaías to the three killers inside the vehicle. His throat tightened. "…with *them.*"

Toño leaned forward, expression flat. "Problem?" "No," Kendall said quickly. "No problem. Just… fuck, man. Y'all look like y'all about to invade a country."

Shadow spoke, barely above a whisper. "We are." Kendall froze. Ruiz elbowed Shadow lightly. "Ay, cálmate, fantasmito. You're scaring him." Shadow didn't smile. Shadow never smiled.

Kendall regained control enough to unzip the duffel. Inside were three pistols, two stripped AR lowers wrapped in rags, and an aftermarket trigger kit still in plastic. "All clean," Kendall said. "Bought over the counter thirty minutes ago. I got receipts if…" "We don't need receipts," Toño said, cutting him off. "We're not returning them."

Kendall swallowed. Isaías counted out a stack of hundreds and handed it through the cracked window. "Half now. The other half when you deliver the scopes and the plates."

Kendall shook his head rapidly. "Nah, man, I need all of it now. Slim said you'd…" Toño pushed open the passenger door and stepped out of the SUV in one smooth, fluid motion. Kendall stumbled backward. Shadow glided out behind him. Ruiz exited last, rolling his shoulders.

The three men surrounded Kendall without touching him. no weapons were drawn, no threats spoken. Just presence.

A presence that said *We decide what happens now.*

Kendall raised both hands, trembling. "Okay… okay… half now is fine. Shit, man. I'm not trying to die here today."

Shadow stepped closer, eyes locking onto Kendall's. His voice was soft but razor sharp. "Then don't lie. Don't short the order. Don't panic. Don't talk to anyone. And don't show anyone our faces." Kendall nodded so fast he nearly lost balance. "I… I won't. I swear." Shadow tilted his head. "You won't swear," he said. "You'll deliver."

Kendall swallowed, nodded again, and backed toward his Civic with the duffel still in his hand. "Next drop… two hours," he muttered. "Same spot. Alone."

He climbed into the Civic, turned the key with shaking fingers, and sped out of the parking lot, tires squealing.

Isaías exhaled. "Damn," he whispered. "Slim wasn't kidding. That kid is one breath away from a heart attack." Shadow slid back into the SUV, movements smooth and silent. "He'll live," Shadow said. "If his fear keeps him loyal."

Toño shut his door with a quiet thud. Ruiz cracked his neck. "So what now?" Isaías checked the time. "We go to the next supplier," he said. "Slim's warehouse man."

Shadow leaned forward once more. "Good," he said. "I want to meet the man who sells guns by the crate."

The SUV pulled out of the parking lot and merged into traffic, blending instantly with the flow of oblivious civilians.

The Murder Team was now armed enough to be dangerous. But they weren't finished. The city still had more to give them. And they were coming to take it.

The warehouse sat along the riverfront, tucked between a scrap metal yard and a half-abandoned seafood distributor. Rusted fencing wrapped the property, the kind of fencing meant less to keep people out and more to hide what was happening inside.

Isaías pulled the SUV to a slow stop at the side gate. A faded sign hung crookedly on the chain links: **MIKE'S PROCUREMENT & STORAGE — BY APPOINTMENT ONLY**

Shadow read the sign once, then turned his eyes to Isaías. "Appointment?" he murmured. Isaías swallowed. "…Something like that."

He honked twice. The response was immediate, a heavy metallic grind as the warehouse door rolled upward halfway, stopping at knee height.

A thick boot slid into view. "Park inside," a voice barked from the dark interior. They rolled forward.

The moment the SUV cleared the threshold, the door slammed shut behind them, sealing out the daylight and muffling the outside world.

Inside, everything smelled of motor oil, sweat, and the faint spice of fried food from a forgotten takeout bag in the corner. The space was massive with concrete floors, metal shelving stretching toward the ceiling, stacks of crates marked with coded symbols, and a forklift parked under a flickering fluorescent tube.

At the center of it all stood **Big Mike**. He matched the name with a massive frame, thick beard, stained LSU hoodie, and hands that looked too big for the cigarette he held between two fingers. His eyes were sharp, though. Too sharp for a man who pretended to be careless.

"Well, well," Mike said, exhaling smoke. "Slim said you were coming. Didn't say you'd bring half a platoon." His eyes drifted over Toño, Ruiz, then landed on Shadow.

Something in his posture changed, like a dog catching scent of a larger predator. "You the boss?" Mike asked Shadow.

Shadow didn't blink. "No." Mike smirked. "Shame. You got the vibe."

Isaías stepped forward quickly. "We're here for the crates." Mike held up a hand. "Slow down, Velasco. Don't rush business. Ain't polite." He flicked ashes to the floor, then motioned toward a tarp-covered section of the warehouse.

"Let's talk hardware." He pulled back the tarp. Underneath were **four crates** stacked two-by-two, unmarked, sealed with steel clasps, and heavy enough that the concrete beneath them was stained from friction drag.

Mike thumped the nearest crate with his knuckles. "Now this right here is the Cadillac package," he said. ".300 Blackout rifles, suppressors, red-dot optics. Not that airsoft shit y'all buy on the street."

Shadow crouched, scraped one glove along the side of the crate, inspecting the metal, the welds, and the weight. "Open it," he said. Mike raised an eyebrow. "You asking or telling?"

Shadow stood. Mike's bravado faltered. "…Alright then," he muttered.

He grabbed a crowbar, wedged it under the latch, and popped the crate open. The lid lifted with a metallic groan.

Inside were Layered foam, Military-grade Wrapped rifles, Magazines stacked with pristine precision, Thermals, Charging handles, Slings, Barrels, and Professional-grade Tools.

Shadow removed one rifle, checked the bolt, inspected the chamber, sighted down the optic, and tested the suppressor threading. Ruiz and Toño flanked him, eyes scanning the warehouse for hidden threats.

Shadow nodded once. "Good." Big Mike exhaled like he'd been holding breath. "Yeah," Mike said with a forced grin. "Only the best. Now… these other crates got armor plates, night-vision shit, bolt carrier groups, you know, stuff people like you need to stay alive."

Shadow's voice came quiet. "We don't need armor." Mike blinked. "…What? Man, this city is…" "Armor slows us down," Shadow said. "We don't plan on getting shot."

Something cold slid down Mike's spine. Isaías cleared his throat. "Prices, Mike."

Mike eyed Isaías, then the team behind him. "Prices went up." Toño stepped forward. "They go down." Mike laughed nervously. "Ain't how business works, amigo."

Shadow stepped closer… not aggressive, not loud… just close. Close enough that Mike had to tilt his head back to meet his eyes. "You charge us more," Shadow said softly, "and you will never do business again."

Mike froze. The cigarette ash trembled at the end of the filter. "…Right," he whispered. "Discount. Sure. Slim shoulda said you boys were… negotiators."

Shadow didn't smile. Ruiz picked up a thermal scope. "We'll take two crates."

Mike blinked again. Two crates was tens of thousands in product. "That's it? Two? Shit, I thought…" "That's all we need," Shadow said. Mike raised his palms. "Fine by me."

He pointed toward a metal hoist. "Loader's over there. Y'all can take 'em yourselves."

Ruiz and Toño moved instantly. Shadow circled the warehouse perimeter once more, checking doors, windows, and possible angles of ambush. When he rejoined the group, Isaías had already sealed the cash into Mike's trembling hands.

Mike pocketed it quickly. "Pleasure doing business. Not a word of this leaves this place," he said, trying to sound firm.

Shadow paused. Then he stepped close, far too close. "Ignore us," he whispered. "Forget our faces. Forget our names. Forget today." Mike swallowed. "Done."

Shadow leaned back, satisfied. Ruiz and Toño lifted the crates into the SUV's rear compartment, slamming the hatch shut.

Isaías gave Mike a small nod. "We appreciate your help." Mike managed a stiff smile. "Just… don't bring that storm back here, alright? I ain't built for that kinda pressure."

Shadow stopped at the warehouse door, hand resting on the metal. His voice cut the air like a blade. "It's already in the city."

Mike's face drained of color. The door rolled open.

Shadow stepped into the vehicle first, head tilted slightly upward as though sensing routes, sounds, threats the others couldn't perceive. He didn't look back.

The rest climbed into the SUV and drove off, leaving the gun runner standing alone in the dim warehouse, surrounded by crates of silence and fear.

The Murder Team was now fully equipped. But the city was not prepared. And far across town, lightning cracked over the skyline as if New Orleans itself shuddered… because tomorrow, **the ghosts begin watching their king.**

Chapter 9

Scouting the Town

Dawn crept into the Kenner safehouse like an intruder; thin, gray light slipping through warped window blinds, dust drifting in slow spirals where it touched. The warehouse felt colder this morning. Quieter, like the city itself sensed something watching it.

The eleven surviving operatives moved around the space with low, deliberate footsteps. A few ate protein bars. Others checked magazines. One practiced adjusting his gait, masking the limp from yesterday's escape. Another shaved his beard down to a civilian stubble. No one spoke unless necessary.

At the center table, **El Silencioso** stood over the spread of maps, street diagrams, and printed schedules. His fingers traced the Garden District boundaries with the same care a surgeon uses when handling organs.

"Three-man surveillance unit," he said without looking up. "Close recce only. Blending in required." The men stopped moving and listened.

He pointed to three of them in silence; **Shadow, Toño, Serrano. There were n**o explanation or justification. There was just selection.

Shadow nodded once. Toño adjusted the cap he'd borrowed. Serrano wiped his hands on his jeans and stepped forward. These were the men who would get closest to the Martello family before the kill.

Velasco approached cautiously, holding a small plastic bag stuffed with clothing. "Disguises," he said. "American casual. Nothing tactical." Silencioso opened the bag and inspected the contents. Inside the bags were Tourist T-shirts, Saints caps, Loose jackets, Cargo shorts in unassuming colors, and Cheap sunglasses.

Shadow held up a shirt with a cartoon alligator on it. He stared at it. Toño cracked a rare smile. "Looks good on you." Shadow lowered the shirt slowly. "No." Silencioso didn't glance up from the maps. "Blend," he said. Shadow sighed quietly and tucked the shirt under his arm.

Serrano tried on sunglasses, checked himself in a dusty window reflection, and muttered, "I look like a contractor who lost his truck." Isaías shrugged. "That's the point. Ordinary and Invisible."

Silencioso tapped the map again. "You will not carry long guns," he said. "Only concealed pistols. No suppressors. Nothing that prints through fabric." Serrano nodded. "Small-frame Glocks, then."

Shadow slid his into the waistband of his jeans, then pulled the oversized T-shirt down over it. Toño pocketed two folding knives before anyone could comment.

Isaías cleared his throat. "Listen carefully. New Orleans is friendly, but it's also… nosy. People watch. Neighbors talk. Tourists film everything. You don't want to end up on someone's TikTok." Serrano grunted. "We don't make videos."

"That's not what I mean," Isaías said, rubbing his forehead. "In this place, people point phones everywhere. That's all." Shadow tilted his head. "Phones are small. People are slow. If someone films us…" "Shadow," Silencioso said without turning. The single word stopped him. Isaías exhaled in relief.

Silencioso circled a neighborhood block with a marker. "This is the target's morning route," he said. "We confirm before nightfall. Vehicle patterns. Guard rotations. Foot traffic." He tapped again. "No contact. No engagement. No curiosity."

Toño frowned. "Define curiosity." Silencioso looked up with eyes that had no softness left in them. "Don't look longer than civilians look. Don't walk where civilians wouldn't walk. Don't act like predators." Shadow replied quietly, "We are predators."

Silencioso held his gaze. His voice did not rise. "And predators survive by pretending they are not."

The room went still. Even the hum of the flickering lights seemed to quiet.

Silencioso turned to the whiteboard Isaías had set up earlier and wrote two words: **BE NORMAL.** He underlined it twice.

Isaías stepped forward. "One more thing. NOPD patrols the Garden District heavily. They don't fuck around. They'll stop you if you look wrong." Toño shrugged. "We'll look right, then." "That's not enough," Isaías insisted. "You need somewhere to duck into. A store. A coffee shop. Anything casual."

Serrano raised a hand, dead serious. "Do we… buy coffee?" Isaías blinked. "Yes." Serrano nodded as he'd just been issued a rifle. "Okay. Coffee."

Shadow muttered, "Tourists." Silencioso didn't smile, but something in his expression barely softened, like the faintest crack in granite.

Then he drew a final circle. Vinny Castenllo Jr.'s mansion. "This is the goal," he said. "But today is not the kill." He tapped the map again. "Today is the eyes." He walked around the table, adjusting the strap of his shoulder bag.

"One hour," Silencioso said. "Dress. Disguise. Move." Toño, Serrano and Shadow nodded as one. Silencioso stopped at the warehouse door. He didn't turn around when he spoke. "If the city sees you," he said, "we abort." A beat. "If the guards see you, we improvise." Another beat. "And if the Martellos see you..." Finally, he looked over his shoulder. "...then you die."

The three men took this in with the calm acceptance of men who had already made peace with dying long ago. The door opened to the gray morning. Shadow slipped out first. Toño followed. Serrano last, adjusting his sunglasses like a man preparing to enter a role. They disappeared into the quiet street.

And the silent and invisible hunt began with three men pretending to belong in a city they had come to destroy.

The Garden District looked exactly the way tourists imagined it with wide oak-lined streets, immaculate lawns, antebellum mansions with wrought-iron balconies, joggers with earbuds, and retirees walking tiny designer dogs.

And completely oblivious to the fact that three killers were moving through it like ghosts.

Shadow walked ahead, wearing the cartoon alligator shirt Slim had given him. He'd tucked it into khaki shorts and paired it with a Saints cap pulled low over his eyes. A coffee cup in hand completed the illusion. Toño and Serrano followed a few paces behind, looking like two contractors on a break with dust-stained caps, sunglasses, and casual backpacks. The trio blended so well that even the homeowners walking their dogs didn't spare them a second glance.

"Eyes open," Shadow murmured without moving his lips. Serrano scratched the side of his face, pretending to adjust his sunglasses. "Copy." Toño sipped from a convenience-store coffee. "Copy."

They walked one block. Then another. Shadow slowed, blending into the foot traffic of a small, gated corner park. "Target perimeter ahead," he said softly.

Through the slats of an ornate iron fence, the **Martello mansion** rose into view. Two guards standing just inside the gate, dressed like upscale private contractors with a professional and well-rested posture.

Shadow didn't look directly at them. Toño pointed with his coffee cup toward a bench across the street. "Sit?" Shadow nodded once. They sat.

A trio of new mothers walked by, pushing strollers. A landscaper trimmed hedges near the mansion's exterior. A tourist couple took pictures of a balcony covered in flowers. And then… The front door opened. A tall man stepped out first. He was dressed in a business suit with Polished shoes, and his Hair slicked back.

He didn't rush. He didn't glance around nervously. He carried himself like a man who believed the world bowed for him. This was clearly Vinnie Castenllo Jr.

Right behind him came a young woman carrying a tote bag and wearing a university hoodie and leggings. She laughed at something her guardian said behind her. A carefree, genuine laugh that drifted over the street like a warm breeze. Sophie.

Serrano muttered under his breath, "She's just a kid." Shadow didn't acknowledge the comment. "Patterns," he whispered.

Vinny Jr. checked his watch. A black SUV pulled to the driveway. A driver stepped out and opened the back door.

One guard followed the family to the vehicle. The second remained at the gate. Shadow watched the positions of both without turning his head. He noted how the gate guard shifted weight onto his left foot. How the SUV guard scanned the street only once. How the driver never checked the mirrors.

Toño murmured, "Security feels light." "Light to you," Shadow replied softly. "Adequate for them."

Sophie climbed into the SUV. Her guardian followed. Vinny Jr. entered last. The SUV rolled out of the driveway and merged onto the quiet avenue.

Shadow stood. "Go." The three men separated slightly, walking parallel to the street but never clustering. They looked like pedestrians with somewhere ordinary to be.

The SUV took a left. Shadow took a left. Toño waited ten seconds, then followed. Serrano waited twenty and trailed last. They drifted through the neighborhood in a loose spiral pattern, never too close, never too far.

Shadow monitored reflections in Store windows and Car mirrors. He also gracefully dodged Puddles left from last night's rain. Toño checked side streets. Serrano scanned rooftops and potential overwatch positions.

The SUV pulled through a traffic circle and onto a busier boulevard. Serrano murmured, "Where are they going?" Isaías's voice hissed through the concealed earpiece they all wore. "GPS tag shows they're headed toward Tulane University," he said. "Same route as last week."

Serrano exhaled, almost amused. "Routine. Rich people love routine." Shadow kept pace with the sidewalk crowd. "Routine kills."

As they moved through the boulevard, the trio ducked into a corner coffee shop, pretending to browse pastries. Shadow stood near the window, subtly angling himself to catch the SUV's reflection as it stopped at a red light.

Sophie gazed out her window, smiling faintly at something on her phone. Her guardian checked messages. Vinny Jr. talked to the driver. Completely unaware.

And yet… Shadow felt something tighten inside him. It wasn't emotion. It was Focus. A predator senses the boundaries of a hunting ground long before it strikes.

Sophie turned her head suddenly… Not toward them, but toward a jogger running past. Still, Shadow's body responded automatically. He lowered his gaze and Shifted his weight. He took a drink from his cup. He was Invisible again.

The SUV rolled forward. Shadow murmured, "Continue the sweep." The three men exited the coffee shop one by one, blending back into the steady thrum of morning life.

Their first contact with the Martello family had lasted less than five minutes. But it was enough. Shadow spoke quietly into the mic. "Route confirmed. Morning habits confirmed. Guard rotation confirmed." A pause. "Move to the second target." And the net began to tighten.

The black SUV carrying Vinny merged onto St. Charles Avenue, slipping into the late-morning traffic with smooth confidence. To anyone else, it looked like a wealthy businessman on the way to a meeting. To the three men following him, it was a moving puzzle of angles, timing, and opportunity.

Shadow didn't follow directly. He never followed directly. He walked one block inland, parallel to St. Charles, keeping pace with the vehicle by watching reflections in shop windows, polished brass streetcar rails, and the occasional glint of sunlight off a windshield.

Toño trailed half a block behind the SUV, disguised as someone reviewing text messages on his phone while actually recording the vehicle's speed and pause points.

Serrano walked opposite the direction of traffic, pretending to sip a smoothie, glancing casually at each passing car, burning the SUV's route into memory.

They didn't speak unless necessary. Shadow murmured, "Isaías. Confirm next stop." Isaías's voice crackled softly through the earpiece. "Financial district. Same building as last week. The one with the mirrored lobby." Shadow didn't answer. He already knew the place.

Vinny Jr.'s patterns were tightening into shape; early departure, drop-off at the mansion gate, family load-out, Sophie's routine, then a business stop. Routine was leverage. Routine was death wearing a wristwatch.

Shadow reached a corner and paused at a newspaper stand, pretending to browse the headlines. He caught sight of the SUV reflected in the storefront window across the street. It slowed and Turned right, Pulling into a private parking garage beneath a seven-story office building.

"Garage entry confirmed," Shadow said softly. Toño rounded the block in time to see it. Serrano approached from the opposite direction, chewing gum to maintain his disguise.

They regrouped on the sidewalk, never standing closer than two feet. Serrano murmured, "High-end place. Cameras from every angle. Lobby guard looks bored but alert." Shadow scanned the area without lifting his head. "Walk the perimeter," he said.

They split into three trails of normalcy drifting in different directions.

Shadow walked past a food truck and glanced over the mirrored windows of the building. He didn't look at the lobby guard. He looked at the reflection. The Guards were bored and the Front desk was inattentive. Most of their attention focused on badge-swiping employees. Perfect.

He glanced at the upper floors. Mirrored glass with No direct line of sight. He continued on.

Toño entered a small café beside the tower, standing behind two office workers ordering lattes. He pretended to scroll his phone, but his eyes flicked toward the building's side door reflection in the stainless-steel espresso machine. The side entrance had a keypad, A loading dock, and a freight elevator entrance. He whispered, "Shadow. They have a service hallway connecting the dock to the garage." Shadow replied, "Noted."

Serrano crossed the street to a newspaper vendor and bought a pack of mints. He used the glass case below the counter to scan the cars entering and exiting the garage. There was a Black SUV, a Government sedan, and a Luxury crossover. Nothing unusual.

But then… One guard stepped out of the SUV's passenger seat, Stretched, and Checked his phone, reentering the garage.

Serrano noted the timing. "Guard rotation fast," he murmured. "Lazy checkpoint discipline." Shadow's voice responded, "Confirmed. Pattern weakness."

Serrano walked away from the vendor, pocketing the mints.

The three operatives reconvened at the corner near a streetcar stop. People moved around them; tourists with cameras, commuters checking watches, and joggers cutting through foot traffic.

Shadow spoke quietly, "Positions. Eyes down." They shifted to form a triangular spacing pattern around the streetcar stop, three men in a crowd, looking at phones, sipping coffee, checking a transit map. Anyone watching would see only ordinary civilians.

Isaías came through the earpiece. "Vinny's inside the building. His GPS tag is stationary." "Guard count?" Shadow asked. "Four total. Two upstairs. Two are staying with the vehicle in rotation." Toño's eyebrow lifted. "Only four? For a man like him?" Shadow didn't look up.

"He feels safe," Shadow said. "That is the most dangerous kind of man." Serrano added, "Safe men make mistakes." Shadow slid a fingertip along the edge of his coffee cup, expression unreadable. "Safe men die," he corrected.

They waited another ten minutes, tracking guard rotations, civilian patterns, choke points, and escape routes.

Everything was recorded mentally, visually, and in the small, encrypted device taped just under Shadow's shirt.

Finally, Shadow turned slightly, giving the smallest nod. "Next pattern," he said. "We follow the daughter." Serrano cracked his knuckles. "Tulane time?" "Toño," Shadow said, "secure transport."

Toño nodded and peeled off toward the car rental desks down the block. Serrano followed, checking behind them casually. Shadow lingered a moment longer at the corner, watching the mirrored tower and the faint silhouette of Vinny Jr. moving through its reflection.

A man who believed himself untouchable. Shadow whispered, more to himself than the others, "We are closer now."

Then he turned and melted into the daytime crowd. The hunt had widened And no one in the city knew it yet.

The Tulane University campus buzzed with late-morning energy with students crisscrossing brick walkways, backpacks bouncing, laughter carrying over manicured lawns. Oak trees draped their branches like green veils, and the warm air smelled faintly of powdered sugar drifting from a nearby café.

No one noticed the white sedan parked near the corner where Broadway met Willow. No one noticed its three occupants blending into the traffic of students and faculty.

Shadow sat in the passenger seat wearing a Tulane hoodie and sunglasses. **Toño** drove one-handed, window down, looking every bit like a dad waiting for his kid. **Serrano** sat in the back pretending to text, occasionally breaking character to scan reflections in passing car windows.

"Target entering campus," Isaías' voice murmured through their earpieces. "Five seconds."

Shadow didn't look up. He didn't need to.

Sophie Castenllo walked near a gated side entrance beside Gibson Hall. Her hair was pulled back. Her backpack was slung lazily over one shoulder. She wore headphones and bobbed her head lightly to whatever she was listening to. Completely unaware of the predator's eyes on her.

Her guardian walked five paces behind here. Same man as earlier that morning. He was scanning the street with bored familiarity. His hand rested near his concealed pistol beneath a windbreaker.

Shadow tracked every angle without lifting his head. His sunglasses hid the micro-adjustments of his gaze. "Guard's attention low," Serrano murmured. "Couldn't pick a tail if it slapped him." Toño scratched his jaw in the driver's seat. "Kid looks happy. No idea what's coming." Shadow said nothing. Emotion had no place here.

Sophie and her guardian disappeared through the security gate.

Shadow finally exhaled through his nose. "Time to walk," he ordered.

They exited the sedan separately. Serrano went first, blending into a knot of students chatting outside an academic building. Toño followed, joining a line of parents visiting campus. Shadow walked last, hands in hoodie pockets, blending with the stream of students heading toward the quad. They moved in loose formation, never too close together, never turning their heads at the same time.

"Eyes on her schedule," Isaías said in their ears. "She has a mid-morning econ class, then an hour break near the student union." Shadow murmured back, "We confirm."

He crossed a footbridge shaded by oaks, passing groups of laughing students. Some sat at picnic tables, some played music, some flirted openly. Normal life. Innocent life. And then he saw her again.

She walked across the quad toward the business building, headphones still in, smiling faintly at a text on her phone.

Shadow paused beneath a tree, pretending to adjust his   shoe.
He scanned the area. Guardian ten paces behind her. Eyes forward, not around. Weak spacing and Predictable pattern.

Toño's voice crackled quietly: "Angle left. I see her too." Serrano added, "Guardian checking his watch every twenty seconds. Routine." Shadow stepped back into the flow of students. "Observe break location," he said.

They followed at distance as Sophie emerged after class and walked toward the Bruff quad, an open plaza filled with tables, people studying, motorcycles zipping past, and a small coffee cart steaming beneath a green awning.

She sat at a metal table under an oak tree. Her guardian hovered near a nearby bench. Not vigilant or disciplined.

Shadow watched from beside a bike rack, sipping a bottled water he'd bought for camouflage. "She is unprotected," Toño murmured from a bench opposite the quad. "Vulnerable," Serrano added, leaning against a railing.

Shadow didn't respond for several seconds.

When he did, his voice was quiet. "She is not the target," he said. Toño nodded once. "Copy." Serrano didn't argue.

They watched for fifteen more minutes as Sophie packed her laptop, throwing away a napkin, and tied her jacket around her waist. Her guardian followed like a man who wished he were anywhere else. She headed toward a secondary building.

Shadow lifted his hand slightly. "Break off." The team melted back into the foot traffic. They walked separate routes back to the sedan.

Once inside, Serrano exhaled, rubbing his forehead. "Feels strange," he admitted quietly. "Watching a kid like that." Toño didn't answer. Shadow stared out the windshield. "Targets do not matter until they matter," he said simply. "Emotion blinds the blade." Neither argued.

Isaías's voice returned to the earpieces. "Good. We've got enough for today. Vinny's schedule matches last week's almost perfectly. Patterns align. We log everything tonight." Shadow nodded.

Then a soft beep chimed in the sedan. A message from Silencioso through the encrypted channel: **DINNER SUNDAY 7 PM. FULL FAMILY.**

Serrano stared at the glowing text. Toño whispered, "He means…" Shadow finished for him. "The window."

Silencioso's second message came instantly after **TOMORROW WE PLAN THE KILL.**

Shadow powered off the device. "Drive," he said. Toño pulled away from the curb, blending into traffic with the indifferent ease of a local commuter.

Sophie Castenllo walked across campus, laughing at a friend's joke.

The killers drove away without a backward glance. The noose around her family tightened another invisible notch.

Chapter 10

The Strategy Session

The storm rolled into Kenner just after nightfall with thick clouds dragging lightning across the sky, thunder shaking the warehouse roof with each passing wave. Rain hammered the corrugated metal like a thousand fists, drowning out the sounds of the sleeping neighborhood outside.

Inside the safehouse, only a single lantern burned. Its dim glow flickered across a long folding table covered in maps, photographs, floor plans, and handwritten notes. Black markers. Compass tools. Three burner phones. A coil of rope. A silenced pistol was placed deliberately at the table's edge like a signature.

Eleven men gathered in a semicircle around it. Breaths were slow and controlled. The air was heavy with a kind of anticipation that bordered on reverence.

Then **El Silencioso** stepped forward. He placed both hands on the table and scanned the room. His face was lit from below by the lantern with shadows cutting harsh lines across his jaw, his cheekbones, and the scar that looked faintly like a second mouth.

"Tonight," he said, voice low but carrying over the thunder,
"We plan the kill." No one reacted dramatically. But something in the room tightened like a muscle preparing to strike.

Isaías Velasco stood nearest to him, clutching a sheaf of printed schedules and route diagrams. He waited, knuckles white around the paper, the pressure of responsibility clinging to him like sweat.

Shadow stood to Silencioso's right, arms crossed, head tilted slightly as lightning flickered behind him. Toño and Serrano flanked him, both silent, both perfectly still. The others arranged themselves by instinct; predators aligning around the apex.

Silencioso unfolded a large street map of the Garden District and weighed down the corners with spare magazines. A gust of wind rattled the warehouse doors. Rain hissed through gaps at the roofline. He didn't look up. "Velasco," Silencioso said. "Begin."

Isaías stepped forward, clearing his throat. "Vinny Castenllo Jr. leaves the house between eight and nine most mornings, returns in the late afternoon." He placed three photos on the table: Vinny entering a building, Vinny shaking hands, and Vinny stepping into his SUV. "Always the same driver. Always the same rotation of guards."

Serrano muttered, "Predictable." Silencioso didn't look at him, but the faintest shift of his jaw indicated acknowledgment.

Isaías continued, sliding a new sheet forward. "Sophie Castenllo's schedule is stable. University classes, short breaks, guardians who don't pay attention." Toño clicked his tongue. "We noticed." "But…" Isaías hesitated before placing the final sheet at the table's center, "…every Sunday at 7 p.m., the entire family meets for dinner. All of them. At the Tony's."

Lightning cracked, illuminating the maps like an omen. "That," Isaías said quietly, "is your window."

Silencioso stared at the sheet for several seconds. Then he traced a fingertip around the perimeter of the mansion. "Entry point," he murmured. Shadow leaned in. "Rear wall. Blind spot near the generator. We walked it twice." "Good," Silencioso said. "Continue."

Shadow pointed to another photo with an aerial view. "Power grid is local. Weak redundancy. Cut from two spots. They'll think it's weather-related." Thunder growled overhead as if agreeing. Serrano stepped closer, pointing with a pencil. "We breach here. Minimal lighting. No civilian line of sight." Silencioso tapped the driveway photo. "Guards?" "Two posted," Toño answered. They don't overlap correctly. There's a six-minute gap."

A slow nod from Silencioso. "Six minutes is eternity."

One of the more senior operatives spoke from the back. "What about neighbors? Anyone likely to interfere?" Isaías shook his head. "Tourists and old money. They don't investigate noises or strangers unless you knock on their door." Shadow's lip twitched. "Then they won't see us."

Silencioso looked at each man in turn, confirming their readiness, reading their faces not for fear but for any hint of hesitation. He saw none.

He moved something small into view. It was aa burner phone. A single line of text was displayed from **Óscar: Do not fail.** Silencioso placed the phone on the table, face-up.

The lantern flickered again, casting the words in trembling shadow. He inhaled once. "Study the maps," he said. "Fix them in your mind. When we strike, we strike without doubt."

He lifted his eyes. "Tonight, we build the plan."

Another crack of thunder shook the warehouse. Rain poured harder, hitting the roof like the footsteps of an approaching army. Silencioso didn't look toward the storm. He looked at his men. "Eleven of us," he said softly. "More than enough." Shadow nodded. Serrano clenched his jaw. Toño tapped the mansion's rear entry point with a finger. And Isaías shivered from the realization that tonight, the killers weren't preparing an attack. They were composing a death sentence. One they were certain they would deliver.

The rain hammered the warehouse roof harder now, each burst of thunder vibrating through the metal beams overhead. Inside, the lantern's light flickered across the table as Silencioso motioned for Isaías to begin the next phase.

"Play it," he said. Isaías set a small, ruggedized laptop on the table and connected a drive wrapped in electrical tape. The screen glowed to life, illuminating the killers' faces in pale blue. "Footage from yesterday," Isaías said. "Street cams. Our phones. Reflections. Shadow's micro-recorder."

The first video opened. It was a shaky reflection from a café window showing the Martello SUV backing out of the driveway. Serrano pointed. "Driver's dominant hand left. Good. He'll open himself when he retreats." Silencioso nodded, filing it away.

The next clip was of Sophie stepping out of a building at Tulane, headphones in, laughing. Toño muttered, "Kid doesn't even see the world around her." Serrano added quietly, "Her guardian doesn't either." Silencioso let the footage play without comment. He wasn't interested in their thoughts yet.

A third clip was Vinny Jr. entering the office tower. Mirrored lobby windows. Shadow leaned in slightly.

"There," he said simply. Silencioso froze the frame. Zoomed.

A guard at the lobby desk laughed at something on his phone. His attention drifted from the entrance. His posture is slack. His sidearm was barely visible beneath his blazer. "Complacent," Shadow said. "Predictable. Weak."

Silencioso added a mark to the map: **LOBBY EASY.**

The Next clip was the SUV stopping at a traffic circle. Toño noticed it immediately. "Brake light delay. Rear signal flickers half a second before illumination." Serrano frowned. "Faulty wiring?" "No," Toño said. "Bad maintenance. That SUV isn't checked nightly. Their security is lazy." Silencioso added another mark to the map: **VEHICLE IS NEGLECTED. DRIVER CARELESS.**

Then came the long clip of Shadow's bodycam capturing Sophie's campus movements. The laptop displayed her walking across Tulane with a crowd around her, her guardian trailing lazily behind. Shadow tapped the screen. "Guard spacing inconsistent," he noted. "He doesn't protect her. He follows her." Isaías flinched. "Meaning?" Shadow's voice was soft. "Meaning he reacts, not prevents."

Silencioso circled Sophie's guardian photo with a slow stroke of the marker. "Harmless," Silencioso said.

Serrano shifted uneasily. Isaías cleared his throat and clicked to the next segment. A panning shot from their walk-by in the Garden District, capturing the mansion's gate, perimeter cameras, and two standing guards.

A lightning flash illuminated the scene in the video and the warehouse at the same time. For an instant, it felt like the storm outside was watching with them. "Pause," Silencioso said. Isaías froze the frame. Silencioso stepped closer, studying every pixel. "Camera angles?" he asked. Toño answered. "Three fixed. Narrow range. No 360° sweep." Serrano added, "Blind spots near the rear generators. Ivy growth on the south wall blocks one angle completely."

Shadow pointed to the two guards. "The tall one leads," he said. "He checks corners. Watches the street. Talks into the mic more often." "And the smaller one?" Serrano asked. Shadow barely glanced at him. "Decoration."

Silencioso underlined the guard section: **TALL IS PRIORITY. SMALL IS NONFACTOR.** Isaías swallowed nervously. The way these men categorized human beings so quickly, so clinically, unsettled even him.

The Next clip was thermal imagery from a borrowed device Slim had arranged. The outlines of heat signatures inside the mansion glowed faintly. "That's the kitchen," Isaías said. "Staff. Movement peaks around five to seven." Shadow murmured, "Irrelevant. Kitchen has no line on the family dining room." Silencioso nodded. "Next," he said.

The final clip began playing street cam footage showing the mansion at sunset, lights turning on inside one by one. Serrano leaned in. "That window. Right side. Light always comes on first." "Office," Isaías explained. "Vinny Jr.'s." Shadow turned his head slightly, listening to the storm. "Routine," he said.

Silencioso circled the mansion again, tightening the marks around the structure like a noose. "No alarms tied to police?" he asked. Isaías shook his head. "Private system. Mostly cosmetic. It alerts guards, not NOPD." Toño smirked. "Rich people love theatrics."

Silencioso capped his marker. "Weak points identified." A roll of thunder shook the table. One of the burner phones buzzed from the vibration alone. Silencioso's voice was almost a whisper beneath the storm: "We have enough."

He looked slowly around the circle of faces, tired and hardened men, killers who had crossed deserts, storms, gunfire, checkpoints, and oceans to stand here in a dim warehouse with a single purpose.

"Tomorrow," Silencioso said, "we shape the attack." Shadow nodded. Toño folded his arms. Serrano swallowed and straightened his shoulders. And Isaías felt something inside him tighten; fear, awe, and inevitability braided together.

The footage on the laptop ended with the final image of The Martello mansion at dusk. Warm lights glowing behind tall windows.

Silencioso closed the laptop with one hand. None of them realized how loud the storm had become until that moment. The storm outside reached a violent rhythm with wind slamming against the warehouse and rain lashing sideways against the metal siding. Every thunderclap felt like a countdown.

Inside, the lantern flickered as Silencioso spread out the enlarged blueprint of the Martello mansion. The men gathered close, shoulder to shoulder, forming a ring around the table. This was not a discussion. This was **doctrine**. Silencioso uncapped the thick marker.

"Entry," he said, drawing a red line along the mansion's south wall, where ivy shrouded the camera's blind spot. "Team Bravo." Toño nodded sharply. He didn't write anything down. He didn't need to.

Silencioso tapped the circle of trees near the rear path. "Team Alpha here. Lock rear egress. No witnesses." Shadow and the last Team Alpha survivor exchanged a glance of agreement without words.

Silencioso pointed to a small square marked *POWER GRID ACCESS*. "Power team," he said. "Serrano. Ruiz. You cut the electricity from both junctions." Ruiz frowned. "At the same time?"

Serrano answered before Silencioso could, Simultaneous blackout. Confusion window is ninety seconds." Silencioso nodded. "Ninety seconds is enough."

He drew a line toward the driveway. "Guard neutralizers." Two men stepped forward, their wounded teammate shifting his stance with a wince. Silencioso looked at him. "You do not engage."

The wounded man opened his mouth to protest and then shut it under Silencioso's stare. "You watch angles," Silencioso said. "You warn us of the approach. That is all." The man nodded slowly, swallowing whatever pride remained.

Silencioso turned the blueprint, reorienting the mansion. Next came the **interior pathing.** He drew three arrows converging on the dining room. "Main entry team moves here. Straight line. No detours. No hesitation."

Shadow traced a finger along one route. "Stairwell here. Guard rotates every twelve minutes." "Cycle ends at 7:03," Isaías added from memory. Silencioso circled the stairwell. "Team Echo intercepts rotation. Silent kills."

The two quietest operatives, men who had spoken less than twenty words since their arrival, stepped forward. Silencioso continued. "We breach dining room at 23:07."

Another thunderclap struck overhead like nature punctuating the sentence. Isaías's breath hitched. Silencioso looked at him.

"We move faster than the clock." No one doubted him.

The lantern flickered again, casting their shadows huge and warped across the walls.

Toño tapped the map. "Family positions?" Isaías quickly spread three printed photos taken from the surveillance feed across the blueprint. "Vinny Jr. goes to bed at 23:00. Wife is right behind him. Children opposite side of the house. Two guards are stationed overnight in the living room."

Shadow leaned over the table, scanning the angles. "Two seconds," he murmured. "To kill both guards." "No," Silencioso said. "One." Shadow nodded, accepting the correction.

Silencioso tapped Vinny Jr.'s photo. "This is the objective. No deviation. We do not chase. We do not improvise. We finish him and extract." Serrano frowned. "What about the wife and kids?"

Silencioso didn't blink. "They live." The calm certainty in his voice chilled the room more than the storm outside.

One operative muttered, "Leaves witnesses." "No," Silencioso said softly. "Leaves a message." A long silence followed as the storm filled it.

Then Silencioso reached into his pocket and pulled out a folded slip of paper that was creased, worn, and handled far too many times. He placed it on the table.

Isaías recognized the handwriting. It was Óscar's. **"Return with his blood on your hands… or don't return at all."**

Silencioso didn't look down at the paper. "Assignments," he said. He pointed with the marker, "**Alpha:** Shadow, Toño, A-Left. **Bravo:** Ruiz, Serrano, secondary entry **Echo:** stairwell neutralization. **Delta:** Guard neutralizers. **Intel/Overwatch:** Isaías **Command:** Me."

He circled all the positions in one continuous stroke turning separate teams into a single, closed loop. "Eleven men," he said. "One mission."

He tapped the living room twice. "All movements converge here." His voice dropped lower. "Where the family sits."

Lightning flickered, illuminating the blueprint in a harsh white flash.

Silencioso set down the marker. "We rehearse until it's instinct," he said. "We memorize until we stop thinking." Shadow inhaled deeply. "And if the plan breaks?" Silencioso met his eyes. "Then we cut our way out."

The storm surged again, shaking the doors. The men leaned closer to the table, absorbing every detail of the kill plan as if absorbing scripture. Outside, the world raged. Inside, the murder began to take shape.

The storm's rhythm shifted, the rain becoming a relentless sheet of white noise against the roof. The lantern flickered as the wind pushed through cracks in the warehouse walls. The men stood closer now, instinctively tightening into a formation even as they surrounded the planning table.

Silencioso uncapped a thinner pen and switched to red ink.

"Contingencies," he said.

The word fell like a stone into deep water rippling across every man's expression. This was the part of the plan where most operations died. Silencioso delivered it without hesitation. He drew three arrows branching away from the mansion diagram. He tapped the first arrow.

"If guards raise alarm too early, we shift to the accelerated breach." Serrano frowned. "Meaning what?" Shadow answered before Silencioso could. "We kill every guard immediately," he said, voice calm as still water. "No rotations. No stealth. Just removal." Silencioso nodded once, confirming it. "Alpha leads. Bravo follows," Silencioso added. "Delta locks the street."

The two guard neutralizers exchanged a grim look.

Silencioso tapped the second arrow. Isaías inhaled quietly, bracing. "NOPD lightning response is four to seven minutes," Isaías explained, pushing forward printed notes. "Garden District even faster. They show up heavy."

Silencioso listened without blinking. "If police arrive during breach," Serrano said, "we abort?" Silencioso answered instantly.

"No."

The storm outside punctuated the word with a violent crack. Shadow's eyes narrowed, not in protest, but in focus.

Silencioso pointed at the mapped escape routes Isaías had taped to the table. "Two vehicles. Two routes. Neither depends on silence or subtlety," he said. "If the police come…" "Toño," Shadow finished softly, "we break them." Silencioso didn't correct him. He simply moved to the final arrow.

This was the scenario most teams hated planning for.

Silencioso marked two hallways on the mansion floor plan. "Echo blocks the left corridor," he said. "Alpha blocks the right. No one escapes. No one runs. We pin them into the dining room." Serrano looked up. "What if they try to hide the target? Rush him upstairs? Panic and split?"

Silencioso's voice dropped to almost a whisper. "Then I find him." Silence coated the room like dust settling. Shadow didn't blink. Toño didn't shift. The others just stared at the map, absorbing the implication; This entire mission might hinge on El Silencioso walking through the mansion alone, hunting a fleeing man through hallways like an executioner stalking a condemned king.

Silencioso re-capped the pen. "Next," he said. "Worst-case." The men straightened. He wrote two words on the map: **HARD FAIL.**

Ruiz grimaced. "Meaning…?" "Everything goes wrong," Silencioso said. "Guards alarm. Police flood the street. Target runs. We lose advantage." Isaías whispered, "Abort?" Silencioso shook his head slowly. "No."

The wind howled outside, rattling the metal siding as if nature itself disagreed.

Shadow stepped closer. "What then?" Silencioso drew one final red line straight through the dining room, kitchen, service hallway, and out the back exit. The kill path. "We take him anyway," he said.

Serrano swallowed. "Sir… even if the house is burning around us? Even if NOPD surrounds the block? Even if…"

Silencioso met his eyes. "Even then." Thunder rumbled.

Isaías looked between the faces of the killers assembled; Some were hardened, Some grim, and yet others were quietly resolute. All were loyal.

Silencioso placed a final mark on the map. It was a small X just outside the mansion's back door. "This," he said, tapping it, "is the point of no return." Shadow murmured, "Define it."

Silencioso lifted his gaze, and when he spoke, his voice carried the weight of a man who had buried mercy long ago. "Once we cross this threshold," he said, "no one runs. No one hides. No one breaks formation." He paused, letting the storm punctuate the silence. "And no one fails."

The lantern flickered, shadows dancing across their hardened faces. "Because failure," Silencioso said, "is death."

Another thunderclap rolled through the warehouse, like a drum signaling the march toward the inevitable. The men absorbed the rule. None objected.

They had stepped into a kind of priesthood, one where the sacrament was violence and the scripture was obedience.

Silencioso uncapped the marker again. "We begin rehearsal," he said. "Five minutes." The killers dispersed, grabbing mock firearms, clearing the floor space, practicing movements with brutal efficiency.

Isaías stepped back from the table, pulse pounding. Because he finally understood This wasn't a plan. It was a prophecy and Silencioso intended to fulfill it.

The storm outside reached a bruised and furious peak. Rain hammered the warehouse roof with relentless force, turning every steel beam into a trembling conductor of thunder. Water leaked through a crack and pattered steadily into a rusted bucket beside the wall.

No one noticed. All eyes were on the map. Silencioso moved his marker one last time, drawing a thick red line that extended from the mansion's rear entry, down the alley, across a side street, and into a two-block radius marked with circles.

Exits. Beside them, in smaller handwriting, he wrote: **BREAK CONTACT FAST.**

Toño stepped closer. "Route Two has lighter police presence." Shadow countered, "Route One has more cover."

Silencioso nodded to both, neither superior nor subordinate, just interlocking pieces of the same lethal design.

"Routes are chosen by moment," he said. "Not preference." He tapped the two exit paths. "If Route One is blocked, we take Two. If Two is blocked, we take One." A beat. "If both are blocked…" Shadow finished quietly, "We make a third."

Silencioso gave the faintest nod. He circled the final mark on the map; an industrial building just outside the Garden District.

"This warehouse is the rally point after exfiltration," he said. "We regroup there for five minutes. Not six. Not four. Five." Ruiz frowned. "Why five?" "Because five is enough to count the living," Silencioso replied.

A hush fell.

Serrano's injured teammate shifted uncomfortably. "And if someone doesn't make it to rally point?" Silencioso didn't hesitate. "We do not go back."

The man swallowed hard. There was no cruelty in Silencioso's tone. Just the weight of necessity.

Toño raised a hand. "Police scanners?" Isaías responded quickly, grateful to contribute. "Slim set up a feed from a cracked NOPD frequency. We'll have thirty-second delay, but it's better than blind." Silencioso nodded once. "Good. Use that time wisely."

He stepped away from the table, facing the semicircle of killers who had become one organism under his command. "Gear ready?" he asked. One by one, the men answered: "Yes." "Ready." "Loaded." "Prepared." Shadow simply said, "Always."

Silencioso turned to Isaías. "You will monitor from here. No contact unless required." Isaías straightened, nerves tight in his throat. "Understood." "You open the channels," Silencioso continued, "but you do not speak unless spoken to." Isaías nodded again. "Yes, Jefe."

The killers returned to the table as Silencioso rolled the map outward to reveal a final sheet beneath it. This one wasn't a plan. It was a promise.

A photograph of the Martello family at a charity event. Vinny Jr. was smiling for cameras, his hand resting on Sophie's shoulder, wife at his side. Silencioso stared at the man's face for several seconds. Every expression in the room tightened; shoulders hunched, jaws clenched, and breaths sharpened.

Silencioso placed one finger on Vinny Jr.'s image. "Tomorrow," he said, voice like a blade sliding free of a sheath, "we take the blood he owes."

Another lightning strike illuminated the warehouse, turning every face stark and hard. Silencioso continued: "We do not hesitate. We do not falter. We do not break. We enter as shadows and we leave as ghosts."

He looked to Shadow. Shadow stepped forward, giving the smallest nod. "It will be done." Then Silencioso picked up the burner phone from earlier. He held it so every man could see the message glowing on its cracked screen.

DO NOT FAIL.

Slowly and deliberately, Silencioso spoke the last words of the night. "Tomorrow," he said, "we end a king."

He powered off the phone. The lantern flickered once… twice… then steadied. The storm outside screamed. Inside, eleven men prepared for murder.

Chapter 11

The Assignments

Dawn broke over Kenner in a dull smear of gray, the kind of color that made the world feel suspended. It was neither alive nor dead, just waiting. The storm had passed, leaving behind wet pavement and a heavy, swamp-scented stillness. But inside the warehouse, there was no calm. There was only preparation. The killers moved like monks in a sacred ritual.

Toño tightened the straps on a black tactical vest with no plates, just pockets for knives and magazines. Serrano wrapped electrical tape around the grip of his pistol, testing the draw with a silent, practiced motion. Ruiz sat on a crate, head bowed, re-tying his boots with slow precision. Shadow stood apart from the others, reassembling his rifle. Every movement was a soft, gentle, and reverent testament to the relationship a killer has with his weapon. As if he wasn't handling a weapon but an instrument he intended to play tonight.

No one spoke. Not because they feared waking someone. Because words felt wrong. The mission had begun the moment they opened their eyes.

Isaías Velasco watched from the doorway, hands trembling around a mug of coffee he no longer tasted. The killers barely acknowledged him now; not out of disrespect, but because they had mentally left the world hours ago. Their bodies were still here. Their minds were already inside the mansion.

Shadow slid a suppressor into his bag. Serrano tucked a map into his jacket. Toño holstered his secondary blade with the absentminded ease of a man who had done it thousands of times.

Then **El Silencioso** emerged from the back room dressed in dark civilian clothing, light enough for speed, heavy enough to hide tools. His face was unreadable, but his eyes… those eyes were colder than the steel laid out before him. He carried nothing at first. Then he set a single item on the table: A folded black cloth. The room stilled completely.

One by one, the men gathered around him. Silencioso unfolded the cloth, revealing the tools of tonight's storm. There were Ropes, Cutters, Signaling mirrors, Two breaching charges, Silenced pistols, and A single red marker.

Silencioso lifted the marker and drew a small dot on the wall map right over the mansion's outline. A blood-red period. Then he looked up. "Assignments in ten minutes," he said quietly. No louder than normal conversation. But the words hit the room like a dropped anchor.

The men straightened. Their breaths synchronized. Eleven killers aligned themselves around the table, waiting for their roles, waiting for the moment Silencioso would carve destiny into their bones. Isaías swallowed hard.

Silencioso moved around the table, his footsteps passing Isaías without acknowledgment. He walked to the rear of the warehouse and opened a small locker. Something metallic glinted inside. The weapon he kept apart from the others, the one only he would carry. Isaías could see just enough to recognize its custom and modified silhouette that had been personalized. Silencioso shut the locker.

His voice drifted through the warehouse, "Eat. Hydrate. Prepare your minds." Toño nodded and grabbed a bottle of water. Serrano stretched his shoulders. Ruiz rotated his wrists. Shadow simply breathed, slow and deep.

Silencioso added, "At eleven tonight… the world changes." A long silence followed.

Then he looked at Isaías. "You monitor us. You keep channels clear. You do not panic." Isaías nodded, throat tight. "Yes… yes, Jefe." Silencioso stepped closer, just close enough to make sure Isaías didn't miss the weight of his next words. "If you panic," he said, "we die." Isaías froze, nodding again, this time more desperately.

Silencioso returned to the center of the warehouse. He scanned his men. He inhaled once, slow and deliberate. "Assignments begin now." And the killers moved toward him like disciples approaching an altar. They had to be shaped into a single, lethal blade.

The killers' boots planted on the cold concrete floor. The lantern cast long shadows behind each man, their silhouettes stretched like dark soldiers of a war not yet declared.

Silencioso stood at the center of the table with the opened black cloth before him. He looked at each man in turn, taking a moment with every face, not to judge but to *weigh*.

When he spoke, his voice was steady and controlled, almost ritualistic. "Alpha Team." Shadow stepped forward first. Silencioso didn't hand him a weapon. He handed him **responsibility**.

"You breach the rear wall," Silencioso said. "You control the northern corridor. If the target flees that direction..." "He won't," Shadow answered. Silencioso nodded once. Shadow stepped back into formation, jaw set, eyes cold.

"Next, Toño." Toño approached, shoulders squared. "You hold Alpha's flank. You cut stragglers. You guard the secondary breach window. If Shadow falls..." Toño placed a fist over his chest. "I step forward." "Good."

Silencioso marked **ALPHA** in red on the map, drawing a line from the rear wall to the dining room.

"Bravo Team." Serrano stepped out. "You take the side entrance," Silencioso said. "Minimal guards. Minimal resistance. But timing is everything. You arrive at the hallway at the same second as Alpha." Serrano nodded. "Understood."

"Ruiz," Silencioso continued. Ruiz stepped beside Serrano. "You manage the junction box. You cut power from the east line. If the second line fails…" Ruiz answered, "I cut it manually." Silencioso didn't smile. But he approved.

He drew a second red line **BRAVO** intersecting the first inside the mansion.

"Echo Team." Two quiet men stepped forward. They were thinner, more peaceful, and ghost-like even among ghosts. "You eliminate the rotating guards if necessary," Silencioso said. "Clean kills. No noise. If the stairwell collapses, you join Alpha from the south corridor." They nodded once. Silencioso circled their entry point in red.

"Delta Team." The next two stepped up; one scarred, one bearded, both with eyes that had watched too many men die. "You hold the driveway," Silencioso said. "No reinforcements. No witnesses. No one enters or leaves through the front door." The bearded one spoke. "Extraction timing?" Silencioso tapped the map. "Six minutes after breach." They nodded and stepped back.

Then Silencioso looked to the wounded man, Team B's survivor with the bandaged shoulder. "You do not fight," Silencioso said calmly. "You watch angles. You warn. You survive." The man's jaw tightened, but he accepted it. "Yes, Jefe." "Live," Silencioso added. It sounded like both a command and a mercy.

Last was Isaías Velasco. He stepped forward reluctantly. "You stay behind," Silencioso said. Isaías nodded. "Yes." "You run the channels. You keep the scanners open. You relay only what matters." "Yes." "And Velasco…" Isaías looked up. "…you do not freeze." Isaías swallowed hard. "I won't."

Silencioso held his gaze one second longer, as if testing the structure of Isaías' fear. Then he turned back to the table.

Silencioso picked up the red marker. With a slow, deliberate motion, he drew a final circle around the mansion's bedroom. "Eleven men," he said. "One strike." He placed the marker down and lifted the black cloth, revealing a row of small, black wristbands made of simple elastic, each marked with a number from 1 to 11. He handed them out one by one.

Finally, Silencioso reached into the cloth and withdrew a band with no number at all. Just black. He slid it over his wrist. Then he lifted his eyes. "These numbers mean nothing," he said. "What matters is your place in the kill."

Another thunderclap rattled the building. Silencioso pointed toward the closed warehouse door. "At eleven tonight," he said, "we move." Shadow murmured, "And if luck fails?" Silencioso answered with the certainty of a man who no longer believed in luck, "Then we do not."

The killers bowed their heads not in worship, but in unity. Assignments were complete. The blade had been forged.

After the assignments ended, the killers dispersed into the warehouse's dim corners, checking gear, repacking bags, adjusting straps, moving with a frightening calm. Every sound felt amplified.

To anyone watching from the outside, it might have looked like preparation. But Isaías Velasco knew better. This wasn't preparation. This was a transformation. Eleven men were turning themselves into the shape of death.

Isaías leaned against the cinderblock wall near the door, palms clammy against the mug he'd reheated three times and barely sipped. His heartbeat thrummed too loudly in his ears, drowning the distant drip of water leaking through the ceiling seam. He tried to swallow but his throat felt too tight.

The city outside was quiet, too quiet. Even the usual hum of traffic on nearby Veterans Boulevard seemed muted, like New Orleans had drawn a breath and held it.

Isaías rubbed his forehead with the back of his wrist. He wanted to speak. To say something. Anything. But the weight of the killers moving through that warehouse felt like walking through a cathedral dedicated to violence. You didn't break that silence. You didn't interrupt gods sharpening their spears.

Serrano approached the table to pick up a magazine. Isaías flinched and looked away before their eyes could meet. Coward, he thought bitterly. But another part of him whispered:

Alive.

Shadow moved next, he was always moving. He crossed the warehouse like a drifting current, silent and omnipresent, passing by Isaías without acknowledging him. It wasn't disrespect, like he didn't deserve anything that human. Shadow simply didn't see Isaías the way he saw the others.

He wasn't a killer or a soldier. He wasn't one of them. He saw him as a useful tool, nothing more.

Isaías forced himself to inhale. The air felt thick and metallic, like the warehouse itself had become an extension of their weapons. He stared at Shadow, at

Serrano, at Ruiz taping his wrists, at Toño checking his sights. Then at **El Silencioso.** Silencioso was standing alone by the planning table, head bowed over the mansion blueprint, one hand resting lightly on its surface.

Lighting flashed behind him, casting his silhouette huge against the far wall. Thunder followed, shaking dust loose from the rafters. Silencioso didn't move.

Isaías felt dread coil in his stomach. *This man… this man is going to walk into the home of one of New Orleans' most feared families and cut it open like a throat.*

A chill crept down Isaías' spine. He turned away, staring at the warehouse door. The only thin barrier between them and the city outside. *New Orleans is not ready for this,* he thought.

He stepped outside into the loading dock. The humid air slapped him across the face, thick with storm residue. The sky was a low, bruised purple, clouds dragging their bellies across the tops of buildings. Puddles collected in cracks along the cement, mirroring the flicker of distant streetlights.

A lone car rolled down the distant street. A dog barked once, then stopped abruptly. Somewhere across the block, a security light flickered. Even the wind felt like it carried a warning. Isaías pressed a hand to his forehead. "Dios… what are we doing?" he whispered to no one.

He knew exactly what they were doing. But saying it aloud felt like tempting fate. He closed his eyes.

When he opened them, the warehouse door was sliding open behind him.

Silencioso stepped into the doorway. His gaze settled on Isaías like a weight being set gently and irrevocably on a scale. "You fear the city," Silencioso said quietly.

It wasn't accusation. It wasn't criticism. It was an assessment.

Isaías swallowed. "Yes." Silencioso stepped fully into the damp, wind-tossed air. "Do not fear the city," he said. "Fear hesitation."

Thunder rolled again, shaking the metal awning above them. Silencioso turned his head just slightly, eyes narrowing on the skyline toward the district where their target lived unaware, warm, safe, and unequipped for death. "The city is only a place," he murmured. "Men create danger. Men remove it."

He looked at Isaías again. "We remove it tonight." Then he stepped back inside the warehouse, leaving Isaías alone on the loading dock with the weight of prophecy pressing down on him.

Isaías took a long, shaking breath. Tonight, New Orleans would bleed. And no one, not the Martellos, not the city, not even Isaías himself, could stop the storm that had already begun forming inside that warehouse.

Back inside the warehouse, the atmosphere had sharpened again. The killers had finished their gear prep and now formed a loose semicircle near the planning table. The lantern's glow spread across their faces, carving shadows under their eyes, across their cheekbones, along the hardened lines of their jaws. Silencioso reached into a side pouch and withdrew a battered metal stopwatch. A relic from another life, but it worked. He clicked the top once. The ticking filled the quiet, a soft metallic heartbeat in the center of the room.

"Everything tonight revolves around timing," Silencioso said. He placed the stopwatch onto the table with reverence, like it was an altar piece.

"Strike window opens at **22:58**," he continued. "We move into position by **23:07**." Toño nodded silently, committing the numbers to memory. "Power cuts at **23:10**," Silencioso said, eyes scanning the group. "Serrano, Ruiz, your synchronization must be exact."

Ruiz tapped his wrist twice. "Two counts, then cut." "Not two." Silencioso lifted a finger. "Three." Ruiz corrected immediately. "Three." Serrano repeated it under his breath, lips barely moving. "Three."

Silencioso clicked the stopwatch again, a sharp snap in the silence. "Alpha and Bravo breach at **23:11**. Echo neutralizes stairwell guards at the same moment. Not before. Not after." Shadow spoke without looking up. "One second early is failure." Silencioso replied, "One second late is death." Shadow nodded.

The storm outside groaned, wind rattling the loose siding like bones shaking in a coffin.

Silencioso pointed to the map again. "Guard check rotation at the mansion shifts at **23:06**. That is when their pattern is weakest. Delta will disable driveway guards at **23:09**, quiet, clean, no alert." One of the Delta men murmured, "Understood."

A flash of lightning lit the warehouse interior completely for a moment. Silencioso didn't even blink. He lifted the stopwatch once more. "Extraction begins at **23:13**. We depart by **23:15**. No delays."

Isaías frowned from his post near the comms table. "That's only two minutes for extraction." "Two minutes is eternity," Shadow murmured. Silencioso nodded. "Two minutes is survival."

Ruiz raised a hand. "What about the police window after the blackout? How fast is…" Isaías answered, voice low and tight. "NOPD will assume storm-related grid failure for ninety seconds. After that, they start rolling." "So we have 90 seconds before the first patrol even thinks something's wrong," Serrano said. Silencioso replied, "We only need sixty." He clicked the stopwatch again. The sound grew louder in the silence, like a countdown only they could hear.

Silencioso raised the metallic relic and let the ticking fill the space before he said, "This watch is the mission." His grip on the stopwatch tightened. "It will dictate when we breathe, when we move, when we kill."

He set it back onto the table with a slow, careful motion. "Memorize the numbers."

He spoke each time point again. Every man repeated them under his breath softly, in unison, like a prayer.

Silencioso watched their lips form the numbers, their eyes fix on the map, their bodies lean subtly forward with purpose.

Then he said, "Adjust gear. Adjust routes. Adjust minds." Shadow looked up. "What about nerves?" Silencioso looked him dead in the eyes. "Nerves are for men with futures."

A chill moved through the warehouse, though no wind touched the room. Silencioso picked up the stopwatch again, thumb resting lightly on the trigger. "We move in less than twelve hours," he said. "Eat. Hydrate. Empty your minds of doubt." The killers all quietly nodded.

Then Silencioso added one final, chilling directive, "From this moment forward… every second matters." He clicked the stopwatch. Tick… Tick… Tick… And every man in the room felt the weight of time pressing down on their shoulders.

Twilight bled across the warehouse windows, staining the concrete floor in bruised purples and dying reds. The storm had drifted east, leaving behind a thick and humid silence. An hour ago, the world outside had felt uneasy. Now it felt *held*. As if the city itself knew something awful was coming.

Inside the warehouse, the lantern still burned. It was the only light. The eleven killers gathered around the planning table once more. Not in chaos. Not in rush. In formation. Each man finding the same spot he had occupied the night before, as though drawn there by instinct.

Silencioso stood at the head, the stopwatch now clipped to his belt. His posture was stronger, stiller, almost carved. The black wristband with no number rested against his skin like a mark of fate.

Isaías Velasco hovered near the comms table, fingers trembling slightly as he tested each radio channel one last time. He felt the moment pressing down on him like a weight he could not set aside.

Something in the room had changed. These were no longer men preparing; These were men waiting for permission to kill.

The first vibration shattered the silence. Every head lifted slightly. The sound came from a single burner phone lying face-down on the table. Its cracked screen glowed white in the lantern light. Silencioso reached for it. He turned it over. There was one message from Óscar. **"The night is yours. Victory is the only language the dead understand."**

The killers didn't move, but the air shifted. It felt like a benediction and a curse wrapped into one. Shadow exhaled once through his nose. Toño lowered his head. Ruiz clenched his jaw. Serrano's fingers tapped his thigh once, then stilled. Silencioso read the message twice. Then he powered off the phone and set it beside the map.

The silence returned. Silencioso looked at Isaías. "Open channel." Isaías's throat bobbed as he swallowed. He flipped the comms switches, felt the static rise into a steady hum, and nodded. "It's open."

Silencioso scanned the men. "You know your assignments." Nods. "You know your timings." More nods. "You know your deaths." No one flinched.

Silencioso reached to the table and picked up a single object The black cloth that had held their weapons, tapes, and tools. He folded it cleanly, precisely, and tucked it under his arm. Then he extended his other hand with his palm open.

Shadow stepped forward first and placed his hand on top. Then Toño. Then Serrano. Ruiz. The stairwell killers. The driveway killers. The remaining survivors. Isaías hesitated and then placed his hand last, knowing he didn't deserve to stand in that circle, but also knowing the circle had already cast its shadow over him.

Silencioso lowered his voice to a whisper that thundered in every man's chest. "The oath." It was not a question. Every voice answered as a low and steady, almost deadly one, **"We do not fail."** Silencioso continued, "What are we?" Shadow answered, **"Ghosts."** Serrano echoed, **"Shadows."** Toño added, **"Judgment."**

Silencioso closed his fingers around the pile of hands, gripping them with calm, terrible strength. "And tonight," he said, "we collect the debt."

He released them. The circle broke. The men stepped back with silent precision, no longer individuals, now a single weapon sharpened to a killing point.

Silencioso lifted the stopwatch from his belt, held it up so they could all see the metal gleam in the lantern's wavering light, then clicked it.

The countdown had begun. "Gear up," Silencioso said. "Load vehicles." "We leave at 22:00." His gaze hardened, voice dropping to the coldest tone Isaías had ever heard from him, "Next stop…" A beat. "…the Castenllo home."

The lantern flickered as if recoiling from the words. And the killers moved at once.

Chapter 12

Sunday Night Out

Marie Castenllo stood at the kitchen counter with her sleeves rolled up, hands dusted in flour, coaxing dough into the shape it had taken every Sunday evening for more than thirty years. The rhythm was muscle memory now: Press, Turn, and Fold.

The restaurant smelled like garlic, simmering tomatoes, and something richer beneath its memory.

Outside, the last of the daylight faded behind the Warehouse District's towering buildings, casting long shadows across the cobblestone streets. Inside, the place felt alive in a way it hadn't for months. Not loud. Not celebratory. Just… present.

Marie wiped her hands on a dish towel and glanced toward the doorway as footsteps approached. "You don't have to hover," she said without turning.

Sophie appeared anyway, leaning against the frame with her arms folded, hair still damp from a shower, Tulane hoodie hanging loose over her shoulders. "I'm not hovering," Sophie said. "I'm supervising."

Marie smiled despite herself. "You supervised when you were six," she replied. "You ate half the dough." Sophie grinned faintly, then let the smile fade into something softer. "It smells like… home," she said quietly.

Marie turned then, really looked at her daughter. There were shadows under Sophie's eyes she hadn't noticed before. Not fear. Fatigue. The kind that came from growing up too fast, from carrying things she didn't talk about. Marie reached out and brushed a loose strand of hair behind Sophie's ear. "That's because it *is* home," she said. "No matter how busy you get. No matter how far you go." Sophie nodded, swallowing.

In the private dining room of the restaurant, Vinny Castenllo Jr. adjusted the cuff of his shirt as he set the table. Another quiet ritual he insisted on, despite the staff's offers to handle it. Crystal glasses caught the light. The silverware was aligned with almost obsessive precision. Control, Marie thought. It was how he survived.

Vinny paused, staring at the long table, then called out, "Ma, you want the red or white tonight?" "Red," Marie answered. "Always red on Sundays." Vinny smiled faintly at that and reached for the bottle Tony Russo had dropped off earlier in the afternoon. A good one. From Sicily. Tony always remembered. Tony Russo had been coming to their house since before Sophie was born. Back when dinners ran long and laughter was louder, before business turned complicated and names like Castenllo carried more weight than comfort.

"Papa's coming too?" Sophie asked from the kitchen doorway. Vinny glanced toward her. "Of course he is." She hesitated. "I didn't know if…" "He wouldn't miss it," Vinny said firmly. "Not tonight."

As if summoned by the words, Vincent Castenllo Sr.'s voice drifted down the hall. "I wouldn't miss what?"

The older man appeared slowly, leaning slightly on his cane, suit pressed but relaxed, his presence filling the space even now. His eyes softened when they landed on Sophie. "There's my girl," he said. Sophie crossed the room and hugged him carefully. "You eating real food tonight?" she teased. "For you?" he said. "Always."

Marie watched them from the kitchen, a tight ache settling behind her ribs. This was what she fought for. What she protected and what she insisted upon. Sunday nights were not business. They were family.

She turned back to the stove, stirring the sauce slowly, deliberately, as if the motion itself could hold the moment together just a little longer.

Outside, a car passed down the street. The place settled into the comforting cadence of a Sunday evening of soft voices, clinking glassware, and the faint hum of music from a radio in the kitchen. For now, there was the fragile illusion that Sunday nights still belonged to them.

Tony's restaurant sat on a quiet corner just off Magazine Street, its neon sign glowing soft red against the deepening blue of evening. The windows were fogged slightly from the warmth inside, and the low murmur of conversation spilled onto the sidewalk every time the door opened. It was the kind of place that felt untouched by time.

Inside, the smell of basil, wine, and fresh bread wrapped around the Castenllos the moment they stepped to the table.

"Vincent!" Tony's voice boomed from behind the bar. Tony emerged, wiping his hands on a towel, silver hair combed back, sleeves rolled up, eyes bright. He crossed the room and embraced Vincent Sr. first, careful of the cane, then Marie, then Vinny Jr., holding him a second longer than the others. "You're too thin," Tony said. "Both of you. That's what power does. It makes men forget to eat." Vinny Jr. smiled politely. "You feeding us or lecturing us tonight?" Tony laughed. "Both. Sit. I have the staff putting the finishing touches on Marie's wonderful meal."

Their table was the same one they'd used for years, tucked into a corner of the private dining room where the noise softened, and the walls were covered in old photographs of Tony as a young man in Sicily, Tony with musicians, Tony with politicians, Tony with Vincent Sr. in better days.

Sophie slid into her seat, glancing around with something like relief. "I forgot how loud it is," she said. "That's how you know it's alive," Tony replied, setting down menus they wouldn't need. "Silence is for hospitals and churches." Marie folded her napkin carefully on her lap. "Let's not tempt fate."

Tony raised an eyebrow. "Still superstitious, Marie?" "Still married to a man who learned the hard way," she replied gently.

Vincent Sr. chuckled, then coughed into his hand, the sound lingering a second too long. Vinny Jr. noticed immediately. "You alright, Dad?" "Fine," the old man said. "Just old."

Tony disappeared toward the kitchen and returned moments later with wine already poured. The first toast came naturally. "To family," Tony said. They echoed it quietly. To family.

Plates arrived in waves. Marie had arranged for antipasti, fresh pasta, and rich sauces that demanded attention and slowed conversation. For a while, no one talked about business. That, too, was tradition. Sophie spoke about classes. Marie talked about a charity event she was considering. Vincent Sr. reminisced about a trip to Palermo decades ago.

Vinny Jr. listened more than he spoke. He watched Sophie laugh at something Tony said, watched Marie reach for Vincent Sr.'s hand without looking, watched the easy rhythm that used to define their lives.

He wanted this back. "You're quiet tonight," Marie said softly. Vinny Jr. blinked. "Just thinking." "About?" He hesitated, then shrugged. "About how lucky we are."

Sophie smiled at him. "You sound like Grandpa."

Vincent Sr. lifted his glass. "Wisdom comes with age. Or regret." The table fell into a comfortable silence for a moment, broken only by the clink of silverware and the low hum of other diners.

Across the room, a man paid his check and left. No one noticed the way he paused just outside the door, glancing back once before disappearing into the night. No one noticed the car idling down the block.

Inside, Tony set down a dessert of cannoli, dusted in powdered sugar. "On the house," he said. "Because Sundays should end sweet." Marie smiled up at him. "Thank you, Tony." He nodded, then hesitated, eyes flicking briefly to the window.

"Don't stay out too late," he said casually. "Storm knocked out some lights earlier. Streets are darker than usual." Vinny Jr. waved it off. "We'll be home soon." Tony watched them a moment longer than necessary, then forced a smile and walked away.

Outside, night fully claimed the city. And somewhere beyond the warmth of the restaurant, the quiet machinery of violence continued to turn a slow and precise churn; almost unstoppable.

The Castenllos left Tony's just after nine. The night air was thick and warm, the streetlights casting amber pools across the sidewalk. Tony stood in the doorway watching them go, hands on his hips with smile lingering until the car doors closed and the engine turned over. Only then did his expression fade into something unreadable.

The black SUV eased away from the curb. Inside, the mood was relaxed and soft in the way that only came after good food and shared memory. Marie sat in the front passenger seat, shoes slipped off, hands folded loosely in her lap. Vincent Sr. rested in the back beside Sophie, his cane tucked carefully between his knees.

Vinny Jr. rode up front in the driver's seat, loosening his tie and leaning back as the city slid past.

"Tony still makes it like your grandmother," Vincent Sr. said. "That sauce... took me back." Sophie smiled. "You always say that." "And I'm always right."

Marie turned slightly, glancing back. "You feeling alright?" Vincent Sr. nodded. "Better than I have all week." That alone made the night feel like a small victory.

The SUV passed through Magazine Street traffic, then turned onto quieter roads leading toward the Garden District. Houses grew larger. Streets grew darker. The city's noise softened to a distant hum.

Vinny Jr. watched it all through the windshield. "You know," he said, almost to himself, "we should do this more often." Marie looked at him. "Do what?" "Be… normal." Sophie laughed softly. "Define normal."

Vinny Jr. smiled, but there was something brittle under it. "Dinner. No phones. No meetings. Just us." Marie reached over and rested her hand briefly on his arm. "We've always been us." He nodded but didn't quite believe it.

The SUV slowed at a stop sign. On the opposite corner, a man stood under a streetlight pretending to scroll on his phone. His posture was loose, casual. He didn't look at the vehicle.

The SUV turned. The man lifted his head just enough to catch the reflection of taillights disappearing down the street.

He touched the small earpiece hidden beneath his cap. "Moving," he murmured.

Three blocks away, another car eased out of a parking space and fell in behind the Castenllo SUV. It did not follow close, nor obvious, just another vehicle heading the same direction.

Inside the Castenllo vehicle, Sophie yawned and rested her head briefly against the window. "I forgot how tiring being around people is," she said. Vincent Sr. chuckled. "That's how you know you enjoyed it." Marie glanced out her window as they passed beneath the arching oaks of the Garden District. Their branches formed a canopy overhead, shadows weaving together like fingers.

Their mansion loomed ahead now, lights glowing warmly through tall windows.

The SUV slowed again. The following car slowed too. Vinny Jr. didn't notice. He was already thinking about the next day; meetings, calls, problems to solve. The way he always did. Control returned like armor sliding back into place.

The driver turned into the driveway. At the far end of the street, a second figure stepped out from between two parked cars, adjusting the strap of a bag slung low at his side. He didn't hurry. Didn't rush. He simply waited.

Inside the SUV, the gate began to open. Marie smiled faintly. "Good night," she said, as if the words themselves were a blessing. The vehicle rolled forward.

Behind them, the street settled back into silence. And above the quiet hum of the engine, no one inside the car heard the soft click of a stopwatch being reset somewhere nearby.

The Castenllo mansion came alive in stages. The front door closed with a soft, final click. The alarm chirped once and then was disarmed. Lights flickered on room by room, warm and golden against the night.

Inside, it felt safe. The kind of safety money bought and tradition reinforced.

Marie slipped off her coat and draped it over the banister. "I'll make tea," she said. "Something to settle after all that wine." Sophie padded down the hallway toward her room, stretching her arms over her head. "I'm going to shower and crash. Early class tomorrow." Vincent Sr. eased himself into the living room chair, sighing as the cushion accepted his weight. "Don't get old," he said lightly to no one in particular. Vinny Jr. smiled and loosened his collar further. "I'll bring you something."

The driver and two guards moved automatically into their evening positions; one inside near the hall, one outside by the front drive. Their posture relaxed now that the family was home.

Outside, the mansion looked as serene as an island of light beneath arching oaks, hedges trimmed to perfection, driveway clean and quiet.

But the darkness around it was no longer empty.

Three houses down, a sedan sat parked beneath a tree, engine cold. Inside, **Toño** adjusted his rearview mirror and scanned the street again. Nothing moved. No pedestrians. No traffic. "Target home," he murmured into the mic.

Static answered. Then Silencioso's voice, low and controlled. "Confirmed."

Across the street, near the rear property line, **Shadow** stood motionless in the narrow shadow between the fence and a thick hedge. The ivy-covered wall loomed ahead of him, just as it had in the photographs. Shadow crouched and touched the ground, feeling vibration through the soles of his shoes.

Inside the trees near the service alley, **Serrano** and **Ruiz** waited with practiced stillness, tools already in hand. Serrano checked his watch. Just instinctive timekeeping. "Grid is quiet," Ruiz whispered. "Always is before it isn't," Serrano replied.

At the far end of the block, **Delta Team** melted into the darkness near the driveway entrance. One leaned casually against the fence, pretending to check his phone. The other stood near a parked SUV, posture loose, eyes sharp. Guard rotation approaching.

Inside the house, Marie poured hot water over tea leaves. The kettle hissed softly. She smiled to herself, enjoying the ordinary domestic sound. Vincent Sr. closed his eyes for a moment in the living room. Vinny Jr. stepped into his office, flicked on the desk lamp, and glanced at the framed photograph on the shelf of the family at a charity gala, all smiles, all whole. He straightened it absently.

Upstairs, Sophie turned on the shower. Water began to run, steam blooming against the bathroom mirror.

Outside, Shadow's earpiece crackled. "All teams in position," Isaías whispered. His voice was tight, controlled, and afraid of being heard even through encryption. Shadow didn't answer. He was watching the rear wall. The ivy stirred slightly in the breeze. Time slowed.

In the driveway, the guard shifted his weight, rolling his shoulders. In the alley, Serrano pressed two fingers together to signal readiness. In the parked sedan, Toño's hand rested lightly on the steering wheel, knuckles white. And somewhere just beyond the mansion's glow, **El Silencioso** stood unseen, stopwatch heavy against his palm.

Inside the house, Marie carried the tea tray toward the living room. "Vincent," she called softly.

"Chamomile." No one noticed the way the generator's hum dipped for just a fraction of a second and then steadied again. No one noticed the shadow passing across the back lawn. The house was settling for the night. The hunters were finished moving.

All that remained now… was the moment.

The house exhaled. That was the only way Marie could have described it later if she ever had the chance. The mansion seemed to settle deeper into itself, as though satisfied that the day was finished and nothing more would be asked of it.

The tea tray clinked softly as Marie set it on the coffee table. Vincent Sr. stirred, eyes half-opening. "Smells good," he murmured. "Drink it while it's hot," she said, smiling.

Upstairs, the shower shut off. Sophie hummed faintly to herself as she wrapped a towel around her hair, steam fogging the mirror until her reflection blurred into nothing.

In the office, Vinny Jr. sat behind his desk for just a moment longer than he needed to, staring at the quiet glow of the lamp, the framed photo beside it. Family. Legacy. Protection. He rose, switched off the light, and stepped into the hallway.

Outside, the street was empty. Too empty.

El Silencioso stood in the darkness behind the neighboring hedge, the mansion framed perfectly between tree trunks and shadow. He didn't move. Didn't blink. His breathing was slow, regulated, almost nonexistent.

The stopwatch rested in his palm. Its face glowed faintly. **22:58.** He pressed the button. **Click.** The second hand began to move.

In the alley, Serrano felt it. Not through the radio, not through sound, but through instinct. His shoulders tightened. Ruiz's jaw clenched. In the parked sedan, Toño straightened slightly, eyes fixed on the driveway. Shadow's fingers brushed the ivy-covered wall.

Inside the house, a light clicked off upstairs. Another followed. The living room dimmed to a warm, amber glow.

Vincent Sr. lifted his cup. "You know," he said softly, "nights like this make a man believe he did something right." Marie reached for his hand.

Outside, the generator hummed. Then… It hiccupped… Just once. Barely noticeable. The porch light flickered.

Inside the house, Marie frowned faintly. "Did you see that?" Vinny Jr. turned. "See what?"

Before she could answer, **The power died.** The mansion plunged into darkness. Sophie gasped upstairs. Vincent Sr. stiffened in his chair. Marie froze, heart stuttering.

Outside, the streetlights along the block blinked out one by one. Silence rushed in to replace the hum of electricity.

Then… A soft voice crackled through multiple earpieces at once.

"Power cut," Isaías whispered. "All grids down." In the shadows, El Silencioso raised his head slightly. His thumb rested on the stopwatch. He didn't look at the house. He looked at his men though they could not see him.

"It begins," he said. And as the second hand swept forward, shadows detached themselves from the darkness and moved toward the Castenllo home; silent, precise, and unstoppable.

Inside, Marie reached instinctively for Vincent Sr. Somewhere upstairs, Sophie called out, "Mom?" And in the blackened halls of the mansion, the night took its first breath.

Chapter 13

Arriving Home

The gate slid closed behind the SUV with a muted mechanical sigh. Vinny Castenllo Jr. barely noticed it anymore. The sound had become part of his internal clock. The driveway curved gently toward the house, headlights washing over trimmed hedges and stonework he'd approved personally years ago. The mansion stood ahead, lights on, warm and expectant.

Home.

The driver brought the SUV to a smooth stop beneath the porte cochère. The engine idled for a beat before cutting out, the sudden quiet settling heavily around them. Vinny Jr. stepped out first, straightening his jacket and inhaling the familiar night air. Somewhere nearby, cicadas hummed lazily. The faint scent of magnolia drifted across the lawn. Behind him, Marie emerged more slowly, one hand resting briefly on the doorframe as she stepped down. Vincent Sr. followed with the help of the driver, cane tapping once against the stone before he steadied himself. Sophie lingered inside the vehicle a moment longer than the others.

"Hey," Vinny Jr. said, glancing back at her. "You okay?" She nodded, forcing a smile as she climbed out. "Just tired." He believed her. Why wouldn't he?

The front door opened almost immediately. One of the guards stepped aside to let them pass, posture relaxed now that the family was home. "Evening, sir," he said. "Evening," Vinny Jr. replied, already shrugging out of the night.

Inside, the house greeted them with quiet order. Lights glowed softly in the hallway. A familiar painting hung exactly where it always had. The faint echo of footsteps bounced off marble and wood.

Marie slipped off her shoes and placed them neatly by the wall. Sophie headed upstairs without being told, calling back, "I'm going to grab my things." "You staying out tonight?" Marie asked. Sophie paused halfway up the stairs. "Just crashing at Mia's. Early study group tomorrow." Vinny Jr. frowned slightly. "This late?" "It's not late," Sophie said gently. "It's Sunday."

Vincent Sr. smiled. "Let her go. She's young. Don't waste it." Sophie leaned over the banister and smiled down at him. "See? Grandpa gets it." She disappeared upstairs, footsteps light and unhurried. Vinny Jr. watched her go, a flicker of something mirroring pride crossing his face. "She's grown," he said quietly. Marie nodded. "She always was."

The living room lights dimmed slightly as Vincent Sr. eased himself into his chair, exhaling in relief. Marie crossed to the sideboard and poured a glass of water, moving with the easy familiarity of someone who knew the house as well as her own body.

Vinny Jr. loosened his tie and glanced down the hall toward his office. "I'm going to check a couple of things," he said. "Just five minutes." Marie didn't look up. "Don't turn it into thirty." He smiled faintly. "I won't."

Upstairs, Sophie reappeared with a small overnight bag slung over her shoulder. She descended quickly, almost lightly, as if eager not to linger. "Keys are by the door," Marie said. "I know," Sophie replied.

She bent and kissed Marie's cheek, then hugged Vincent Sr. carefully. "Don't stay up too late," he said. She smiled. "You either." Her eyes met Vinny Jr.'s. "I'll text you when I get there," she said. He nodded. "Be safe." Sophie stepped outside, the front door closing softly behind her.

The house seemed to settle again, reshaping itself around the three who remained.

Vinny Jr. turned toward his office. Marie carried her water into the living room. Vincent Sr. closed his eyes for a moment, listening to the quiet.

Outside, the driveway lay empty again. Down the block, unseen, a man adjusted his stance in the shadows and murmured into a concealed mic: "Family home. Daughter departing." There was a pause. Then a calm voice answered, steady as a metronome: "Copy."

Inside the house, Vinny Jr. flicked on his desk lamp. The light snapped on. He sat down, unaware that somewhere nearby, a stopwatch had already begun to tick.

Sophie's car pulled out of the driveway with a soft crunch of tires over gravel. She drove slowly at first, one hand on the wheel, the other resting on the overnight bag beside her. The gate slid shut behind her, sealing the mansion away with a mechanical finality she barely noticed.

The night felt cooler beyond the property line. Less controlled. Streetlights cast uneven shadows across the pavement, and the neighborhood stretched wide and quiet around her. Freedom, she thought. Or something like it. Her phone buzzed as she turned onto the main road. **Mia:** *You almost here?* Sophie smiled and tapped out a reply at the next stop sign. **Sophie:** *Five minutes.* She glanced in the rearview mirror out of habit. Nothing there. Just her own taillights receding into the darkness.

She turned up the radio, letting music fill the car with the sound of something familiar and light. Her shoulders loosened as the distance between her and the house grew. She didn't see the parked sedan two blocks down, engine off, lights dark. She didn't notice the man inside lift his head slightly as she passed. "Daughter clear," he murmured into his mic. Static answered for a beat. Then the reply came, low and precise: "Confirmed."

Sophie turned onto Magazine Street, traffic sparse now, storefronts mostly dark. She yawned and rolled down the window, letting humid air rush in. Her thoughts drifted to class, deadlines, and to the small, ordinary concerns of someone whose life still belonged to tomorrow.

She slowed at a red light and glanced at her phone again. A text from her father waited unread. She opened it. **Vinny Jr.:** *Text me when you get there.* She smiled softly. **Sophie:** *Always do.* She sent it and slipped the phone back into her bag as the light changed. The car moved on. Behind her, the city swallowed the sound of her engine.

At the mansion, the house absorbed her absence without complaint. Marie stood in the kitchen rinsing a cup, listening to the water run a little longer than necessary. When she shut it off, the silence felt heavier than before.

"She's gone," Marie said, not really to anyone. Vincent Sr. stirred in his chair. "She's young. Nights like this belong to her." Marie nodded, though unease tugged faintly at her chest.

Vinny Jr. sat at his desk, reviewing documents he'd already reviewed twice. Numbers blurred together. His thoughts kept drifting back to Sophie's voice on the stairs. *I'll text you when I get there.* He glanced at his phone. No message yet. "She'll text," he muttered to himself.

Outside, the street remained quiet. The guard by the driveway shifted his stance, hands resting loosely at his belt. He glanced down the block, then back toward the house. Normal.

Farther back, near the ivy-covered wall, a figure remained motionless in shadow, eyes tracking windows, doors, patterns. Waiting.

The house settled into its nighttime rhythm. Lights dimmed automatically in unused rooms. The air-conditioning whispered through the vents. Somewhere deep in the walls, pipes ticked as they cooled.

Vincent Castenllo Sr. slept lightly in his chair, breath slow, uneven but steady. Marie moved quietly through the kitchen, wiping already-clean counters, straightening objects that didn't need straightening.

Vinny Castenllo Jr. stood in his office doorway, phone in hand, staring at the darkened hallway beyond. "She'll text," he said again, as if saying it twice made it law. He returned to his desk and sat, the chair creaking softly beneath him.

Outside, the mansion glowed like a ship at anchor.

Two houses down, **Toño** adjusted the angle of his rearview mirror for the third time. He didn't look directly at the house. He didn't need to. He could feel it.

"Street is dead," he murmured. In his earpiece, Isaías answered quietly from the Kenner safehouse. "NOPD scanner clean. No patrols diverted. The neighborhood is quiet." "Copy." Toño's hand rested near the door handle now, not gripping it, just ready.

Behind the mansion, **Shadow** stood inches from the ivy-covered wall. He could smell damp earth, crushed leaves, the faint metallic tang of the generator nearby. He closed his eyes briefly and listened. The house spoke if you knew how to hear it. He lifted his wrist and checked the small, dark face of his watch. 9:48. Shadow touched his earpiece. "Rear wall secure," he whispered. "Cameras unchanged. Blind spot intact."

Silencioso's voice came back instantly, calm as breath.

"Hold."

Near the service alley, **Serrano** and **Ruiz** crouched behind a low utility structure, tools laid out neatly on a cloth between them. Ruiz flexed his fingers once. "Feels too easy." Serrano didn't look at him. "That's because it's already over." Ruiz frowned slightly. "You don't believe in luck." "I believe in timing," Serrano said. "And timing's on our side." He glanced at the junction box, dark and silent. Waiting.

At the front of the property, **Delta Team** watched the driveway. The guard leaned against the stone post, posture relaxed, weight on one leg. His partner paced once, then stopped, checking his phone before slipping it back into his pocket.

They were bored and bored men died quietly. One of Delta murmured, "Rotation in two minutes." "Plenty," the other replied. Neither sounded excited.

Inside the mansion, Marie carried a blanket and draped it gently over Vincent Sr.'s shoulders. He stirred but didn't wake. She brushed his hair back with her fingertips. "Rest," she whispered. She turned toward the hallway.

As she did, the lights flickered. Just once. Barely enough to notice. Marie paused.

Her heart gave a small, sharp jump. "Vincent?" she called softly. Vinny Jr.'s voice floated back from the office. "Yeah?" "Did you see that?" "See what?" The lights steadied. Marie hesitated, then shook her head. "Nothing. Probably the storm earlier."

Vinny Jr. frowned but said nothing. He checked his phone again. Still nothing from Sophie. 9:49.

Outside, Shadow's eyes narrowed slightly. He'd felt it too. He pressed his mic. "Stand by," he said quietly. Silencioso answered without hesitation. "Stand by."

Somewhere nearby, unseen, **El Silencioso** raised the stopwatch and watched the second hand sweep forward. Every man was in place. The night had drawn a clean line around the Castenllo home. And with each passing second, the space for doubt narrowed
until soon, there would be none at all. Time slowed the closer it came to the hour.

Inside the mansion, the house had grown quieter; not the peaceful quiet of sleep, but the expectant hush of a place that believed it was safe. The kind of quiet that came from locks turned, routines followed, guards posted.

Vinny Castenllo Jr. stood in the doorway of his office, phone in his hand, thumb hovering uselessly over the screen. He stared down the hall toward the staircase, listening for Sophie's footsteps out of habit before remembering that she was gone.

A flicker of irritation passed through him, quickly followed by something less defined. Unease, maybe. He pushed it aside and set the phone face down on the desk.

In the living room, Marie sat on the edge of the couch, hands folded in her lap, eyes drifting toward the darkened windows. The blanket on Vincent Sr.'s shoulders rose and fell with his breathing. She listened to the sound of it; steady, fragile, precious. The house creaked softly as it cooled. Somewhere in the distance, a dog barked. Then stopped.

Outside, the night tightened. Behind the ivy-covered wall, **Shadow** adjusted his stance by a fraction of an inch, redistributing his weight so that every muscle was ready without tension. His breathing slowed further, syncing with the cadence he'd learned years ago. He watched the rear of the house not as a structure, but as a system.

His earpiece came alive with a whisper. "Delta, guard rotation complete," one of the driveway men reported. "Two stationary. Both relaxed." "Copy," came Isaías' voice, thin but controlled.

Two houses down, **Toño** rolled his shoulders once and let them settle. His gaze tracked the end of the street, then the mouth of the driveway, then the windows glowing on the second floor. "Traffic zero," he murmured. "Street belongs to us."

Near the service alley, **Serrano** glanced at his watch again; not the time, but the *space* between seconds. Ruiz crouched beside him, fingers resting lightly on the insulated cutters. The junction box waited. "Thirty seconds," Serrano said quietly. Ruiz nodded once.

Inside the mansion, Marie rose and crossed the room, turning off a lamp near the window. The living room dimmed further, shadows stretching across the floor. She paused by the window and looked out. The street was empty. Her reflection stared back at her from the glass, pale and uncertain.

A sudden, irrational urge took hold of her. She turned and called softly, "Vinny?" "Yes?" His voice came immediately, closer now. "Lock the office door tonight," she said. "Just… for me." He frowned slightly but nodded. "Of course."

He closed the door behind him with a soft click and turned the lock. The sound was small, but it settled something in her chest. She didn't know why.

In the darkness beyond the property line, **El Silencioso** stood utterly still. The stopwatch was warm in his hand now. He watched the second hand approach its mark. 9:53.

His voice moved through the channel without urgency, without emotion. "All teams… ready." One by one, acknowledgments came back. "Alpha ready." "Bravo ready." "Echo ready." "Delta ready." Silencioso didn't respond.

Inside the house, Vincent Sr. shifted slightly in his sleep and murmured something unintelligible. Marie covered his hand with hers. "Shh," she whispered.

Outside, the generator hummed steadily, its sound unnoticed by the family, catalogued by the men waiting to silence it. The night held its breath. The distance between intention and action shrank to a razor's edge.

And as the second hand crept forward, the city itself seemed to lean away, as if it already knew what was about to be taken from it.

The stopwatch ticked softly in El Silencioso's hand. Each second landed with absolute clarity.

The mansion glowed in the darkness like a living thing, unaware that it had already been measured, mapped, and condemned.

Inside, Vinny Castenllo Jr. sat at his desk, fingers steepled, staring at his phone again. Still no message. A faint crease formed between his brows.

In the living room, Marie brushed her thumb across the back of Vincent Sr.'s hand, grounding herself in the feel of skin, bone, and warmth. The house creaked softly around them, the familiar language of settling wood and cooling stone.

Outside, Shadow's eyes never left the rear wall. Behind him, the ivy stirred in the breeze.

Serrano crouched at the junction box, cutters poised but not yet touching metal. Ruiz's breath came slow and steady beside him.

Toño's hand tightened on the door handle of the parked sedan, muscles coiled.

Delta Team watched the driveway guards of two silhouettes beneath soft exterior lighting, bored, relaxed, doomed.

Silencioso raised the stopwatch. The second hand reached its mark. **23:10.**

He didn't raise his voice. The words moved through the channel like a blade sliding free of its sheath. "Cut the power."

Serrano closed the cutters. Metal met metal. The generator coughed once and then died.

The mansion went black. Lights snapped out room by room, plunging halls into sudden darkness. Marie gasped.

Vincent Sr. jolted awake, confusion sharp in his eyes. "What the…?"

Vinny Jr. stood abruptly in his office, heart hammering as the desk lamp vanished and shadows swallowed the room.

Outside, the streetlights failed in sequence, plunging the block into near-total darkness. Silence rushed in, heavy and unnatural.

Inside the house, Marie's voice trembled. "Vinny?" "I'm here," he called back, already moving toward the door.

Upstairs, a startled noise echoed as something fell in the dark.

Guards shouted outside with confused disorientation. And in the blackness beyond the rear wall, shadows began to move.

El Silencioso lowered the stopwatch. The count had ended. The hunt had begun.

Chapter 14

The Raid

Darkness slammed into the mansion like a physical blow. It wasn't the gentle dimming of a power outage, but a hard, instant erasure. The light vanished and sound sharpened. Time fractured.

Inside the house, Marie gasped as the room disappeared around her. The familiar shapes of furniture dissolved into nothing, replaced by a suffocating void that pressed in from every direction. "Vinny!" she called, panic cracking her voice. Vincent Sr. lurched upright in his chair, disoriented, his cane clattering to the floor. "What's happening?"

In the office, Vinny Castenllo Jr. froze mid-step as the desk lamp cut out, plunging him into pitch black. His hand went instinctively to the drawer beneath the desk.

Outside, the driveway lights snapped off. The garden illumination died. Finally, the security floodlights along the rear wall vanished in a single breath. The Castenllo estate ceased to exist as a visible object.

At the edge of the property, **Delta Team** moved. They didn't rush, they didn't need to. They flowed.

The guard nearest the driveway frowned and took a step back, squinting into the darkness. "What the…" A hand clamped over his mouth. A blade flashed once, quick and precise, and the guard folded soundlessly to the ground.

Ten feet away, his partner reached for his radio. He never finished the motion. Two bodies hit the stone almost simultaneously. The front of the house was sealed.

Behind the mansion, **Shadow** was already in motion. The blackout was his signal. He crossed the lawn in a low sprint, boots whispering through grass damp with evening dew. The ivy-covered wall loomed ahead, exactly where it had always been. The blind spot swallowed him.

To his left, Toño mirrored the movement. To his right, Alpha's third man slid into position. Three silhouettes at the rear wall. Perfect spacing.

Shadow raised a clenched fist. They stopped as one. He pressed his earpiece. "Rear clear," he whispered. Silencioso's voice answered instantly, cold and absolute. "Proceed."

Shadow drew a small breaching charge from his pack. It wasn't explosive enough to announce itself, just enough to open flesh and bone. He placed it carefully against the service door seam and counted. One… Two… The door *thumped* inward with a muted crack, hinges surrendering quietly. The smell of burned metal and old paint bled into the night air. Shadow slipped inside.

Inside the house, Marie fumbled blindly, her heart pounding so loudly she could hear it in her ears. "Vincent!" she cried again, fear tearing through her composure. "I'm here," Vinny Jr. shouted from the hallway. "Stay where you are!"

He slid the drawer open. His fingers closed around cold steel. The pistol came free.

Outside the office door, the house was utterly silent… Too silent.

There were no alarms. No shouting guards. No footsteps running toward help. Just darkness. And somewhere deep within the house…

A floorboard creaked.

Vinny Jr. turned toward the sound, weapon raised. "Who's there?" he shouted. No answer. Only the faintest whisper of movement, barely louder than breath.

From the darkness of the service corridor, **El Silencioso** stepped inside the mansion. He didn't pause to adjust. Didn't listen in panic. He already knew where everything was.

The stopwatch clicked softly in his pocket. **23:11.** He pressed his mic once. "Inside," he said. Around the house, shadows advanced.

The raid had begun. The blackout did what it was meant to do. It stole context.

Inside the mansion, sound became treacherous with every breath too loud, every footstep a betrayal. Outside, the estate disappeared into the Garden District's deeper shadows, indistinguishable from the trees and hedges that ringed it.

At the front drive, **Delta Team** worked without haste. One man dragged a body behind the stone planter, checked the radio clipped to the guard's vest, then removed it and crushed it under his boot. The other stepped to the wrought-iron gate, slid it shut, and looped a thin steel cable through the latch. Sealed. "Front secure," he murmured. "Copy," came Silencioso's reply. No praise. No confirmation beyond the word.

Behind the house, **Echo Team** ghosted along the rear wall toward the service stairwell. They moved in file, each man tracking a separate plane, floor, midline, ceiling, covering angles that never overlapped.

A door handle rattled softly ahead. A guard stepped out, confused, his flashlight sweeping the dark. He saw nothing. Echo closed the distance in two steps.

The flashlight clattered to the tile and rolled, its beam spinning once before going still against the baseboard. The guard slid down the wall and stopped moving. "Stairwell clear," Echo whispered.

Inside the house, **Shadow** signaled Alpha forward. The breached service door yawned open behind them, a black mouth swallowing sound. Toño slipped left, weapon up; the third man flowed right, checking corners with the economy of men who had done this too many times. They paused at the threshold to the main hall.

Shadow listened. The house answered. A man was breathing too fast. A woman calling a name. An old man is shifting in a chair.

Shadow raised two fingers. *Three targets. One priority.* Toño nodded.

From the far end of the corridor, **Bravo Team** reached the side entrance. Serrano tested the handle, felt the lock give, and eased the door inward just enough to slide through. "Bravo inside," Serrano breathed.

In the living room, Marie's voice trembled in the dark. "Vincent, where are you?" Vinny Jr. moved down the hall with the pistol tight to his chest, using the wall to guide his steps. His mind raced. *Guards, alarms, why nothing?* Training kept his movements deliberate.

He reached the corner. A shadow shifted at the far end. He raised the gun. "Stop!" he shouted. The shadow didn't stop. It *split*.

Two shapes moved where there had been one. Vinny fired. The shot cracked the night open. The sound was thunder in the dark.

Alpha froze for a fraction of a second and then flowed. Toño ducked, the round passing overhead. Shadow surged forward, closing the distance with terrifying calm.

"Gunshot inside," Isaías whispered over the channel, panic barely leashed. "Continue," Silencioso replied.

Outside, the neighborhood slept. The gunshot echoed through the mansion, ricocheting off walls and stairwells, tearing the silence apart like fabric.

Marie screamed. Vincent Sr. shouted her name, panic snapping him fully awake as he fumbled for his cane in the dark. Vinny Jr. staggered back half a step as the recoil punched into his shoulder. His ears rang. Smoke curled from the barrel, the smell sharp and metallic.

He hadn't seen what he'd hit. Only that something had moved and now it was closer. Too close.

Toño hit the wall hard, shoulder first, breath exploding from his lungs as plaster burst beside his head. He rolled, came up kneeling, weapon already tracking. "Contact confirmed," he hissed. Shadow didn't slow. He *advanced*.

Vinny Jr. fired again, the muzzle flash briefly painting the hallway in stark white. The second round shattered a picture frame inches from Shadow's head. Shadow dropped low, sliding across the polished floor like a blade skimming water. Distance collapsed.

Vinny Jr. felt it then. It was not fear, not yet, but the sudden, awful realization that whoever was coming for him **was not retreating**. He fired a third time. Click… Empty. The sound was deafening in its finality.

Vinny's eyes widened. Shadow was already on him. The impact drove Vinny Jr. back into the wall, knocking the air from his lungs. The pistol clattered to the floor, skidding into darkness. Vinny swung wildly, catching Shadow's shoulder.

Shadow didn't flinch. Toño was there now, grabbing Vinny's arm, twisting it behind his back with brutal efficiency. Vinny cried out in fury and drove his elbow backward, catching Toño in the ribs. Toño grunted but held on.

"Jesus… Vinny gasped. "Who the hell are you?" Shadow answered by slamming him into the wall again, harder this time. The impact rattled the hall, pictures jumping on their hooks. Down the corridor, footsteps thundered.

Marie. "Vinny!" she screamed. Shadow's head snapped toward the sound. A shape burst from the living room. Marie, wild-eyed, rushing toward them in the dark. "No!" she cried. Shadow's hand came up. Toño froze. Before anyone else could move, **El Silencioso** stepped into the hall.

His presence cut through the chaos like cold water. "No." The single word landed heavy and absolute. Shadow stopped instantly.

Marie skidded to a halt, breath hitching, staring at the figure she could barely see. Silencioso looked at her once but only once. Then back to Vinny Jr.

Vinny struggled, rage and desperation bleeding together. "You think this ends anything?" he spat. "You think killing me…" Silencioso struck him. A precise blow to the throat. Vinny choked, collapsing to his knees, hands clawing at his neck as air refused to return.

Silencioso crouched in front of him, close enough that Vinny could feel his breath. "This ends *you*," Silencioso said quietly.

Behind them, Vincent Sr.'s voice cracked through the darkness. "Vincent…?"

Silencioso didn't turn. He raised a hand, signaling Alpha to hold positions. The house seemed to shrink around them as walls pressed in, shadows deepening, time slowing to a crawl.

Marie stood frozen, one hand clamped over her mouth, watching her husband gasp for breath at the feet of a stranger whose face she could barely see.

Vinny Jr. looked up at Silencioso, eyes burning, defiant even now. "You won't…" he rasped. Silencioso leaned closer. "You are already finished."

Vinny Castenllo Jr. collapsed forward, coughing violently, hands clawing at his throat as air refused to come back to him. His body betrayed him with his muscles spasming, and knees striking the floor hard enough to echo through the hall.

Marie cried out his name. "Vinny… please… please…" She took a step forward.

Shadow moved instinctively. Silencioso raised two fingers. Shadow stopped.

Marie froze where she stood, breath hitching, terror hollowing her face as she watched her Vinny struggle on the floor like a man drowning in plain sight.

Vincent Sr. appeared at the edge of the hallway, cane abandoned somewhere behind him. His eyes adjusted slowly to the dark, then widened as the shapes resolved into meaning.

His son was on his knees, surrounded by strangers. "Vincent…" he whispered.

Silencioso did not look at him. He focused only on Vinny Jr., whose defiance still burned even as his body failed him. Vinny forced air into his lungs in broken gasps, one hand braced against the floor as he tried to rise.

"You don't…" he rasped. "You don't get to…" Silencioso placed his palm flat against Vinny's chest and pushed him back down with controlled force, not to dominate, but to *position*. "You were chosen," Silencioso said calmly.

Vinny coughed again, blood flecking his lips. "For what?" he spat. Silencioso leaned closer, his voice low enough that only Vinny could hear it. "For consequence."

He drew his pistol. Marie let out a broken sob. "No… no… please… he's my…"

Silencioso spoke without raising his voice. "Take her." Toño moved immediately, stepping between Marie and the hall, gripping her arms gently but firmly, preventing her from rushing forward. "Don't hurt her," Vincent Sr. said hoarsely. Silencioso finally looked at him. He held the old man's gaze for one measured second. "We won't."

Then he returned his attention to Vinny Jr. Vinny's breathing was ragged now. He looked up past the gun, past the shadowed figure holding it, and for the first time, fear cracked through his composure.

"You think this ends it?" he whispered. "You think this saves anyone?" Silencioso answered him honestly. "No."

Silencioso pulled out the custom K-Bar knife from its sheath on his belt, which he had placed there back at the warehouse. He immediately leaped for Vinny like a puma attacking its prey. Once on top of Vinny Jr., he grabbed him by the back of his hair and yanked his head back, fully extending his neck. With one fluid motion, he plunged the knife deep into his throat and cut across his neck. Vinny's body jerked once, then went slack, collapsing sideways onto the floor.

The sound rang through the house, bouncing down halls and staircases, tearing through the last illusions of safety.

Marie screamed. Vincent Sr. staggered backward, his legs giving out as he fell into the wall, hands shaking, eyes locked on the still form of his son.

Silencioso lowered the weapon. He didn't look at the body again. "Target down," he said quietly into his mic. Across the property, acknowledgments came back in clipped whispers. Silencioso turned. "Restore power," he ordered.

Behind him, Alpha and Bravo teams shifted automatically, beginning the withdrawal without a single wasted motion.

Marie sagged in Toño's grip, her strength leaving her all at once. "Vinnny..," she sobbed. "My Vinny…"

Silencioso paused once more. Not for mercy, but for control. He looked at Marie, then at Vincent Sr., two people still breathing, still present, still very much alive in the wreckage he had just created. "This is finished," he said. Then he turned away. The killers moved. And behind them, the house held its breath around a single, irrevocable absence.

There was no pause to look. No breath taken in triumph. No lingering. Doctrine replaced emotion.

"Echo, clear stairwell," Silencioso said, already turning away from the body. "Clear," came the reply. "Delta, status." "Front sealed. No movement," Delta answered. Silencioso nodded once and pressed his mic again. "Restore power."

Behind the mansion, Serrano flipped the switch. The generator coughed. Then caught.

Lights snapped back on throughout the house.

The hallway flooded with brightness, revealing everything the darkness had hidden. Vinny Castenllo Jr.'s body lay twisted on the floor, eyes half-open, blood spreading beneath his head in a slow, obscene bloom. The wall behind him was scarred, a darkening spot where blood had splattered from Vinny's neck.

Marie screamed a raw, animal, tearing at the back of her throat. Toño loosened his grip just enough for her to collapse to her knees beside her husband. She clutched at him, shaking, whispering his name over and over as if repetition might undo physics. Vincent Sr. stared, frozen, his mouth open but silent now. His hands trembled violently at his sides.

"Alpha, move," Silencioso he ordered. Shadow and Toño flowed past the office doorway, weapons up, eyes scanning. Bravo peeled off toward the side entrance. Echo disappeared up the stairwell one last time to confirm no movement. The house was secured.

Outside, the Delta Team stepped away from the driveway, leaving the guards where they lay, out of sight, out of mind. One man clipped a small device to the inside of the gate control box. A camera blinked once. Recording stopped. "Exterior clear," Delta said.

Silencioso crossed the threshold at the rear service door, the cool night air washing over him like absolution. He didn't slow. Didn't look up at the stars or the trees or the house he had just broken open. He simply walked.

Behind him, Shadow emerged last, pausing for half a second to glance back through the open door. Marie's wail followed them out into the night. Shadow turned away.

Down the block, Toño slid into the driver's seat of the SUV, engine turning over without a hitch. Shadow took the passenger seat, already removing gloves, dropping them into a sealed bag. Serrano and Ruiz peeled off in the opposite direction, disappearing into darkness that closed behind them like water. The vehicles pulled away in staggered silence.

Inside the mansion, power fully restored, Marie rocked back and forth beside Vinny's body, her hands slick with his blood, her voice breaking into hoarse fragments of grief. Vincent Sr. sank into a chair, his legs failing him completely now, eyes never leaving the floor where his son lay.

The house, which was so warm and so certain just minutes ago, now felt enormous and empty.

A place hollowed out. Somewhere outside, sirens began to rise.

And miles away, moving through the city like smoke, the Murder Team vanished into the night, leaving behind light, life, and order restored…

…except for the one thing that would never be repaired.

The sirens arrived in layers. Red and blue light washed across the Castenllo mansion, slicing through the warm glow that had been restored only minutes earlier. Patrol cars skidded to a stop at the gate. Radios crackled. Boots hit gravel.

Inside the house, Marie knelt beside her Vinny, her hands pressed uselessly against a wound that no longer bled the way it should. Blood had soaked into the rug, into her sleeves, into the knees of her dress. "Stay with me," she whispered, voice shredded. "Vinny, stay with me. Please."

But Vinny Castenllo Jr. was already gone. His eyes stared past her at nothing.

Vincent Castenllo Sr. sat slumped against the wall, breath shallow, chest rising and falling in uneven jerks. His world had collapsed inward, decades of power and calculation reduced to a single, unbearable absence on the floor in front of him.

A guard burst into the hallway, weapon raised, then stopped dead. "Oh God," he breathed.

Another followed. Then another. No one spoke. They didn't need to. The truth was laid out in blood and silence.

An officer stepped carefully around the body, eyes already cataloging angles, trajectories, the impossibility of it all. He looked at Marie, who finally sagged backward into a pair of arms as medics arrived and pulled her gently away from her husband. "Get her out of here," he said. As Marie was lifted, her gaze caught on something near the doorway; a faint scuff on the floor where boots had turned, a mark she would never stop seeing in her mind.

The last footprint of the men who had taken her world.

Across the city, far from the Garden District, a vehicle rolled to a quiet stop beneath a dead streetlight.

El Silencioso stepped out first. He removed his gloves and dropped them into a burn bag, sealed it, and handed it off without comment. Shadow did the same. Toño wiped blood from his knuckles and exhaled once, long and slow. The mission was complete.

Silencioso checked the stopwatch one last time.

23:17. On schedule.

Isaías's voice crackled through the channel, tight and reverent. "Target confirmed deceased. Media hasn't broken yet. NOPD response ongoing." Silencioso nodded, though no one could see it. "Good," he said.

He turned and walked away from the car, disappearing into the narrow gap between buildings, the city swallowing him as easily as it had sheltered him. Behind him, engines started and doors closed. The Murder Team scattered into separate streams flowing back into the darkness, leaving no wake behind them.

Back at the mansion, a sheet was drawn over Vinny Castenllo Jr.'s body. The room felt smaller with it there. Heavier. Vincent Sr. stared at the covered form, something inside him finally breaking loose. His hand shook as he reached out, stopping just short of touching the sheet. "They took my son," he whispered. No one answered.

Outside, cameras flashed. Neighbors gathered at a distance. Whispers spread like an infection. A powerful man had been killed in his own home. Safest place in the city. Which meant only one thing: No one was safe anymore.

And somewhere far away, a message appeared on a secure phone. **DONE.** The reply came minutes later. **RECEIVED.**

The kind work that could never be undone.

Chapter 15

Disappearing Into the Wind

The city slid past in fragments of light and shadow. Streetlamps flickered across the windshield in steady intervals, each one briefly illuminating the inside of the van before surrendering it back to darkness. The engine hummed at a disciplined, even pitch. There was no sudden acceleration, no nervous braking. Just motion. and distance. No one spoke.

The Murder Team sat exactly where they had planned to sit, spacing preserved, gear stowed, weapons broken down and sealed in cases beneath the bench seats. Blood had been wiped away. Gloves placed in burn bags. Evidence erased down to muscle memory.

The violence was already receding into procedure. In the passenger seat, **El Silencioso** stared straight ahead, hands resting loosely on his thighs. His breathing was slow, deliberate. If anything was happening behind his eyes, it didn't show.

Behind him, **Shadow** cleaned his blade with a cloth soaked in solvent, methodical, reverent. He inspected the edge once, then slid the K-Bar back into its sheath and locked it away.

Toño drove. Both hands on the wheel. Eyes forward. Speed was fast enough to move, slow enough but not to be remembered.

The radio scanner crackled softly between bursts of static.

"…possible homicide… Garden District… officers en route…" No names yet. No details. Just noise.

Isaías's voice came through the earpiece from miles away, tight but controlled. "NOPD has the scene. Media's circling but no confirmations yet." Silencioso nodded once, though no one could see it. "Good," he said.

The van merged onto the highway, tires thumping rhythmically over seams in the concrete. The city skyline receded in the rearview mirror, shrinking into something abstract and distant.

Shadow glanced out the side window as the lights thinned and the dark stretches of road grew longer. "It was clean," he said quietly. Silencioso didn't respond. Clean wasn't the objective. Completion was.

Toño adjusted lanes without looking back. "Plate change in five." "Copy," Serrano replied from the rear, already reaching for the alternate tag. The van exited briefly, dipped into a dim industrial stretch, and rejoined the highway moments later with a different identity.

The world accepted the lie without question. The scanner chirped again. "…victim confirmed deceased… spouse in critical shock…" No names yet. Just confirmation.

Shadow's jaw tightened almost imperceptibly. Silencioso closed his eyes for a single second, then opened them again. "Phones," he said.

One by one, burner devices were powered on, checked, then powered off again. No messages yet. No incoming signals. Silencioso waited.

The van pushed north, leaving sirens, lights, grief, and questions behind. Ahead there was distance, borders, and… silence.

The job wasn't finished yet, but it was moving exactly as planned.

The van stayed steady at sixty-five as the highway opened into long, unlit stretches. Pine and scrub blurred past the windows, swallowed by night. The scanner fell silent for a few precious minutes, replaced by the low, constant rush of tires on asphalt.

Silencioso lifted one hand. Toño eased the van onto the shoulder beneath a dark overpass and killed the engine. The sudden quiet pressed in, thick and intimate. "Two minutes," Silencioso said.

Shadow didn't ask why. He reached under the bench seat and withdrew a small, hard case. Inside, nested in foam, was a phone no one else touched. No apps. No contacts. No history. Just a camera and a single encrypted channel. Shadow powered it on.

The image on the screen was clinical. Cropped. Tight. No faces but one. No background that could be traced. Just proof, framed to remove doubt and nothing more.

A single photograph.

A man's throat, opened cleanly with a precise and fatal K-Bar. No gore beyond necessity. No flourish. The edge of a collar visible. The suggestion of a body without context. Completion.

Shadow adjusted the exposure by a fraction. No shadows that could hide. No highlights that could distract. Silencioso leaned in once, inspected the frame, then straightened. "Send," he said. Shadow's thumb hovered for a beat, not out of hesitation but ritual, and then he tapped.

UPLOADING... The progress bar crept forward. Outside, a semi roared past on the highway above them, the concrete vibrating faintly. Dust drifted down in the overpass lights. **SENT.** The phone chimed once.

DELIVERED. No celebration followed.

Shadow powered the device off and slid it back into the case. He sealed it, snapped the latches, and passed it forward. Silencioso took the case and set it on the floor between his feet. He didn't open it again.

"Time?" he asked. "On schedule," Toño replied.

The scanner crackled back to life as the engine restarted. "…identity confirmed… body of…" Static swallowed the rest.

Silencioso reached into his jacket and removed another burner. This one was already warm in his hand, as if it had been waiting. It vibrated once. Then again. He answered without speaking.

A voice came through, distant and controlled like it was filtered by distance and authority. "Received."

Silencioso said nothing. A pause stretched. Not awkward. Measured. "Remain dark," the voice continued. "Routes as planned. Do not surface." "Understood," Silencioso replied. The call ended.

He powered the phone off, removed the battery, and handed both to Serrano, who dropped them into a sealed bag marked for destruction.

The van pulled back onto the highway, disappearing into the dark ribbon of road. Behind them, the message had landed.

Ahead of them, borders waited. And somewhere far south, a man had seen what he demanded to see and knew, without question, that the debt had been paid.

The highway narrowed as they pushed farther north, traffic thinning until the van seemed alone with the dark. Mile markers slid past at measured intervals, ticking away distance like a metronome.

Silencioso sat unmoving. The case with the phone rested at his feet. Untouched. Forgotten already.

The burner in his jacket vibrated, Once, Twice. This one mattered.

He removed it, powered it on, and answered without preamble.

"Yes." Óscar's voice came through the line, older and heavier, carrying the weight of distance and certainty. There was no anger in it. No satisfaction either. Just acknowledgment. "I have seen it." Silencioso said nothing. "That was my son's blood," Óscar continued. "And my granddaughter's future."

A pause. It wasn't grief. It was Calculation.

"You were precise," Óscar said. "That is why I chose you." Silencioso looked out the windshield as the van passed beneath another stretch of unlit road. "Precision was required," he replied.

Another pause. Longer this time. "You did not touch the wife?" Óscar asked. "No." "And the old man?" "Alive." Óscar exhaled slowly. The sound carried something close to memory, but it passed quickly. "Good," he said. "They will understand the message better this way."

Shadow's jaw tightened in the back of the van.

Óscar continued, his voice dropping. "You are no longer safe on American soil." Silencioso's eyes narrowed slightly, not in surprise, but in recognition. "Expected," he said. "There will be noise," Óscar added. "There will be investigations. Names whispered. Questions asked." "None will reach us."

Óscar allowed a thin, humorless sound that might have been agreement. "Good. You will move as ghosts now. No contact. No visibility." Silencioso nodded once. "Understood."

"One more thing," Óscar said. Silencioso waited. "When the time comes," Óscar said, "there will be more work."

Silencioso didn't ask when. He didn't ask who. "There always is," he replied. The line went dead.

Silencioso removed the battery, broke the phone in two with a sharp, practiced motion, and handed the pieces back without comment. Serrano sealed them away. The van continued north. No one spoke. The call had done what it was meant to do.

The job was no longer just complete. It was **acknowledged**. And that acknowledgment carried a new weight. One that followed them like a shadow across state lines.

Óscar sat alone in the study. The room was dim, lit only by a single desk lamp that cast a tight circle of light across polished wood and leather-bound books. Outside the tall windows, Mexico City breathed with distant traffic, muted horns, and the low, ceaseless murmur of a city that never truly slept.

Óscar did not look out at it. His attention was fixed on the phone in his hand. The image filled the screen. He studied it the way a man studies a ledger entry. With fact, not emotion.

The cut in the throat was unmistakable finality. A K-Bar. Clean. Professional. No excess.

Óscar nodded once. "Efficient," he murmured to the empty room. He powered the phone off and set it carefully on the desk, screen down. For several seconds, he simply sat there, hands folded, posture rigid, absorbing the permanence of what had been done.

Then he reached into a drawer and removed an old photograph. It showed Carlos as a boy smiling, too confident even then, standing beside Óscar with a soccer ball tucked under one arm. A future that had once felt infinite. Óscar's thumb traced the edge of the photograph. "One mistake," he said quietly. "One." He placed the photo face down beside the phone.

Another drawer opened. This time, he withdrew a small object; a child's toy, worn smooth at the edges. Something his granddaughter had left behind during her last visit. Bright. Innocent. Entirely out of place in the room. Óscar stared at it longer than he had stared at the photograph.

This time, something did move behind his eyes. "They crossed too far," he said softly. "And they forgot who remembers."

He leaned back in the chair, the leather creaking faintly beneath his weight. The message had not just been received. It had landed.

The Guillen name had been answered in blood and now it demanded silence, fear, and obedience in return.

Óscar reached for the phone again, this time dialing a different number. One that did not ring. It simply connected. "Begin Phase Two," he said. No response came back. None was needed. Óscar ended the call and sat motionless, the lamp's light carving his face into planes of shadow and resolve.

Outside, the city continued, unaware that a new current had just been set in motion that would reach far beyond New Orleans, far beyond borders.

The message had been delivered. Now it would spread. The Gulf Cartel would use this murder to solidify its position in the Gulf South drug market.

The van reached the outskirts of the city just before dawn. The sky had begun to pale at the horizon, the darkness thinning into a dull gray that flattened the world into silhouettes of warehouses, exit signs, and power lines cutting across the sky like scars. Traffic thickened slightly, enough to blend into, not enough to slow them down.

Toño took the exit without signaling and guided the van into a low industrial district where nothing opened early and no one watched closely. The vehicle slipped into a fenced lot behind a shuttered logistics depot and rolled to a stop beneath a broken security light. Engines turned off and silence returned.

Silencioso stood first. "Two minutes," he said. No one rushed. They moved with the same discipline that had carried them through the night. Bags lifted, cases passed hand to hand, nothing dropped, nothing forgotten. Each man took only what he would keep. Everything else was left behind to be erased.

Shadow handed Silencioso the final sealed case. Inside: blades, cloths, fragments of a job that no longer existed. Silencioso nodded once and handed it back. "Burn it."

Shadow turned and disappeared into the depot. The faint smell of fuel followed. Serrano and Ruiz stripped the van of plates, decals, anything that could be traced. Within seconds, the vehicle looked like a dozen others in the lot, anonymous and forgettable.

Isaías's voice came through one last time, distant now. "Border routes are clear. Flights staggered. No connections between you." Silencioso acknowledged him with a single word. "Good." One by one, the men split off.

Toño walked toward a waiting sedan at the far end of the lot, hood already warm. Serrano and Ruiz vanished down opposite streets. Shadow emerged briefly, the smell of smoke clinging faintly to his clothes, then turned and melted into a line of early-morning foot traffic.

Within minutes, the team no longer existed as a unit. Only individuals. Only ghosts.

Silencioso lingered alone for a moment beneath the broken light. He removed the black wristband from his arm, the one without a number and dropped it into a metal barrel beside the fence. He struck a match, watched the flame catch, then turned away before it burned out completely.

Across the city, televisions flickered on in kitchens and bedrooms. **BREAKING NEWS** banners crawled across screens. A powerful man dead in his own home. Security was breached. No suspects. No motive yet.

Marie's face appeared briefly blurred, distraught, ushered past cameras by police. Silencioso did not watch.

He stepped into a waiting car, closed the door, and became another commuter heading toward an airport that didn't know his name.

As the car pulled away, his phone vibrated once. A single message. **WE DON'T EXIST FROM THIS POINT ON.** He powered the device off and removed the battery. The city swallowed him. Behind him, New Orleans woke up to what had been done. Ahead of him, the began to move.

Chapter 16

The Callout

Detective Matthew Kaiser was already late. Not disastrously late, just enough to irritate him. The kind of late that came from a knee that didn't like humidity and a coffee machine that chose that morning to sputter instead of brew.

He limped through the front doors of the NOPD building on Broad Street, one hand gripping a paper cup that was already leaking through the seam. "Morning Moonpie," the desk sergeant called out. Kaiser lifted two fingers in acknowledgment without slowing.

"Pelicans won last night," someone said from a nearby desk. "Don't jinx it," Kaiser muttered, easing himself into his chair and setting the coffee down before it betrayed him completely. He rolled his knee once, grimaced, then reached for the folder he'd left on his desk the night before.

It was a B&E, so it wasn't anything major. A domestic that would end in paperwork and disappointment. A city doing what it always did.

Zoe Babineaux appeared at the edge of his desk, hair pulled back tight, notebook already in hand. "You're late," she said. "You're early," Kaiser replied. "That's worse." She smirked and slid into the chair opposite him. "Traffic?" "Knee," he said. "And I didn't want to come." "That tracks."

He flipped open the folder and skimmed it, eyes already glazing. "Anything good?" he asked. "Define good," Zoe said. "Because if we're talking about productive, no. If we're talking about depressing, always." Kaiser snorted. "That's New Orleans for you."

She hesitated, then added, "My mom had another round this morning." He looked up at her. "How bad?" Zoe shrugged, but it was a careful shrug, practiced. "She's tired. More than usual." "That's the worst part," Kaiser said. "The waiting." She nodded once, grateful he didn't try to dress it up.

The bullpen hummed around them with phones ringing, keyboards clacking, and someone arguing quietly with a printer.

Kaiser leaned back in his chair, wincing as his knee protested. "Remind me again why we don't work bank robberies," he said. "Because you hate masks," Zoe replied. "And enthusiasm," he added. She smiled faintly.

The desk phone rang.

Neither of them moved at first, then it rang again Kaiser reached for it. "Detective Kaiser." He listened. His posture changed immediately.

Zoe noticed it before he said a word. "Yes," Kaiser said slowly. "Where?" A pause, and his jaw tightened. "How many?" he asked. Another pause, this time it was longer.

Zoe's smile faded. Kaiser exhaled through his nose. "We're on our way." He hung up and stood, favoring his knee but moving fast now. "What is it?" Zoe asked, already grabbing her jacket. "Garden District," he said. "High-end residence." "How bad?" Kaiser didn't answer right away. "Bad enough they called us directly," he said finally.

He grabbed his badge, clipped it on, and nodded toward the door. "Lights on," he said. Zoe followed.

Behind them, the bullpen noise kept going, unaware that somewhere in the city, normal had just been permanently broken.

The Garden District was already awake when Moonpie and Zoe arrived. Not awake-awake, but alert in that distinctly New Orleans way, where curtains twitched, and neighbors lingered just long enough to see without being seen. Red and blue lights splashed against white columns and manicured hedges. Too many units.

Kaiser clocked it instantly. "Jesus," Zoe muttered. "That's a lot of uniforms." "That's a lot of money behind a gate," Kaiser replied, easing the car to a stop. He killed the engine and sat for a beat, watching the scene settle into his bones.

There were two patrol cars, a crime scene van, an unmarked supervisor's unit, and a small knot of people held back by tape. Mostly neighbors, staff, maybe one or two who didn't belong but had nowhere else to be at that hour.

Kaiser stepped out, his knee barking in protest. He ignored it. A uniform approached immediately. "Detective Kaiser?" "Yeah." "Officer Bellamy. We got the call at 23:22. Power outage was reported first. Then…" He swallowed. "Then a body."

"One?" Zoe asked. Bellamy hesitated. "One confirmed deceased. Two surviving witnesses in shock. Guards neutralized outside. No gunfire reported by neighbors." Moonpie's eyebrow twitched. "Neutralized how?" Bellamy shook his head. "Medical hasn't finished yet. But… quiet." Kaiser nodded once. Quiet was never good.

They passed under the tape and through the gate. Kaiser took in details automatically, the scuffed stone near the driveway, the way one hedge was bent where it shouldn't be, and the faint metallic smell still hanging in the air. Blood had a way of announcing itself even when you couldn't see it.

The front door stood open. Inside, the house was too bright. Every light on. As if someone had tried to erase what happened by flooding it with electricity.

Zoe stepped in behind him, eyes moving, cataloging. "No forced entry up front." "No," Kaiser agreed. "They didn't want attention."

A crime scene tech nodded to them from the hallway. "Detectives." Kaiser followed the sound of low voices toward the living area. He saw it before he registered it fully, the shape on the floor, the dark stain that didn't belong against the polished surface. He stopped.

Zoe stopped beside him. The body lay just off the hallway, sheet drawn up to the shoulders but not high enough to hide the damage. The wound at the throat was unmistakable.

Just violence applied with purpose. Zoe swallowed. "Knife." "Yeah," Moonpie said quietly. "Big one." A K-Bar, he thought, or something close.

A woman sat on the couch nearby, wrapped in a blanket that wasn't helping. Marie Castenllo stared at nothing, hands clenched so tightly her knuckles had gone white. A paramedic hovered nearby, speaking softly, being ignored. An older man sat rigidly in a chair across the room, eyes fixed on the sheeted body. He hadn't moved since Kaiser entered. "Vincent Castenllo Sr.," Bellamy whispered. "Victim's father."

Zoe's jaw tightened slightly. She made a note. Kaiser crouched carefully beside the body, staying outside the taped boundary. He leaned just enough to see the wound clearly. It was a single cut. "That wasn't rage," he murmured. "That was intent."

Zoe glanced around the room. "Power outage?" "Brief," Bellamy said. "Backup kicked in. Looks like it was cut deliberately." Kaiser straightened slowly, knee protesting again. "Any cameras?" "System was disabled during the outage," Bellamy replied. "Came back online after. No footage."

Kaiser exhaled through his nose. He looked at the house again; not as a home, but as a space someone had entered, altered, and exited without leaving themselves behind.

"Where are the guards?" he asked. "Two outside," Bellamy said. "Deceased. Quietly." Zoe looked at Kaiser. "This isn't a robbery." "No," Kaiser agreed. "This is a message."

He glanced at Marie again, her hollow stare and the way she didn't look at the body anymore because she didn't need to. "Let's talk to the wife," he said. "Not yet. But soon."

He turned back toward the hallway. "And I want every camera, every neighbor, every license plate within five blocks." Zoe nodded. "On it."

As Moonpie took one last look at the wound, a familiar thought settled in his chest. Whoever did this hadn't been surprised by the house. They'd already known it.

Kaiser stood in the hallway and let the house talk to him. He followed the path instinctively from the front door to the living room, then back toward the hallway where the body lay. He watched where officers had stepped, where they hadn't. He listened to the quiet spaces between sounds.

"Timeline," he said. Zoe was already flipping pages in her notebook. "Power outage reported at 23:10. Backup kicked in less than a minute later." "Neighbors notice anything?" "Some lights flickered on the block," Bellamy said. "Nobody called it in. They thought it was weather." Kaiser nodded. "That's not an accident."

He crouched again near the hallway wall, pointing at a faint scuff mark just above the baseboard. "See that?" he asked Zoe. She leaned in. "Boot?" "Yeah. Hard sole. Tactical tread."

Bellamy frowned. "We get that kind of footwear all the time." "Not in a living room," Moonpie said. "And not without breaking anything."

He stood and moved toward the back of the house. The service door showed signs of forced entry, but only if you knew what to look for. A stress fracture along the frame. Paint scorched so lightly it could be mistaken for age. Zoe exhaled slowly. "That's clean." "Too clean," Moonpie said. "They didn't want noise. Or time."

He glanced at his watch. "How long between outage and death?" Bellamy checked his notes. "Roughly three minutes." Zoe looked up sharply. "Three minutes to breach, move, kill, and exit?" Kaiser nodded. "Which means they already knew where everyone was."

He turned back toward the living room. "Who was home?" he asked. Bellamy replied, "Victim. Wife. Father. Daughter had already left." Zoe's pen paused. "Left when?" "Just before nine," Bellamy said. "Confirmed by gate log." Kaiser stopped walking. "Say that again." "The daughter left before nine," Bellamy repeated.

Kaiser's jaw tightened. "They waited," he said quietly. Zoe looked at him. "For her to leave." "Yeah," Kaiser said. "Which means they were watching." The realization settled over the room like humidity.

This wasn't opportunistic; it was patient.

Kaiser returned to the body and crouched again, this time studying the wound more carefully. "One cut," he said. "Deep. Clean. No struggle." "Medical says he died in under ten seconds," Bellamy added. Zoe swallowed. "Execution." Kaiser straightened slowly.

"Not quite," he said. "Executions are public. This was… instructional."

He turned toward the front of the house, where crime scene techs worked quietly. "Guards?" he asked. "Both killed outside," Bellamy said. "No gunshots. Likely blades."

Moonpie closed his eyes briefly.

He opened them again. "This wasn't a crew," he said. "This was a unit." Zoe nodded. "Military?" "Or something that learned from them," Kaiser said.

He looked around the room again, at the wealth, the power, the belief that this place was untouchable. "And whoever sent them," he added, "wanted us to find it exactly like this." Zoe's voice dropped. "Why?" Moonpie met her eyes. "Because fear travels faster than bullets."

He glanced toward Marie again, still silent, still hollow. "And this," he said quietly, "is how you teach a city to listen." Marie Castenllo sat exactly where they had left her. The blanket was still around her shoulders, though it had slipped halfway down one arm. A paper cup of water sat untouched on the table beside her. She hadn't asked for it. Someone had simply put it there, hoping routine might anchor her.

It hadn't.

Her eyes were open, but unfocused. Fixed on a point somewhere past the wall, past the house, past the night that had already taken everything from her. Kaiser approached slowly. He crouched a few feet away, careful to stay in her line of sight without forcing it.

"Mrs. Castenllo," he said quietly. "I'm Detective Kaiser. This is Detective Babineaux." Zoe nodded gently. "We're very sorry for your loss." Marie didn't respond.

Kaiser waited. Seconds passed that felt like minutes. Finally, Marie blinked.

"My husband," she said. Her voice barely carried. "Yes," Kaiser said. "Your husband."

She nodded once, as if confirming it for herself. "They didn't shout," she said suddenly. "That's what keeps bothering me." Zoe's pen paused, then resumed. "They moved," Marie continued. "But they didn't yell. They didn't panic."

Kaiser felt something tighten in his chest. "Did you see them?" he asked carefully. Marie swallowed. "Not clearly. It was dark. But they weren't… frantic." She shook her head slowly. "They knew where he was," she whispered. Zoe looked up sharply. "They went straight to him," Marie said. "No hesitation."

Moonpie nodded once. "How many?" Marie closed her eyes. "Three," she said. "Maybe four. But one of them…" She hesitated. "One what?" Zoe asked gently. "One was in charge," Marie said. "I could tell."

Kaiser leaned forward slightly. "What makes you say that?" "The way he spoke," Marie replied. She opened her eyes and looked directly at Kaiser now. "And when he did, everyone stopped, just the way they did when Vinny spoke."

The room felt smaller. "Do you remember what he said?" Kaiser asked. Marie shook her head. "Just… 'No.'" Zoe wrote it down anyway. Kaiser exhaled slowly.

"Did your husband say anything?" he asked. Marie's jaw tightened. "He tried," she said. "Even when he was… even then." Her voice broke, but she pushed through it. "He thought it was a warning," she said. "Not the end." Kaiser let that sit.

"Did he mention anyone recently?" Zoe asked. "Any threats? Problems? Names?" Marie laughed once, sharp, humorless. "Every day," she said. "There's always someone who wants something."

She looked down at her hands, noticing the faint stain still beneath her nails. "But this," she said quietly, "this was different." Kaiser nodded. "How so?" "They weren't there for money," Marie said. "They didn't touch anything."

She looked up again, eyes clearer now with focused. "They wanted him dead," she said. "And they wanted us to live with it." The words settled into the room like dust.

Kaiser stood slowly, his knee aching, his thoughts racing. "Thank you," he said. "That helps." Marie looked at him, something raw and sharp flickering beneath the shock. "You're going to find them," she directed more than she asked. Kaiser didn't answer right away. He met her eyes and chose his words carefully. "We're going to try," he said.

Marie nodded once. "Good," she said. "Because they left something behind." Zoe looked up. "What?" Marie's gaze drifted toward the hallway where her husband had died. "A message," she said.

Kaiser stepped away from Marie and into the front hallway, rubbing his knee with one hand as if the ache might anchor him. It didn't. Zoe followed, closing her notebook halfway but not putting it away. She had learned that cases like this didn't like being put down.

"What kind of message?" she asked quietly. Kaiser shook his head once. "The kind that doesn't come with a return address."

They paused near the front door, where a crime scene technician was photographing a faint scuff mark on the floor. Moonpie waited until the flash finished, then spoke. "Any phones recovered yet?"

The tech nodded. "Victim's phone was in the office. No damage. Wife's phone too. Daughter's already off-site. Guards' radios were destroyed." Zoe frowned. "Destroyed how?" "Crushed," the tech said. "Deliberately."

Kaiser closed his eyes briefly. "That's not panic," he murmured. "That's cleanup."

A uniform hurried up, breathless but trying not to look it. "Detective, NOPD Command wants an update. And" he hesitated, "FBI called. They heard about the outage and the guards." Zoe's head snapped up. "Already?" Kaiser's expression darkened. "Yeah," he said. "That didn't take long."

He stepped aside and took the phone the uniform offered. He listened without speaking, his jaw tightening incrementally with each sentence. "Yes," he said finally. "Yes, I understand. No, we're not calling it anything yet."

He hung up and handed the phone back. "Federal?" Zoe asked. "Watching," Kaiser said. "Not in yet. But they're circling."

He looked back down the hallway toward the living room, where Marie sat alone again, wrapped in silence and loss. "This thing reaches past New Orleans," Zoe said quietly. Kaiser nodded. "Past Louisiana."

A second uniform approached, this one older, more careful. "Sir, we've got neighbors asking questions. Media's stacking at the corner." Moonpie sighed. "Of course they are."

He turned to Zoe. "Get canvass teams in every direction. I want cameras from stores, traffic lights, doorbells, ATMs; anything that blinks." Zoe nodded. "Already queued."

"And Zoe," Kaiser added. She looked up. "Rerun the victim's recent contacts. Not just business. Personal. International if we have to." Her pen hovered. "International?" Kaiser didn't smile. "People who do this don't stop at borders," he said.

A faint buzz cut through the air. Kaiser's phone vibrated in his pocket. He checked the screen. It was an unknown number. He stared at it for a long second before silencing it.

Zoe noticed. "You expecting that?" "No," Kaiser said. "But I was waiting for it." He slid the phone back into his pocket.

Outside, the crowd had grown louder. A helicopter thumped somewhere overhead. Cameras flashed against the front of the mansion, capturing nothing and everything at once.

Moonpie looked back at the house. "They didn't just kill a man," he said quietly. "They destabilized a system." Zoe closed her notebook with a soft snap. "And they wanted us to know it," she said. Kaiser nodded.

The living room no longer felt like a crime scene. It felt like a negotiation space. Kaiser recognized the shift the moment the suits arrived.

Two men entered without announcing themselves. They wore dark jackets with no visible rank. Their posture was relaxed in a way that only came from authority that didn't need permission. One flashed a badge too quickly for politeness. The other didn't bother.

"Detective Kaiser," the taller one said. "Special Agent Callahan. FBI." Kaiser didn't offer his hand. "Morning," he replied flatly. Callahan glanced past him, eyes already scanning the room, cataloging blood patterns, camera placements, and personnel density.

"Hell of a scene," Callahan said. "Professional work." "That's our working theory," Kaiser replied. "You're early." Callahan smiled thinly. "You're late."

Zoe stepped closer to Kaiser's side, her notebook tucked under her belt now. She wasn't writing. She was watching. "What brings the Bureau?" she asked.

Callahan tilted his head slightly, measuring her. "Private security neutralized. Infrastructure sabotage.

Execution-style homicide tied to organized crime." He shrugged. "We get curious."

Kaiser folded his arms carefully, mindful of his knee. "Curiosity doesn't equal jurisdiction."

The second agent finally spoke. His voice was softer. More dangerous. "Not yet," he said. "But it will." Kaiser held his ground. "This is a local homicide," he said. "Victim was a New Orleans resident. Crime scene's ours." "For now," Callahan replied. "But if this connects to transnational actors this goes federal fast."

Zoe's jaw tightened. "You have evidence of that?" Callahan met her eyes. "Not yet." Kaiser nodded. "Then you're observers." A beat passed. Callahan smiled again. "We'll see."

He turned, already losing interest, and walked toward the hallway where techs worked the scene. The second agent followed without another word.

Zoe leaned in, voice low. "They're not wrong." "I know," Kaiser said. "I just don't like being told I'm temporary." His phone vibrated again with the same blocked number. He stared at it this time. He didn't answer, nor did he silence it.

Across the room, a uniform whispered something to another cop, who glanced toward the doorway where the agents stood. The room felt crowded now.

Kaiser exhaled slowly. "This case is already bigger than us," Zoe said quietly. "Yeah," Moonpie replied. "And that's exactly what scares me."

He looked down the hallway once more at the bloodstain now half-covered by evidence markers, at the place where the message had been delivered. "They didn't just plan the murder," he said. "They planned the aftermath." Zoe nodded. "Including us."

Kaiser's phone vibrated a third time. This time, a notification appeared beneath the blocked number. Kaiser's eyes narrowed. "They don't want to talk," Zoe said. "No," Kaiser replied. "They want us to listen." He slipped the phone back into his pocket and straightened, pain flaring briefly in his knee as he did. "Let's finish our work," he said. "Before someone else decides it for us."

Outside, the press noise grew louder. Inside, the lines between local justice and something far larger began to dissolve. Kaiser stood alone for a moment in the front hallway.

The house buzzed behind him now with agents murmuring, radios chirping, cameras clicking. Procedure had taken over. That was always the signal that grief was being packaged into something manageable. He hated that part.

He stepped just outside the front door, past the threshold where the tape fluttered lightly in the morning breeze. The Garden District looked almost offended by the intrusion. Sunlight touched white columns and flowerbeds as if nothing had happened.

Across the street, neighbors pretended not to stare. Across the corner, media vans jockeyed for position. And somewhere above it all, a helicopter traced a lazy circle, filming tragedy from a distance that made it palatable.

Zoe joined him, holding out two cups of coffee she'd commandeered from somewhere inside. "Cream?" she asked. "No," Kaiser said. "I don't trust things that try to soften the truth." She handed him the cup anyway.

They stood there in silence for a few seconds, watching the city absorb the shock. "You know what bothers me most?" Zoe said. Kaiser took a careful sip. "Only one thing?" She huffed quietly. "They could've done this a dozen different ways. Bomb. Drive-by. Accident. Poison." Kaiser nodded. "But they didn't."

"They wanted the knife," Zoe said. "They wanted proximity." "And witnesses," Kaiser added. Her eyes shifted back to the house. "Marie," Zoe said. "The father." Kaiser nodded. "Survivors carry stories."

They watched a crime scene tech wheel a cart past the tape. Evidence boxes were stacked neatly. Lives reduced to inventory.

Kaiser's phone vibrated again. This time, it didn't stop. He stared at it, feeling the weight of choice settle in his chest. Zoe noticed. "You going to answer?" Kaiser shook his head slowly. The phone went silent.

Kaiser looked back at the house; at the bloodstain that would never fully come out, at the wife whose life had been split in half, at the father who would never sleep again.

"This was about revenge," he said. "It wasn't about money. Or territory." Kaiser's jaw tightened. "Demonstration," he said. "They wanted the city, the mob, the cops, and anyone watching to understand the message." He folded the phone and slipped it into his pocket. "They wanted everyone to understand the same thing at the same time." Zoe's voice dropped. "Which is?"

Kaiser looked out over the street, the cameras, the crowd, the waking city. "That power still answers to something darker," he said. "And it doesn't care where you live."

A siren wailed somewhere down the avenue, distant now, almost routine. Kaiser exhaled. "This case doesn't end with an arrest," he said. "It ends when someone else decides to speak."

Zoe wrapped her arms around herself. "And until then?" Kaiser finished his coffee and dropped the cup into a nearby trash can. "Until then," he said, "we listen very carefully."

Behind them, the Castenllo house stood open and exposed. It was no longer a fortress, no longer private. Just another place where a message had been delivered.

And somewhere in New Orleans, the people it was meant for were already deciding how to answer.

Chapter 17

The Crime Scene

The Garden District glowed with the wrong kind of light. Red and blue strobes bounced off white-pillared mansions and manicured hedges, turning the quiet, historic street into a fever dream of motion and color. Uniforms swarmed the front yard like ants on sugar. There were officers stringing tape, securing perimeters, and directing a growing crowd of stunned neighbors who had gathered in robes and pajamas among other things.

Detective Kaiser stepped out of the mansion, his knee complaining the moment his foot hit the pavement. He ignored it, inhaling the thick, humid air spoiled by generator fumes and the scent of blood carried faintly from somewhere deeper on the property.

Beside him, Zoe tightened her ponytail and scanned the scene with sharp, steady eyes. "Jesus," she murmured. "Every cop in the city showed up." "Wouldn't miss a party like this," Kaiser said, the words dry enough to crack.

A uniform jogged over. "Detectives! Moonpie, over here!" Kaiser winced at the nickname but didn't fight it. He waved the officer on. "Walk and talk."

They passed clusters of police and crime scene techs, stepping over a coil of cable someone had dragged across the lawn. "What's the situation?" Zoe asked. "Still unfolding," the uniform said breathlessly. "Neighbors heard screaming right after the power came back on. Multiple 911 calls. The Chief has just arrived and is talking to the FBI now." Zoe and Kaiser exchanged a look.

As they approached the porch, a familiar figure emerged from the doorway. He was a thick-set man in a gray suit, his sleeves rolled up, tie loosened, and a face carrying irritation like a second skin. Assistant Chief **Dominic Carlucci was finishing up a very animated discussion with the two agents in FBI windbreakers**. "Kaiser," Carlucci barked. "Babineaux." "Morning, Chief," Kaiser said. "Don't," Carlucci snapped. "Not today. We've got a goddamn circus on our hands. Press is stacking at the corner, neighbors are losing their minds, and half my officers look like they're about to piss themselves."

Zoe lifted her chin slightly. "Who called the feds?" "Not me," Carlucci growled. "Which means someone upstairs heard 'Garden District, multiple bodies' and hit the panic button."

Kaiser looked past him into the brightly lit foyer. Crime scene techs moved like ghosts, silent and focused, already photographing, dusting, marking.

"Who's running point inside?" he asked. "You are," Carlucci said. "Congratulations. This is your shitshow now." Kaiser blinked once. "Appreciate the vote of confidence." "It wasn't confidence," Carlucci said. "It was delegation. Now get inside before somebody with a windbreaker tries to take my damn scene."

Zoe gave Kaiser a quick, thin smile. "Moonpie saves the day." He grunted. "If this is saving, I want a refund."

They stepped up onto the porch. Flashbulbs popped across the street as reporters tried to shoot around the tape. "Detectives! Over here!" "Kaiser! Is it cartel-related?" "Is the family alive?" Zoe stiffened. Kaiser didn't even turn his head.

Once back inside the foyer, he exhaled slowly. The chaos outside muffled to a dull roar behind the walls.

He felt the heavy hush of a sense that the building itself was holding its breath. He glanced at Zoe. "You ready to take on the FBI?" he asked. She nodded once. "You?"

Kaiser rolled his aching knee and stepped forward. "No," he said. "Let's go anyway."

A sergeant met Kaiser and Zoe halfway down the foyer, his face tight and pale under the harsh indoor lighting.

"You're going to want to see what we found in the backyard," he said quietly. Kaiser exchanged a glance with Zoe. "Lead the way," Moonpie said.

They followed him through the kitchen, past a row of shocked household staff being questioned by two officers. A woman in an apron sobbed softly into her hands. Another kept whispering, *"This can't be happening,"* over and over.

The sergeant pushed open the back door. The humid air rolled in. The backyard was a scene carved out of a nightmare. There were string lights still glowing weakly, hedges rustling in the early morning wind, and the two bodies of the guard lying face down in the grass, boots angled unnaturally, hands slack. Kaiser's jaw set hard.

The two Castenllo guards were sprawled where they had fallen, one near the stone path, the other by the generator housing. Both had dark, spreading stains beneath them, and both had unmistakably fatal wounds.

"The bodyguards were caught by surprise," the sergeant said. "We found them like this when units arrived." Zoe crouched near the closest guard but didn't touch him. "Slashed," she murmured. "Same blade?"

"Medical says no," the sergeant replied, "But we won't know for sure until the autopsy is complete."

Kaiser didn't crouch. He scanned. Eyes moving deliberately. Lines forming in his head. "Positions are wrong," he said. Zoe looked up. "Wrong how?" Kaiser pointed with two fingers. "They didn't run. They didn't reach for anything. They were taken exactly where they stood."

He stepped farther into the yard, ignoring the damp of the grass clinging to his shoes. He circled the area once, then twice, tracing footprints, disturbances in the hedge, the faint gouge left on the stone path. "This wasn't an ambush," he said finally. "This was a sweep."

Zoe's throat tightened. "They moved like a team." Kaiser nodded once. "A good one."

A radio crackled behind them. "Medical coming through!" Kaiser turned. Paramedics were guiding a stretcher out of the house with Marie Castenllo on it, wrapped in a blanket, eyes wide and empty. Her lips moved, but no sound came out. One medic murmured something soothing; Marie didn't react.

"Jesus," Zoe breathed. Kaiser stepped toward the stretcher, but the medics shook their heads. "She's nonverbal," one said quietly. "Shock. We're taking her straight in."

Marie's gaze drifted to Kaiser for half a moment and then past him, like she was looking through the air at something only she could see. The stretcher rolled on.

Zoe swallowed hard. "She saw it, Moonpie. She saw everything." Kaiser didn't answer. He was staring at the second guard's body; at the angle of the fall, the clean, efficient kill, the lack of hesitation.

He exhaled through his nose. "The city's not ready for this," he said. Zoe nodded. "Neither are we."

Another officer approached, breath visible in the early chill. "Detectives, the inside is stable. Chief Carlucci says whenever you're ready." Kaiser looked back at the house with the warm light pouring out, incongruous with the violence it now contained. "We're ready," he said. But the way he said it sounded more like a promise he wasn't sure he could keep.

Kaiser stepped back into the house, Zoe close behind him, and immediately felt the atmosphere shift. Outdoors had been chaos wrapped in humid air and confusion. Inside was something else entirely.

The foyer looked untouched at first glance with clean tile, tasteful rug, and framed photographs aligned on the wall. But the quiet hummed wrong. Like a note struck just slightly off-key. A crime scene tech waved them over toward the front door. She said, "We've got forced entry, but not at the front door," she said. Kaiser frowned. "Where then? Did they break a window or slip past the guards?" "See for yourself."

She led them to the side service entrance. Zoe leaned in. "That's not kicked." "No," the tech said. "It's punched."

Kaiser crouched, knee grumbling, and ran two fingers lightly along the metal, careful not to disturb anything. The lock plate had a deep, surgical indentation, the kind created by a specialized tool, not brute strength. A red smear traced the outer edge, barely visible. "Thermal breach tool," Kaiser said. "Heated. Fast. He knew exactly where to hit it."

Zoe exhaled. "Three seconds or less." Kaiser pushed to his feet.

He turned toward the living room, spotless except for the lingering sense that someone had moved through it quickly and with purpose. A pillow knocked slightly askew. A coaster on the floor. A chair angled wrong. It wasn't a struggle. It was a path.

"Living room is clean," Zoe said, reading his expression. "No overturned furniture. No defensive marks." "They didn't waste time," Kaiser replied. "They didn't explore the house. They went straight." He walked toward the hallway.

It was brighter here with crime scene lights flooding the space, bouncing off the polished flooring. The air smelled faintly of bleach patches where techs had begun mapping out blood trails.

A tech approached them. "Breakers were cut manually from the outside. Not tripped." Zoe nodded, jotting it down. "How'd they get to the box?" "They knew exactly where it was," the tech said. "No hesitation. We checked the switch. Thumbprint smears, but nothing usable. Gloves, we think."

Kaiser rubbed his jaw. "They cut power first," he muttered. "Not to hide the kill. To control timing." He stepped deeper into the hallway.

A faint smear on the wall caught his eye, not blood, but a dark mark, almost soot-like. "What's that?" Zoe asked. "Impact," Kaiser said. "Gear scraping during entry. Someone brushed the wall while moving fast."

He followed it a few inches farther down. Boot prints began to emerge; faint impressions where the polish had dulled under pressure. Not wild scuffs or desperate lunges. Perfectly spaced. Uniform stride. A team moving as one.

Zoe stood beside him, her face tightening. "Moonpie… they weren't guessing where to go." "No," Kaiser said. "They were navigating." He glanced back toward the foyer, mentally drawing the path. "This house isn't huge," Zoe said, "but it's not small either. They had a map." "Or reconnaissance," Kaiser said. "Or someone who'd been here before."

Zoe's pen froze mid-stroke. "That's… bad." Kaiser nodded grimly.

He moved closer to the hallway intersection where the blood had begun to pool earlier, though techs had cleaned enough to keep it from spreading. "This is where it happened," he said. The air felt heavier here. Colder. As if the violence had left an imprint deeper than the blood.

Zoe stepped back instinctively. "Moonpie," she said quietly. "This wasn't just efficient. It was rehearsed." Kaiser stared at the floor. "No," he said. "Rehearsed means mistakes the first few times." He looked up, eyes dark. "They were perfect."

Dominic Carlucci stepped fully into the hallway, the soles of his dress shoes stopping just short of the plastic sheeting. He stared down at the bloodstain, at the evidence flags, at the violence carved into the space like a signature.

For the first time that morning, his face cracked. "This is bad," he murmured. Kaiser nodded once. "Yeah."

Dominic turned toward him, color rising into his cheeks. "Give me something, Moonpie. Anything. Tell me this was a robbery gone sideways. A local beef. Some personal grudge we can wrap in a press release."

Zoe Babineaux stood beside Kaiser, silent, watching them both. Kaiser crossed his arms. His knee ached. His back was tight. But his voice was steady. "This wasn't local." Dominic blinked. "What?"

Kaiser gestured toward the floor, the walls, the trail of perfect boot prints. "This wasn't amateurs. This wasn't street-level. It wasn't a mob beef across town or some idiot crew making a name for themselves."

"Then who?" Dominic demanded. "Who does something like this?" Kaiser hesitated just long enough for Dominic to feel it. "People who plan," Kaiser said finally. "People who rehearse." "People who don't panic." His gaze dropped to the blood. "And people who don't miss."

Dominic swallowed hard. Anger flared, covering fear. "Moonpie, Matthew, this city is a powder keg. Are you telling me we have *professionals* running kills in the Garden District? That someone sent a damn strike team into a mob house?" "Yes," Kaiser said. Dominic's eyes widened. "Jesus."

Zoe spoke up softly. "And they left survivors on purpose." Dominic jerked toward her. "To send a message?" Kaiser shook his head. "No. To make sure it spread."

Dominic scrubbed a hand over his face. "This is going to explode. Politicians, press, the feds; they're already circling."

"Let them circle," Kaiser said. "Won't change what happened." Dominic stepped closer, lowering his voice. "I need to know if this is cartel." Kaiser met his gaze. "I think it's something worse."

The hallway seemed to tighten around the three of them, the air heavier now that the words had been spoken. Dominic exhaled sharply. "God help us." He turned and stormed out of the hallway, already barking orders at whoever came closest.

Kaiser and Zoe remained where they were, standing over the place where a man's life had been ended with surgical precision. Zoe broke the silence first. "So… what kind of people do this?" she asked quietly.

Kaiser didn't answer right away. He reached into his pocket, took out a cigarette, and lit it despite the "NO SMOKING" sign posted five feet away. Zoe didn't call him on it. He stared down the hallway as smoke drifted upward. "The kind," he said finally, "that don't miss…"

He inhaled slowly. Exhaled even slower. "…and don't stop." The truth hung between them, sharp and bitter as the scent of smoke.

And outside, the early morning light crept across the Garden District, revealing a city already beginning to tremble under the weight of what had been done.

Chapter 18

The Witness

The elevator doors slid open onto the fourth floor of Ochsner Hospital, releasing a wash of air and the low, constant hum of machines. The ICU wing always carried a strange, quiet weight, but never a peaceful one.

Detective Matthew Kaiser stepped out first, his knee stiff after the ride up. He adjusted his jacket, scanning the hallway automatically. Nurses moved between rooms with soft, clipped efficiency. Families clung to plastic chairs. The lights overhead hummed with a sterile brightness that no one could ever quite get used to.

Babineaux walked beside him, notebook tucked under her arm, expression composed but not hardened. Her gaze moved across the tired and shell-shocked faces lining the hall. "This place always smells like endings," she murmured. Moonpie nodded. "And sometimes beginnings we don't want."

They moved toward the waiting area where a small knot of uniformed officers stood posted. Their presence alone told Kaiser that the hospital considered Marie Castenllo more than an ordinary patient. One of the uniforms, a young officer named Talbot, straightened when he saw them.

"Detectives," he said, voice lower than usual out of respect for the space. "Lieutenant said you'd be stopping by."

"How is she?" Zoe asked. Talbot hesitated. "Bad. She's conscious, but she's... not all here. Keeps asking for her husband, then forgetting we answered." Moonpie's jaw tightened. Trauma did strange things to the mind. Grief did worse. "Any visitors?" he asked. "Just medical staff," Talbot said. "We've kept everyone else out." Kaiser nodded. "Good."

A nurse in pale blue scrubs approached from the ICU doors, her expression guarded. "Are you the detectives?" she asked. "Yes," Kaiser replied. "We need to speak with Mrs. Castenllo." The nurse exhaled slowly. "You can try. She's awake, but she's drifting in and out. She's medicated, grieving, and confused. Don't push her." Kaiser gave a slow nod. "We won't." Zoe's gaze flickered toward the double doors. "She's our only witness." "And a fragile one," Kaiser said quietly.

The nurse gestured them through. As they stepped past the threshold into the ICU wing proper, the hum of machines grew louder, more intimate. Every sound mattered here. The beeping of monitors, the soft hiss of oxygen lines, and the rustle of sheets all had a purpose.

Moonpie felt the shift in Zoe beside him; the subtle bracing of someone preparing to walk into the emotional crossfire. "She saw it," Zoe said softly. "Yeah," Kaiser replied. "And whether she wants to or not, she's going to remember some of it." He paused at the corner before the final stretch of hallway. "Let's move slow," he said. "We're not here for a statement. We're here to keep her tied to the world long enough to talk." Zoe nodded. "Got it." They followed the nurse toward Room 417. Marie Castenllo waited on the other side of the glass door. She was alive but shattered.

The room was dim, the blinds half-drawn to soften the morning light. Machines beeped in measured intervals a steady indifference to human suffering. A bag of saline dripped slowly into the IV line running into Marie Castenllo's arm. She looked impossibly small in the hospital bed. Her hair was tangled, streaked with dried tears. Her hands still showed faint signs of where she'd clutched at her husband's blood. Her eyes were open, unfocused, drifting like she was somewhere between waking and drowning. The nurse spoke softly. "Mrs. Castenllo? You have visitors." Marie blinked slowly.

Kaiser stepped forward, stopping at the edge of her bed. Zoe remained just behind him, hands clasped in front of her notebook.

"Marie," Kaiser said gently. "How are you feeling?" Marie's gaze slid toward him, landing for the first time on something real. "Moonpie…" she whispered. Kaiser's eyebrows lifted slightly. "You know my nickname?" She nodded weakly. "Vinny… talked about you once or twice. Said you weren't like the others." Kaiser swallowed that down quietly. "I'm sorry you have to see me under these circumstances."

Her breath shook. "My husband," she whispered. "Vinny… he… he…" Her face crumpled, and for a moment Kaiser thought she might slip under entirely.

Zoe stepped softly to the other side of the bed. "Marie, we're not going to make you relive anything you're not ready for. We just want to help you." Marie nodded faintly, as if remembering how. Kaiser pulled a chair closer and sat patiently. "You're safe now," he said. "No one is going to hurt you. Not here. Not with us."

Marie's fingers twitched. Her eyes finally focused on Kaiser's. "They… they came in the dark," she said. "When the lights died… everything went quiet… like the house… stopped breathing." Zoe's breath hitched, but she said nothing. Marie continued, her voice thin as a thread. "I didn't see their faces. Only… shadows. Shapes. The way they moved." Kaiser leaned in slightly. "What way was that?"

Marie blinked again, slower this time. "Together. Like they'd done it before." Kaiser nodded gently. "We think so too." Marie reached up suddenly, gripping his sleeve with surprising strength. "One spoke," she whispered.

Kaiser froze. Zoe stepped closer. "The one in charge?" Marie nodded, trembling. "All he said was 'No.' One word. And they stopped. Like… like he controlled the air." Kaiser felt something cold settle in his gut. Zoe's pen hovered, unmoving.

Marie's grip loosened, her eyes drifting again, but not all the way. Not this time.

"They didn't want me dead," she said, voice barely audible. "I don't know why. But I knew… I *knew*… it wasn't mercy." Kaiser swallowed hard. "Marie… is there anything else you remember? Anything at all?" Her brows knit. A flicker of something surfaced, something she had buried deep the moment it happened. "There was a sound," she whispered.

Kaiser leaned closer. "What kind of sound?" Marie's eyes unfocused again, searching the memory. "A click," she said finally. "Metal… small… like a stopwatch." Zoe's breath froze. Kaiser didn't move, didn't blink.

Marie continued in a trembling whisper:, "He held it in his hand… the man who said 'No.' I heard it… click… and everything happened after that." Her voice broke. "That sound… I hear it in my sleep already."

Zoe stepped back, stunned. Kaiser sat very still. A stopwatch. A small detail.

Kaiser exhaled slowly, steadying his voice. "Marie," he said quietly, "what you just gave us is important." She didn't respond. Her eyes drifted closed, exhaustion pulling her under. The nurse moved in. "That's enough for now."

Kaiser and Zoe stepped away, the weight of the clue heavy between them. Zoe whispered, "Moonpie… that's military." Kaiser didn't look at her. "It's worse," he said.

They both knew what he meant. The killers weren't just trained. They were timed.

Kaiser let the ICU door ease shut behind them, careful not to let it click. The hallway outside Room 417 was quiet in that strange hospital way, but nothing about what they had just heard felt ordinary.

Babineaux walked at his side, her notebook open but forgotten in her hand. She kept glancing down at the scribbled line. **"A click… like a stopwatch."** She shook her head. "Moonpie… that can't be nothing." "It's not," Kaiser said.

They stopped near a window facing the hospital parking lot. Pale morning sunlight spilled across the tile, warm in a way that didn't match either of their faces. Zoe turned to him fully. "Okay. Let's talk about the obvious. Who the hell uses a stopwatch during a murder?" Kaiser rubbed a hand over his jaw. "Someone who trains with precision timing." "Special forces?" Zoe asked. "Could be." "Private military contractors?" "Maybe." "A cartel strike team?"

Kaiser paused at that. Zoe noticed immediately. "What?" "Cartels don't usually work with timers," he said. "Not like this. They're brutal, not precise."

"But the Gulf Cartel has hired ex-military before," Zoe said. "And the Castenllos aren't exactly small-time." Kaiser didn't argue. He stared out the window, watching a nurse wheel a patient's breakfast tray down the sidewalk below. "Zoe… what she described isn't just training," he said finally. "It's discipline."

Zoe raised a brow. "Moonpie, they killed three men in under three minutes. I'd call that discipline." "No," Kaiser said. "That's efficiency. I'm talking about something else."

He tapped his finger against his thigh, thinking it through. "A stopwatch means synchronicity," he said. "It means choreography. It means they weren't just executing a plan, they were executing it on a schedule." Zoe went still. "You're saying they timed the murder." Kaiser nodded slowly. "Or the whole operation."

Zoe closed her eyes for a moment, letting that sink in. "That's… insane," she whispered. "Or practiced," Kaiser replied.

Zoe flipped to a blank page in her notebook, writing quickly now. "Okay, so we have: multiple trained assailants, silent kills, clean entry, coordinated movement, and now timed execution." Kaiser glanced over her shoulder at the list. It looked worse written down.

She added the final words: **'Purposeful survivors.'** He exhaled through his nose. "Yeah. They wanted the wife alive. Maybe the father, too." Zoe turned the notebook toward him. "This looks like a professional hit team, Moonpie." "Not looks like," Kaiser corrected. "Is."

Zoe stared at him, weighing something serious behind her eyes. "Then we're not dealing with what killed Vinny Castenllo." "We're dealing with who sent them," Kaiser said. Heavy silence stretched.

Zoe finally spoke. "What do we tell Carlucci?" Kaiser huffed a humorless breath. "Nothing yet. He'll panic." Zoe considered. "FBI?" "Not yet. They'll claim jurisdiction the second they smell foreign involvement."

Zoe leaned back against the window ledge, tapping her pen against her notebook. "So what do we do?" Kaiser looked back down the hall toward Marie's room. "We find out who the man with the stopwatch is," he said quietly. "And fast."

Zoe nodded. "Okay. We follow the timing angle. Military supply shops? Tactical forums? Anybody caught on camera in the neighborhood holding something that size?" Kaiser didn't smile, but something like approval flickered behind his eyes. "More than that," he said. "Stopwatches are for training. For drills. Routines. We find drills like this? We find the unit."

Zoe tucked her notebook under her arm. "Then that's where we start." Kaiser rubbed his knee absently. "This wasn't a hit. It was a performance." Zoe frowned. "For whom?" Kaiser didn't hesitate. "For whoever sent them."

NOPD Headquarters was a different kind of chaos when Kaiser and Zoe returned. It was humming, tense, and charged in a way that meant whispers were spreading faster than facts.

Detective Bullard from Robbery brushed past them, lowering his voice as he murmured to another officer, "A whole damn hit squad." Zoe shot Kaiser a look. "That didn't take long." "Rumors outrun bullets," Kaiser said. "Always have."

They moved down the hallway toward the Homicide bullpen. Phones rang. Printers jammed. Officers clustered around computer screens, trying to get first access to whatever intel was trickling in from the Garden District.

As soon as Kaiser stepped into the bullpen, heads turned. Moonpie Kaiser was not easily rattled, and today, everyone could see the weight in his shoulders.

Lieutenant Gravois appeared from his office like he'd been waiting for them. "You two," he barked. "Report." Zoe started, "We spoke to the widow. She's…" Gravois held up a hand. "I don't need emotional status. I need intel."

Kaiser handed him the folder with preliminary notes. "You're not gonna like it." Gravois flipped it open, eyes skimming the top lines. He stopped halfway down the page, brow creasing. "A stopwatch?" he said. Zoe nodded. "Marie heard it. Multiple clicks. Right before the team moved." Gravois stared at her. "Who times a murder?" "No one," Kaiser said. "That's the point." He stepped closer. "They weren't reacting to the environment. They weren't improving. They were following timed intervals."

Zoe added, "Choreography." Gravois shut the folder. "So, what, this is some ex-military fantasy camp? A cartel special ops spin-off?" Kaiser shook his head. "Not fantasy. Not cartel muscle either. These guys trained somewhere real. And they're used to timing." "Used to?" Gravois repeated. Zoe answered for him. "You don't bring a stopwatch if you're guessing."

Gravois paced once, rubbing a hand over his jaw. "Alright. Fine. What's our next step?"

Kaiser glanced at Zoe, then back at the lieutenant. "Training," Kaiser said. "Find the units that use timed silent entry drills. Could be military. Could be mercenary. Could be foreign. But it narrows the field."

Zoe slid into her chair and started pulling up her computer. "We'll cross-reference any recent reports of tactical contractors operating stateside. Also look for former special forces with ties to organized crime." "Or private training outfits," Kaiser added. "The kind with enough money and enough secrecy to run drills that require precision."

Gravois sighed. "This is a nightmare." Kaiser agreed. Zoe's keyboard clacked as she built a search matrix.

"Anything else from the widow?" Gravois asked. Kaiser hesitated for the first time. He thought of the way Marie's eyes had unfocused, then sharpened at that last memory. He thought of her whisper: *'He said 'No.' And everything stopped.'* "She remembers the leader," Kaiser said. "Not his face. But his control."

Gravois frowned. "Meaning?" "Meaning he didn't force the others into formation. They were already in it." Zoe turned in her chair. "They're a working team. Not hired shooters scraped together for one job." Kaiser nodded. "A real unit."

The bullpen grew quiet around them and the attention coming into focus on them. Officers nearby pretended to work but were listening closely.

Gravois blew out a slow breath. "Okay. You two keep digging. Stay ahead of the feds if you can. I'll buy you time." Kaiser and Zoe nodded. They turned back toward their desks, but before Kaiser sat, Zoe asked, "You think they're still in the country?" Kaiser paused, one hand on the back of his chair. "They were timed on entry," he said. "They're timed on exit." Zoe swallowed. "Meaning?" Kaiser met her eyes. "Meaning they're already gone."

Zoe stared at him, the reality settling like a cold weight in her lungs. "Then what are we chasing, Moonpie?" He sat, finally letting his knee rest. "The leftovers," he said. "And maybe… if we're lucky… one mistake."

The bullpen had settled into the low, grinding hum of focused work. Kaiser and Zoe had fallen into their rhythm: she combing through digital breadcrumbs, he sorting physical evidence with the quiet intensity of someone listening for a whisper in noise. For twenty minutes, nothing surfaced. Then Zoe froze. A sudden stillness. The kind Kaiser had seen enough times to know meant something had shifted. She zoomed in on her screen. "Moonpie…" she said softly. "Look at this."

Kaiser rolled his chair over, ignoring the jab in his knee.

Zoe tapped the monitor. "It's a traffic cam on Prytania," she said. "Caught a few seconds when the power flickered on that block. Most angles went dark, but this one had residual battery."

A grainy nighttime image filled the screen of a side street, low light, a wash of static. "Watch the corner," Zoe said. She played the footage. Two seconds of nothing… Three seconds… Four… A shape moved in the lower right of the frame.

The figure stepped from between two hedges and crossed the boundary of the camera's view. Their head was down, hood up, silhouette tight and compact like someone carrying gear under a jacket.

But that wasn't what caught Kaiser's attention. It was the glint. There was a brief flash of metal in the figure's right hand, catching ambient light from a distant porch lamp. Zoe paused the footage, zoomed again. The resolution wasn't friendly. The pixels warped at the edges. But the shape was clear enough to see. A small, round metal object that was palm-sized. Thumb resting on a top-mounted plunger. A thin strap or lanyard looped over the wrist. Kaiser inhaled through his teeth. "A stopwatch," he said.

Zoe nodded. "Marie wasn't imagining it." Kaiser leaned closer. "Rewind ten seconds." She did. The figure reappeared, stepping with controlled urgency. He moved like the world around him belonged to him.

Zoe glanced at Kaiser. "He's calm." "Too calm," Kaiser said. "A man leaving a murder scene shouldn't look like he's coming back from errands." Zoe typed rapidly. "I'll run enhancement. See if we can stabilize the outline."

Kaiser rubbed the back of his neck. "There's something else here." "What?" Zoe asked. He pointed at the timestamp. "Power wasn't fully restored yet." Zoe blinked. "You're right." "He wasn't fleeing after the kill," Kaiser said slowly. "He was *finishing a task*." Zoe swallowed. "Which means the timing wasn't just for the entry." "No," Kaiser said. "It was for the exit too."

Zoe leaned back in her chair, absorbing the implications. "Moonpie… if this guy was timing the whole operation…" Kaiser finished the thought for her. "Then we're looking for someone who's done this before. Many times."

Zoe saved the frame, printed it to the evidence board, and wrote beneath it: **UNSUB #1 'Stopwatch'** Kaiser stared at the grainy and distorted image that was barely more than a shadow holding a metal circle. But a shadow was still *shape*. And a shape could become a face.

He straightened. "This," Kaiser said, tapping the printed image, "is our way in." Zoe met his eyes. "Our first real lead." The hum of the bullpen continued around them. But Kaiser felt something else beneath the noise; a faint, electric shift in the air.

The bullpen didn't quiet after the cam still was pinned to the board. If anything, it sharpened. The kind of tension that used to ripple through units when a case turned its face toward them but was not fully revealed, nor fully hidden, but enough to say: **Come find me.**

Babineaux was already pulling up maps of the surrounding blocks, layering traffic cams, private security feeds, and doorbell networks. Lines of data streamed down her screen like digital rain. Moonpie stood in front of the evidence board, hands on his hips, knee throbbing, eyes flicking between the bloody hallway photos and the blurry image of the man with the stopwatch.

Zoe looked up. "I'm triangulating his angle of movement. If he crossed Prytania at that time, he could've exited on…" "Philip Street," Kaiser finished. She blinked. "Yeah. How'd you…?" "Footwork," Kaiser said. "The stride. He wasn't in a sprint or a retreat. He was in an exit pattern. Philip's the cleanest path out. No cameras at the corner store, either, they've been busted for months."

Zoe almost smiled. "Moonpie, you're psychic." "No," Kaiser said. "I've just run away from enough things in my life to know how a man moves when he's done running."

Before she could answer, Lieutenant Gravois re-emerged, holding a file with the kind of grip that meant *don't ask what's in it unless you want bad news.* "Detectives," he said, tossing the folder onto Kaiser's desk. Moonpie opened it.

A black-and-white investigative summary. Stamped with **FEDERAL REVIEW UNRESOLVED.** A list of "possible foreign contract operators." Three names redacted. One unit designation visible: **Sombra Unidad, 'The Shadow Unit.'** Unofficial. Unconfirmed. Rumored.

Zoe's eyes widened. "Sir… where did this come from?" Gravois didn't answer at first. He leaned against a desk, crossing his arms. "A friend at the Bureau slid it over," he said. "Said if we're seeing the kind of precision you described, this is one of the only units on record with matching technique."

Zoe leaned closer. "Special operations?" "Unofficial special operations," Gravois corrected. "Trained for cross-border extractions. Silent kills. Timed breaching patterns." Kaiser's jaw tightened. "Ghost stories. I've heard of them." "Well," Gravois said, "ghosts or not, someone used their playbook." Zoe tapped the photo of the stopwatch man. "And one of them was here."

Kaiser felt a slow, cold realization start at the base of his spine and crawl upward. If this unit was real… If they had been contracted… Then this wasn't a one-off hit. This was a message delivered by men who didn't miss, didn't hesitate, didn't leave evidence… Except the single glint of metal in a traffic cam.

Zoe closed her notebook with a soft snap. "So what now?" Kaiser stepped back from the board. His voice was quiet. "Now," he said, "we stop treating this like a murder." Zoe nodded slowly. "And start treating it like… what? A paramilitary operation?" Kaiser's eyes lifted to the still on the board. "No," he said. "Like we're hunting the kind of men who time their breathing while they kill."

The bullpen went still for a heartbeat. The case no longer felt local. It felt like the beginning of something that would stretch far beyond New Orleans.

Zoe exhaled. "Moonpie… this is going to get worse." Kaiser nodded once. "It already has."

The sky outside the DCX building that housed the NOPD Headquarters had faded to a flat, bruised gray by the time Kaiser and Zoe finally stepped out onto the front steps. The building buzzed behind them with phones still ringing, officers still moving, the case still breathing down everyone's neck, but out here the world felt strangely muted.

Zoe hugged her arms against the cooling evening air. "Longest day of my life," she said quietly. Kaiser cracked his knee once, wincing as he descended the steps. "You're young," he said. "Give it time." She snorted, but it didn't reach humor.

They reached the bottom of the stairs, where a line of police cruisers idled, ready to roll out on their own sets of emergencies. Zoe paused. "Moonpie… that woman's face is going to stay with me."

Kaiser didn't look at her. He lit a cigarette he shouldn't have been smoking on city property and watched the smoke rise into the early night. "That's part of the job," he said. Zoe shook her head. "No. Some cases get inside you. This feels like one of them." Kaiser took a slow drag, thinking. "Cases don't get inside you," he said finally. "People do." She was quiet for a moment, considering that. "And the man with the stopwatch?" she asked. Kaiser blew out a ribbon of smoke. "He's already inside all of us. He made sure of it."

Foot traffic trickled past as officers went home and others arrived on shift. A patrol car pulled out of the lot, its headlights sweeping across their faces before disappearing into traffic. Zoe opened her car door but didn't get in. "Do you think we'll actually find them?" she asked.

Kaiser looked out over the city with the soft sprawl of lights, the distant sirens, and the quiet threat humming beneath the surface. "Maybe," he said. "But not because they slipped. Men like this don't leave crumbs."

"Then how?" Zoe asked. "Because they want something," Kaiser replied. "Everyone wants something." She absorbed that, nodding slowly. "Go home," Kaiser said. "Get some sleep. Tomorrow we start pulling every timed-entry training record we can find. Contractors. Foreign units. Anyone who drills by the second." Zoe slid into her car. "See you in the morning, Moonpie." He made a small salute with his cigarette. "Bright and early." She drove off, taillights fading into the city's night-glow.

Kaiser remained where he was, staring at the sky, the smoke, the creeping dark. His knee throbbed, his back ached, and exhaustion pressed down on him like a weight he couldn't shake. But beneath all of that there was a spark. The kind of feeling he only got on cases that mattered. The ones that didn't end until something broke.

He flicked the cigarette, watched the ember die out on the concrete, and murmured to no one, "Alright. Let's see what time does to you."

Then he turned and walked back inside. Because the day wasn't done. And neither was he.

Shadow's eyes narrowed. "Who else?"

The city felt hollow when Kaiser finally pulled into his driveway. The kind of hollow that came not from absence, but from knowing something had moved through the world and left a space nothing else could fill.

His porch light flickered due to the cheap wiring he kept forgetting to repair. He shut the car door carefully, not wanting to wake the neighbor's dog, and stood for a moment beneath the humid night sky.

Normal sounds. Except Kaiser knew normal had already been taken behind the shed and buried.

He walked up the steps, knee aching, joints stiff. The screen door protested when he opened it, which was another thing he'd kept meaning to fix. Another thing that didn't matter.

Inside, the house greeted him with the familiar smell of old wood and coffee grounds left in the machine. He dropped his keys in the bowl by the door. The silence settled in. It felt like a silence that knew something.

Kaiser loosened his tie, sat on the edge of his couch, and stared at the blank TV screen. His reflection looked older than yesterday. More tired. More aware.

His phone buzzed on the cushion beside him. He didn't reach for it immediately. He already knew what the message would say before he even looked. A single text. Just two words: **"KEEP DIGGING."** Kaiser stared at it, unmoving. The message was from Carlucci. He deleted it out of understanding.

He leaned back, exhaling into the quiet. "Alright," he murmured to the empty room. "We'll dig."

Outside, a breeze stirred the magnolia leaves in the yard.

Somewhere far away, too far for sound, but not too far for consequence, a stopwatch clicked.

A second passed.

Chapter 19

The Investigation

Kaiser sat hunched over his desk, rubbing the ache out of his knee while the first cup of reheated coffee barely steamed beside him. The bullpen wasn't quiet; Homicide never was. but there was a different tension in the air this morning. Every detective could feel the Castenllo case vibrating through the building like a live wire too close to water.

Zoe Babineaux came in fast, ponytail swinging, laptop tucked under her arm. "Moonpie! Tony's here." Kaiser looked up. "Russo?" "Yeah. He says he brought something."

Before Kaiser could stand fully, a familiar figure stepped into the bullpen. **Tony Russo came strolling in.**

"Kaiser," Tony said quietly. "Tony." Kaiser gestured him over. "You said you had something?"

Tony pulled his hand from his jacket. In it was a small, black USB drive. "This is from the house," he said. "Exterior cams. I pulled the footage from the night Vinny was killed."

Zoe blinked. "I thought your system was offline after midnight." "It is," Tony said. "But the backup system? The one Vinny insisted I install after that attempted break-in last year? That one runs on its own loop." Kaiser exchanged a look with Zoe. "Let's take a look," he said.

They moved to Zoe's workstation. She slid into her chair, inserted the USB, and waited as the files loaded. The grainy footage came up and was timestamped just after 10PM on the night of the murder. Tony leaned over and pointed. "There," he said. "That one. Play that section."

Zoe dragged the slider back ten seconds. The SUV carrying the Castenllo family pulled up in front of the house. The family got out. Vinny, Marie, Sophie, and Vincent Sr. all talking, laughing lightly.

Then, as the camera continued recording, something else emerged at the edge of the frame. A car.

Not unusual by itself. It was an older model sedan, dark, unobtrusive. But it didn't park. It slowed, just enough to notice. Then the vehicle continued down the street and disappeared. Zoe narrowed her eyes. "Play that again." She looped it. Same thing.

Kaiser leaned closer, jaw tightening. "That wasn't an accident," he said. Tony folded his arms. "I thought so too. That's why I brought it."

Zoe ran the playback another time, slowing it to 50%. "There," she said, pointing. "The slowdown isn't caused by braking. It's manual. Someone flicked the lights." Kaiser exhaled through his nose. "A relay check." Zoe nodded. "Someone signaling someone else 'They're here.'"

Tony looked between them, disturbed. "You think that's the team?" "Maybe," Kaiser said.

Zoe clicked to the next file, which was timestamped twenty minutes later. The same sedan appeared again, this time passing in the opposite direction. Then gone. She sat back in her chair. "They tracked the family's movements." "More than tracked," Kaiser said. "They confirmed arrivals. Timed departures. The hitters didn't improvise at the house. They had eyes on them all evening."

Tony swallowed. "Jesus… Vinny never saw it coming." Kaiser rested a hand briefly on Tony's shoulder, a rare gesture from him. "We're gonna use this," he said. "It's a good lead."

Zoe was already exporting the clip. "I'll run plate enhancement. The image is trash, but I might get shape recognition. Maybe even a partial." Kaiser nodded. Tony hesitated.

"There's one more thing," he said. Kaiser turned. "What is it?" Tony's face tightened. "It wasn't just the shadows," he said quietly. "That car? It was there earlier too. Afternoon, after lunch. I didn't think anything of it. Now…" He shook his head. "I think they'd been watching them the whole day."

Zoe looked at Kaiser, eyes wide. Kaiser looked at the screen. "Yeah," Moonpie said quietly. "They were."

The tech lab at NOPD always felt too bright. Walls were humming with servers, monitors stacked three high, wires coiled like snakes across metal tables. It was the kind of place where evidence got stripped down to its bones.

Kaiser stepped inside with Zoe, close behind him. Two analysts were already waiting: **Reggie Tran**, thin and sharp-eyed, and **Kendra Moss**, who could pull clarity out of pixel mush like it was a party trick. Reggie spun in his chair. "Detectives. Heard you brought us a present."

Zoe handed him the USB. "Costenllo family backup footage. We need to isolate and track a sedan seen signaling the night of the murder." Kendra leaned forward. "What kind of signal?" Zoe replicated the movement with her hands. "Dip in speed. Twice. Not from braking, but manual." Reggie raised an eyebrow. "Communications signal?" Kaiser nodded. "Looks like surveillance relay."

"Well," Kendra said, cracking her knuckles, "let's wake the beast." She pulled up the footage Zoe imported, freezing the frame where the car entered the edge of the feed. Grainy pixels, deep shadows, and minimal identifying features. Just the type of footage cops hated… and analysts lived for. Reggie zoomed in. "Older model sedan. Four-door. Can't get the make or model yet, but the wheelbase is long. Ride height's too low for recent American builds."

Kendra tapped her pen against the desk. "Okay. Let's do a light sweep. Pulling frame layers." The pixelated mess separated into segments of contrast maps, luminance spreads, and edge-sharpening overlays.

Kaiser watched silently, arms folded. Zoe leaned in. "Can you pull the plate?" "Not from this angle," Kendra said. "But headlights tell me plenty." Kaiser frowned. "How?" "Pattern," she said. "Every headlight filament burns uniquely. Watch."

She overlaid a spectral mapping of two oblong white clusters representing the headlights. They weren't perfectly symmetrical. One had a small crescent-shaped darkening on the right edge. "That shadow pattern," Kendra said, "means the headlight glass is chipped. Probably from gravel. And the bulb is old… older than what you'd find on a modern ride."

Reggie typed rapidly. "Running headlight spectrum characteristics across citywide traffic footage." Zoe raised her eyebrows. "We can do that?" Reggie grinned. "We can do anything if the budget people don't find out." Kaiser huffed once. "Just don't tell them, then."

The system whirred, monitors scrolling through thousands of captured vehicle profiles. After nearly a minute, the computer pinged. "Got something," Reggie said. "Two possible matches. "Kaiser stepped closer as the images popped up:

Camera 1 St. Charles & Amelia Sedan. Same low profile. Same right-side headlight crescent shadow. Timestamp: *5:07 PM, day of the murder.* **Camera 2 Washington & Magazine** Same vehicle. Same headlights. Timestamp: *9:12 PM four minutes after Castenllo family arrived at Tony's.* Zoe circled the second one. "That's right before they left dinner." Kaiser nodded slowly. "Which means the car wasn't just watching. It was following intervals."

Kendra pulled both images up side-by-side. "Now watch this." She activated thermal layering. The driver's window glowed faintly yellowish with residual heat signature. Someone was in the car.

Reggie shook his head. "We still can't see the face, but…" "But we know he was alone," Zoe finished. "A lone spotter." Kaiser rubbed his chin. "Spotter relays to the team. Team executes based on timing."

Kendra pointed at the timestamps again. "Guys… this isn't stalking." Zoe looked at her. "Then what?" Kendra's voice dropped. "This is choreography." Kaiser leaned back, absorbing that. Internally, the gears shifted. Moonpie exhaled slowly.

"We're not just hunting ghosts," he said. "We're also hunting the man who keeps time for them." Zoe stepped closer to the screen, staring at the blurred image of the driver, which was just a silhouette, a faint shape under a streetlamp. "The spotter," she whispered. "The first link." Kaiser nodded once.

"Pull every camera on his route. Streetlights, store fronts, private feeds. If this car followed them all day, it left a trail." Reggie cracked his fingers. "Now you're speaking my language."

Back in the Homicide bullpen, a whiteboard had been dragged into the center of the room. Kaiser stood before it with a marker in hand, Zoe Babineaux at his side, and Reggie and Kendra hovering over printouts like vultures waiting for movement. The surveillance stills were already pinned to the board. Zoe drew a horizontal line across the board. "Okay," she said. "We map the day. We start from the earliest sighting."

Kendra flipped through her clipboard. "5:07 PM," she said. "St. Charles and Amelia. Spotter's car is northbound." Moonpie marked it on the line. Zoe added, "Family dinner arrival at Tony's is around 9:08 PM." Reggie tapped the screen. "Spotter drives past at 9:12 PM. Same vehicle, same headlights." Kaiser stepped back a bit, arms folded, reading the line like a pulse. "Four hours between sightings," he said. "Long gap. Could mean nothing... or everything."

Tony, who had stayed to watch the process unfold, spoke up quietly. "Vinny had meetings all afternoon. If someone knew his schedule…" "They could tail him without being close," Zoe finished. Reggie moved to another monitor. "I'm pulling all available private business cams along St. Charles and Magazine from 2 PM forward. With Castenllo money, he hit at least three restaurants, two offices, and probably a few cash-only stops."

Kaiser rubbed his jaw. "Spotter didn't need to be on top of him. Just needed confirmation points." Zoe circled the two confirmed timestamps. "Which means if we find more timestamps, we can recreate the entire surveillance pattern." "And maybe see where they staged," Kaiser said. "Where they synchronized with the team."

Kendra appeared beside them with a new sheet. "We already found another one." Zoe raised her eyebrows. "Already?" Kendra nodded. "Camera on Felicity Street. 3:42 PM. Same crescent-shaped headlight shadow." Zoe marked it on the line. Kaiser's eyes hardened. "Three points," he said. "Beginning to look like a route."

Reggie swiveled in his chair. "Spotter wasn't following the family in real time. He was moving ahead of them. Confirming stops. Confirming departures." Zoe froze. "That means…" "They had Vinny Jr.'s schedule," Kaiser said. "And they were predicting his next moves before he made them."

Kendra bit her lip. "Detectives… I don't think this was surveillance for opportunity." Zoe looked at her. "Then what was it?" Kendra swallowed. "It was surveillance for *timing*. They were building a countdown."

Kaiser stepped closer to the whiteboard. "This was the choreography you mentioned earlier," he said. "The spotter wasn't just watching. He was pacing the day." Zoe nodded slowly. "If we keep pulling footage, we might find the moment the spotter communicated the final confirmation. The point of no return."

Kaiser capped the marker. "We need the whole day. Start to finish." Zoe turned to Reggie and Kendra. "Pull everything from noon to midnight. Every block. Every traffic cam. Every private feed within half a mile of any Castenllo-associated property." Reggie saluted with exaggerated formality. "On it." Kendra was already typing. "If the spotter slipped even once… We'll catch it."

Tony stood silently, staring at the timeline. "My friend was dead before he sat down to dinner," he murmured. Kaiser looked at him, not unkindly, but directly. "No," he said. "Your friend was dead before he woke up that morning." Tony closed his eyes.

Zoe added one final note on the board: **SPOTTER = FIRST WAVE KILLERS = SECOND WAVE TIMING = THE KEY** Kaiser nodded. "Now," he said, "we find the gaps." "Why the gaps?" Zoe asked.

Moonpie looked at her with a grim spark of certainty. "Because that's where the truth hides."

After Tony left the bullpen, the team moved back to the lab, The hum inside the tech room had shifted from curiosity to anticipation. Reggie and Kendra had thrown half the city's footage into a processing queue. Moonpie and Babineaux stood behind them, watching the lines of time build themselves on the whiteboard like a heartbeat developing its rhythm. One by one, the spotter's appearances stitched themselves across the city map. Kaiser traced the movement with a finger. "Look at this," he said. "He's not tailing them. He's orbiting them." Zoe nodded. "He's always ahead. Always waiting."

Kendra printed another sheet and hurried over, excitement edging her voice. "Another location," she said. "Canal Street. 6:21 PM. Same headlight signature." Zoe marked the new point on the timeline. Kaiser stared at the board. "Felicity at 3:42… St. Charles at 5:07… Canal at 6:21… Magazine at 9:12…"

Zoe connected the dots with a straight line. It curved around the Castenllo family's known movements with eerie precision. "This is pre-knowledge," Zoe said quietly. "He knew where they'd be before they arrived."

A tech assistant called out from another terminal. "Detectives! Got something else." They moved quickly across the room. The assistant brought up a split-screen comparison of two different camera angles. One from a gas station lot at 2:16 PM, the other from a street pole at 2:53 PM. Same slow glide, never stopping. But what mattered wasn't the car. It was the way it moved. Zoe leaned in. "That's… the same turn radius." "Same driver behavior pattern," Reggie said. "Someone trained to maintain a uniform pace. Not casual driving." Kendra added, "And the sedan appears to be using secondary streets to avoid main cameras."

Moonpie exhaled slowly. "He wasn't hiding," he said. "He was avoiding clutter. Giving the team clean signals." Zoe looked at him. "Meaning?" "Meaning he didn't care if someone caught footage of him in the background. He cared about clarity. Efficiency." He tapped the board. "He didn't want to be lost in traffic or crowds. He wanted a clean line."

Reggie's voice lowered. "A clean line to what?" Kaiser turned to him. "To the hour of death." The room went quiet.

Zoe swallowed. "Moonpie… this isn't just surveillance. It's sequencing." "Yes," Kaiser said. "Someone spent an entire day timing the family's movement like a piece of choreography."

Kendra hesitated. "Detectives… there's something else." She pulled up an enlarged still of the spotter's sedan at 6:21 PM near Canal. The driver's face was still obscured, but on the dashboard, a faint glint of metal was visible. Zoe's breath hitched. "Is that…" Kendra zoomed again. Pixels blurred, but the outline was unmistakable; **A round, metallic object resting on the dash.**

Kaiser felt his stomach tighten. "That's him," he said. "The same man Marie heard." Zoe whispered, "The timekeeper." Reggie wrote it on the board: "Find him," he said.

Kaiser didn't answer. He didn't have to. Zoe was already typing. "Cross-referencing the vehicle's movement pattern with parking lots, gas stations, and pay-to-park garages. He had to stop at some point during the day." Kendra jumped in. "And if he stopped, he was caught on at least one static camera. Maybe multiple."

Kaiser thought of Marie's trembling whisper. *I heard a click… like a stopwatch… and everything happened after that.* The line between planning and killing was the width of a thumb's press on a button. "Keep pulling," Moonpie said. "He wasn't a ghost. Nobody's a ghost." Zoe met his eyes. "If we find the car," she said, "we find him." Kaiser nodded. "And if we find him," he said, "we start to understand the team."

The tech room had shifted from tense to electric with every station humming, monitors flickering with grids of traffic feeds, street maps, and timestamps. Even the air felt charged.

Zoe hovered over Kendra's workstation, eyes darting across the developing timeline. Kaiser stood with Reggie by the front table, scanning each newly uploaded clip before it was slotted into the board.

Kendra typed rapidly. "I'm widening the camera pull radius. Not just the Castenllo orbit, but also anything within a half-mile of each timestamp." Zoe nodded. "Good. He wasn't tailing them directly. He was running parallel routes. That means intersections, feeders, service roads; any place he could maintain visual without being obvious." Reggie added, "Or where he had a vantage point to signal the hitters."

Kaiser didn't look away from the screen. "That's what we need, his vantage points."

Kendra's monitor beeped. "I've got movement correlation," she said. "Multiple clips showing the spotter car crossing paths with… something." Zoe leaned in. "With what?" Kendra pulled up a split screen. On the left side was the Timekeeper's sedan passing under a streetlamp. On the right side was a second vehicle, caught barely a minute later, moving in the opposite direction on another street. Zoe frowned. "Different make. Different plate. Not our guy." "No," Kendra said. "But watch the timestamps."

She synchronized them. The two vehicles appeared in alternating sequence on different cameras, which indicated a leapfrog pattern.

Reggie whistled. "That's coordination." Zoe blinked. "A second surveillance vehicle?" Kendra nodded. "Same timing intervals. Same route orbit. And look here, this one hangs back farther. Way farther." Kaiser rubbed his jaw. "Long-range tail. First car confirms location. Second car confirms departure."

Moonpie exhaled sharply. "Son of a bitch. How many were watching them?" Zoe pointed at the board. "At least two. Maybe more." Reggie chimed in, "Look at the vehicle spacing. They're maintaining timing, not distance. That's military doctrine. One signals, one monitors drift, one adjusts pacing."

Kaiser stepped closer to the screen, studying the second vehicle's movement. "No headlight dip," he said. Zoe nodded. "Right. Because he wasn't signaling. He was copying intervals. Meaning this wasn't just surveillance," she said. "This was *calibration.*"

Reggie pulled up a new file that was timestamped 7:04 PM, near a small strip mall parking lot. The second vehicle pulled in for twelve seconds, then exited. Kaiser's eyes narrowed. "Stop. Zoom the entry frame." Reggie enhance-and-zoomed the moment the second car entered the lot.

A figure stepped briefly into frame. It was just a sliver of shoulder and torso, silhouetted against the glow of a convenience store window. "Who's that?" Zoe asked. Reggie zoomed again, though resolution degraded. Kaiser leaned closer. Zoe whispered, "That's training. Even just standing still." Moonpie rubbed his forehead. "This is insane. They were everywhere."

Kendra brought up another synchronized pair of clips. "This confirms what we suspected," she said. "Wherever the Castenllos went, the spotter team was already there or just leaving."

Zoe scribbled a new note on the board: **TWO SPOTTERS COORDINATED TIMEKEEPER = PRIMARY SHADOW DRIVER = SECONDARY**

Kaiser inhaled slowly. Everything about this felt too big, too organized, too practiced. But big things had cracks. And they had just found one. "Keep expanding the radius," Kaiser said. "Every feed within the orbit, every clip that even hints of movement outside normal traffic flow."

Zoe turned to him. "Moonpie… what exactly are we looking for now?" Kaiser pointed at the blurred silhouette in the parking lot. "That," he said. "Because if he stepped out of the car even once, then somebody saw him."

The hum of the tech room had become a kind of heartbeat pulsing through the building like the city itself knew something was about to crack.

Reggie's fingers flew across the keyboard. Kendra's eyes darted between monitors. Zoe hovered over the data stream, waiting for a flicker or a mistake.

Kaiser stood with his arms folded and weight shifting off his bad knee. He watched the timeline on the whiteboard expand with each new sighting.

Then… A chime. A **flag** chime. Kendra froze. "Oh… wait." Zoe leaned over her shoulder. "What is it?" Kendra enlarged a frame from a traffic cam on Napoleon Avenue with a timestamp 4:18 PM. The screen brightened, pixelated, and then sharpened.

The spotter's sedan was there gliding through the intersection. But this time… Zoe inhaled. "There's someone else in the car." Kaiser came closer. "Show me." Kendra zoomed the passenger side. The silhouette was faint, but unmistakable. There was a second figure sitting in the front seat.

Reggie frowned. "That's new. We haven't seen a passenger in any earlier footage." "No," Zoe breathed. "This is the first time." Kaiser's jaw tightened. "Timeline?" Zoe ran her finger across the board. "4:18 PM… that's hours before the family went to dinner. Hours before the evening surveillance."

Kendra switched screens. "Here's the full clip." The sedan rolled to a stop at a red light. Passenger leaned forward toward the driver. A subtle exchange of movement. Kaiser narrowed his eyes. "What are they doing?"

Reggie rewound. Played again. Slowed it to 30%. Something passes between them. Zoe whispered, "They're syncing." Kaiser nodded slowly. "Spotter to secondary. Secondary to… who knows." Kendra layered a motion tracker over the clip. "Watch the passenger's shoulder," she said.

On the monitor, a faint shift of two distinct movements; the passenger's hand lifts and the driver nods once. Kendra tapped the screen. "That's communication." Zoe wrote on the board. Kaiser stared at the screen. Running a coordinated timing grid across the city. Meaning the killers didn't improvise anything, they were operating off a synchronized, continuous relay. Kaiser said quietly. "This is above military planning. This is contract precision. They had a system."

Kendra highlighted the timestamp. "Detectives… the passenger disappears from all later footage." Zoe blinked. "Meaning what?" "Meaning," Kendra said, "he got out of the car after this clip. Somewhere in that four-minute block before the next camera." Reggie muttered, "And if he got out, he walked. And if he walked…" Zoe finished it, "…then he might have crossed a storefront camera."

Kaiser pointed at Reggie. "Pull everything from two minutes before to ten minutes after. Shops, bars, street corners." Reggie cracked his knuckles. "Fishing for a face." "Fishing for a mistake," Kaiser corrected.

Moonpie stared at the freeze-frame of the second silhouette. "We won't find him first," he said. "We'll find where he went." He tapped the timestamp on the screen. "Because mistakes don't start at the kill, they start hours before." Zoe nodded. "And this is hours before." Kendra smiled faintly. "Then let's make him famous."

Kaiser watched the shadows on the screen; two shapes in a car that had spent a day marking the Castenllos for death. Finally, he said, "Run it all. The whole city. I want every frame from every angle." He turned toward the board. "And if he stepped into daylight even once, we'll see his face."

The tech room lights dimmed automatically as Kendra executed a multi-camera sweep. Twelve screens flickered at once with storefront angles, apartment lobby cams, bar entry feeds, crosswalk sensors. Each one searched for the same thing, **A man who had only existed as a shadow.** Zoe leaned forward. "What's our radius?" "Quarter-mile from the intersection where the passenger disappeared," Kendra said. "If he got out of the car, he had to cross at least one of these angles." Reggie muttered, "Unless he vanished into thin air…" Kaiser didn't look away from the screens. "Nobody vanishes," he said. "They just pick cameras we haven't found yet."

A ping. One screen brightened. A grainy convenience store feed, timestamp 4:19 PM, just one minute after the sedan clip. Zoe inhaled sharply. "There." A figure stepped into frame from the very edge that matched the silhouette from the car. A figure with short hair, dark jacket, a medium build, calm gait came into frame. "Side profile," Zoe said. "Look at the ear shape. And the jawline." Kaiser nodded slowly. "That's our passenger."

Moonpie stepped closer, tension radiating off him. "Can you get the face?" "Working on it…" Kendra fused two adjacent frames, stabilized the motion, and sharpened the edges. A soft outline of a face emerged. Reggie whispered, "Jesus… we've got him."

Zoe grabbed a sticky note and wrote **UNSUB #2 WALKER** beneath the still image before pinning it to the board. Kaiser stared at the screen. The man wasn't young, nor was he old.

Kendra zoomed further. The passenger paused outside the convenience store. He turned slightly. Looked across the street. Zoe narrowed her eyes. "What's he looking at?" Kendra rewound and played it again. This time slower.

Walker lifted a hand subtly, almost invisible, and tapped his ear. Then nodded once. Communication gesture. Clear as daylight.

Reggie gasped. "He was wearing an earpiece." Kaiser exhaled. "So the spotter car wasn't the only relay. They ran comms the whole day." Zoe murmured, "This… this is a military operation. Timing, relay, comms, coordination; this is a unit."

The footage continued. Walker crossed the street, disappearing out of frame. That's when Kendra caught it. "Hold up! There's another angle!" A city-owned maintenance camera caught the same man crossing the next block, a full-body shot this time. Zoe sucked in a breath. "Moonpie…" His stride was smooth and **deliberate.** A man perfectly comfortable walking through daylight after orchestrating surveillance that would lead to blood.

Kendra printed the image immediately. Zoe pinned it under the first one. Reggie spoke quietly. "He's not hiding. He's blending. That's worse." Kaiser stepped back.

"We can run this," Zoe said. "Face recognition, gait analysis, body proportion match, this is enough to start a real hunt." Kaiser nodded, but his expression didn't shift.

Because something wasn't right. Zoe noticed. "What is it?" Kaiser pointed at Walker's hand. "Zoom." Kendra did. Walker was holding something at his side. Zoe whispered, "Is that another stopwatch?" Kaiser stared. "No," he said quietly. "That's something else."

The shape was different; oval rather than round. A tiny antenna protruding from the top.

Zoe frowned. "What is that?" Kendra brought up a comparison overlay. Reggie's eyes widened. "Holy shit." Zoe realized it at the same time: "That's a **signal repeater.**" Kaiser nodded slowly. "Yeah," he said. "He wasn't just receiving instructions." Zoe finished the sentence for him. "He was *transmitting them.*"

The room went silent. Not because they'd found a face. But because they'd seen the man who had been, all day long. **keeping the killers connected.**

Kaiser finally spoke. "Print every frame. Pull every angle. This man is the key to the whole damn operation." Zoe nodded. Reggie nodded. Kendra nodded. And Kaiser looked at the timeline again, feeling the shape of the case change under his feet.

The image of **UNSUB #2** sat pinned to the center of the evidence board now, flanked by timestamps and route   maps.
Every detective walking past slowed, looked, then kept going with a new tension in their shoulders.

Zoe Babineaux uploaded the enhanced still into the city's recognition database, fingers flying over the keyboard.
Reggie stood behind her, already prepping federal and interstate data links. Kendra sifted through other

angles to refine the composite. Moonpie didn't sit; he paced.

Zoe hit ENTER. The automated voice of the database system chimed, **"Image processing. Please wait."** Reggie smirked. "Please wait. The three worst words in police work." Zoe didn't look away from the screen. "It's running through local first. Then driver's licenses. Then mugshots. Then employment IDs. Then military discharge records."

Kaiser stopped pacing. "If he's ever been in a government office, I want it found." Zoe nodded. The progress bar crawled. **24%... 37%... 49%...** "C'mon," Reggie muttered. Kendra added softly, "The face isn't clean, but the gait match might hit." "If it's all we have," Kaiser said. **73%... 84%... 92%...** A soft *ding*.

Everyone leaned in. The screen flashed: **NO DIRECT FACIAL MATCH FOUND.**

Reggie groaned. "Damn it."

But another line appeared beneath it: **POTENTIAL GAIT MATCHES: 14 RESULTS. FILTERING... 7 RESULTS... 3 RESULTS...** Zoe's pulse quickened. "We might have something..." The results finalized: **2 POSSIBLE MATCHES One local One international** Kaiser stepped closer. "Pull both."

Zoe clicked the first one. A DMV ID photo appeared. It was a blurry and outdated picture of a man who vaguely resembled the silhouette, but not exactly.

Reggie shook his head. "No rhythm match on the walking pattern. Toss it." Zoe clicked the second. A different ID popped up, this one cleaner. Late 30s. Neutral expression. Civilian clothing. Eyes that didn't quite smile the way ID photos often forced people to try.

Zoe frowned. "Doesn't look exactly like the footage…" Kendra slid in. "Flip the angle. Rotate five degrees." Zoe adjusted it. When the image shifted, the jawline aligned, the ear shape matched, and the proportion of skull to neck tightened into place. Reggie whispered, "Holy shit, that's him."

The system pinged again. **GAIT CONFIRMATION: 87% MATCH. ANTHROPOMETRIC MATCH: 81% OVERALL LIKELIHOOD: HIGH**

Zoe exhaled. "This is our guy." Kaiser stared at the screen. The name that was listed: **Miguel A. Ramos and his age was listed as** 38. Last known residence: was listed in Mexico. His Employment history was listed as unknown. Previous service: **Mexican Marines, 7th Infantry Regiment** (AWOL)

Kaiser's eyes darkened. "Mexican Marines," he repeated. Reggie swallowed. "So he wasn't cartel. He wasn't mob. He was military." Zoe's voice came low. "A soldier? A soldier did this?" "No," Kaiser said quietly. "A former soldier. A trained operative. Someone who learned precision and discipline long before the wrong people got a hold of him. He is probably Cartel now."

Zoe clicked into his last documented employer, **Aurelius Protective Services** with a Specialty in Overseas operations, extraction support, and counter-surveillance. Zoe looked up. "This guy is a professional." Kaiser nodded. "More than that." He tapped the board where "TIMEKEEPER" was written. "He was part of a system. And now we have a name."

Zoe printed the composite and pinned it next to the Timekeeper's image. The board now had two faces. One that was still blurry and one that sharpened into a man.

Zoe said quietly, "We're close, Moonpie." Kaiser didn't smile. "We just found the thread," he said. "Now we pull it."

The moment Miguel Ramos' name hit the printer, the bullpen changed in the way every detective suddenly spoke a little softer, leaned a little closer, and moved a little quicker.

Before Zoe could pin the printed sheet fully to the board, Lieutenant Gravois' office door flew open.

"Moonpie! Babineaux! Inside. Now." Kaiser and Zoe exchanged a look, then followed him in. Gravois shut the door behind them harder than necessary. He jerked a thumb toward the phone on his desk. "That's the Bureau," Gravois said. "They want the case file you just built." Zoe stiffened. "Already?"

Gravois stabbed a finger toward the window overlooking the bullpen. "They caught the same ping from the facial rec system you did. They know we hit a name. And now they want to swoop in like they've been doing the damn work." Kaiser leaned against the desk. "What did the Bureau say exactly?"

Gravois mimicked a clipped monotone, "*We believe this case may intersect with an ongoing federal inquiry. Please forward all materials for review.*" Zoe rolled her eyes. "That means take it away from us." "Damn right it does," Gravois barked.

Kaiser stayed calm. "How long do we have?" Gravois blew out a breath. "They're sending an agent over in the morning. Callahan."

Kaiser's jaw twitched. "Of course it's Callahan." Zoe looked between them. "...That bad?" "Arrogant," Kaiser said. "Possessive. Treats locals like interns."

Gravois slammed his hand on the desk. "This is *our* city. *Our* homicide. And I'll be damned if we hand over our first real lead because some fed got itchy."

Zoe crossed her arms. "So we stall?" "No." Gravois leaned in. "You accelerate." Zoe blinked. "Meaning?"

Kaiser answered for him. "We use the time before they walk in the door. We run Ramos' background. We find where he trained, who he's worked with, and who has paid him." Gravois nodded sharply. "Exactly. Once the Bureau takes over, they'll bury half the file under national security red tape."

Zoe looked at Kaiser. "Moonpie… what if the feds were aware of Ramos already? What if he wasn't a ghost to them?" Kaiser didn't hesitate. "He was. Until he started killing people in my city."

A soft knock at the door interrupted them. Reggie poked his head in. "Uh… detectives? You might wanna see this." Gravois waved him in. "What now?" Reggie held up a tablet. "We pulled Ramos' last known cell activity. The signal's dead, like he ditched the phone months ago. But…" He handed the tablet to Kaiser.

A map came up with a scatter of old pings from three years back, then nothing. Except one. There was a single, isolated, recent hit.

Zoe's heartbeat kicked. "When was that?" she asked. Reggie swallowed. "Three days before the murder." Kaiser narrowed his eyes. "Where?"

Reggie zoomed as the map enlarged and coordinates sharpened. A warehouse district in Kenner near the airport pulled up.

Zoe whispered, "That's abandoned property." Reggie nodded. "Most of it. Except that block." Kaiser's voice dropped. "That's where he staged." Gravois nodded once, decisive. "Then that's where you go."

Zoe looked at him. "Tonight?" "No," Kaiser said. "Right now." Gravois looked between them, jaw tight. "I'll stall the Bureau. You two move." Kaiser handed the tablet back to Reggie. "On it." Zoe grabbed her jacket. "Let's go."

As they stepped out of the office, the bullpen parted instinctively with detectives sensing something escalating.

Moonpie and Babineaux headed for the door, the city humming beneath them and the investigation turning its first real corner.

The warehouse district near the airport always felt half-abandoned, half-waiting for trouble. Old buildings slumped against each other, windows dark, alleys clogged with weeds and rusted chain-link. Somewhere far off, a jet engine moaned across a runway. Kaiser and Babineaux pulled up beside a long-defunct shipping bay. The air smelled like oil and river mud. "This is where the ping hit?" Zoe asked, scanning the desolate stretch. Kaiser held up his phone with a screenshot of Reggie's tablet. A single red dot on the map; exact coordinates tied to Miguel Ramos' last known activity. "Right here," Kaiser confirmed. "Three days before the hit."

They stepped out of the car. The quiet wasn't normal. It was a *vacancy*, the kind that came after movement had stopped but not long enough for the world to forget it. Zoe swept her flashlight across the asphalt. "Doesn't look like much." "That's the point," Kaiser said.

The beam caught on something faint but deliberate. A set of fresh tire impressions at the edge of an overgrown loading ramp. The imprints were not deep enough for rain to have filled them, nor old enough to have cracked. Zoe crouched down. "Definitely a vehicle. Heavy."

Kaiser's gaze drifted to the warehouse door. He knelt, lifted the edge, and shined his light inside. "Someone was here," Kaiser said. "Recently." Zoe stepped inside with him, boots crunching lightly.

Half the warehouse lay in darkness, the rafters disappearing into black rafters. But the area near the back wall had a disturbance: footprints in the dust and drag marks where something had been moved. "Staging area," Zoe murmured. "This is where they prepped." Kaiser nodded, shining his light over the faint outline of a rectangle on the floor that was cleaner than the dust around it. "A table used to sit here," he said. "Or a crate."

Zoe's beam found something else. A scrap of torn tape stuck to the concrete. It was bright red marking tape. Exactly the type used to label equipment in tactical kits. She held it up. "They didn't miss much. But they missed this." Kaiser slipped it into an evidence envelope. "And more importantly…" he pointed at the disturbed dust trails "…they moved as a team. Even here. Patterned footsteps. Coordinated spacing."

Zoe followed the tracks deeper into the shadows until she found a small metal object wedged against the wall. "Moonpie," she called quietly. "Look at this." He crossed to her.

She held up a tiny magnetic clip designed to hold comm wires or secure tactical gear to a vest. His expression tightened. "What were they doing here?" Zoe asked. "Prepping loadouts," Kaiser said. "Coordinating timing. Syncing comms." Zoe frowned. "So they came back after the job?" He shook his head. "No. This was before."

Something in his tone made her look at him sharply. "You sure?" "Yeah," he said quietly. "Look at the dust. Undisturbed near the entrance. Heavy patterns here. They came once. Prepared. Then left for the hit." Zoe exhaled. "So this was their safehouse?" Kaiser nodded.

But then he stopped. Because something didn't fit. He scanned the room again. "Zoe," he said slowly, "count the tracks." She pointed. "One, two, three sets."

Kaiser tilted his head. "Now count the pattern." Zoe did. Her face shifted. "There are four."

Zoe straightened. "Moonpie… someone erased their tracks on purpose." Kaiser's stomach tightened. "Yeah," he whispered. "The fourth doesn't want to be found."

Before either could say more, Zoe's radio crackled. "Dispatch to Detective Babineaux, urgent message. FBI en route to HQ. Repeat, en route. Immediate transfer request." Zoe's eyes widened. "They're coming for the case." Kaiser didn't move. He looked at the erased tracks, ghosts of a ghost, and understood this wasn't just a kill team.

Moonpie rose slowly, voice low, resolute. "We're not giving this case up." Zoe nodded. "Then we'd better move fast."

Kaiser took one last look at the warehouse with the shadows, the erased footprints, the hint of something bigger lurking beyond the visible. "Let's go," he said. They stepped out into the night, the warehouse echoing behind them. The airport wind howled through the loading bay. And unseen in the rafters, a thin scrape of metal whispered in the dark.

Chapter 20

The Funeral

The bells of **St. Louis Cathedral** tolled slowly and heavy across Jackson Square, rolling over the crowds gathered in the early afternoon heat. The sound felt older than the city itself. Black cars filled the entire block with every seat inside the cathedral taken. The steps outside overflowed with mourners dressed in crisp suits, dark dresses, veils, and rosaries. This wasn't just a funeral, it was a **statement.**

Detective Kaiser stepped out of the unmarked sedan with Zoe Babineaux at his side. The moment his foot hit the pavement, he felt every pair of eyes shift toward them. "Quite the turnout," Zoe murmured. Kaiser looked over the crowd with faces from every corner of New Orleans' shadowed underworld, a few faces Kaiser knew from old case files. Behind them, ordinary citizens came simply to witness the spectacle of a fallen Castenllo. "So many people loved Vinny Jr.," Zoe whispered. "Loved?" Kaiser said quietly. "Some of them feared him. Some depended on him. Some hated him. And some are here because showing up is part of staying alive." Zoe scanned the crowd again, absorbing the weight of it.

Sophie Castenllo stood near the cathedral steps, surrounded by a protective ring of family and men loyal to the Castenllo name. Her black dress was immaculate. Her chin was high. Eyes red, but dry. She wasn't breaking. Marie Castenllo was not present. Grief and trauma kept her confined to the hospital. Vincent Castenllo Sr. stood just inside the cathedral entrance, hands clasped in front of him, staring down at the polished marble floor like he might fall straight through it. The Archbishop waited beside him. Overhead, the bells finally fell silent.

Kaiser adjusted his jacket, glanced at Zoe. "Ready?" "No," Zoe said. "Let's go anyway." They stepped past the threshold into the cathedral's cool interior.

The shift was immediate, from humid noise to sacred quiet, from street chaos to ordered reverence. Sunlight poured through stained glass, scattering jewel-toned patterns over the pews. The coffin rested at the front, closed and adorned with white lilies and a black ribbon.

Sophie's eyes flicked briefly toward Kaiser and Zoe as they entered, just long enough to acknowledge them. Then she looked forward again, expression carved from stone.

Detectives were not welcome here, but they were tolerated. Because information traveled in strange ways and today was not a day to make enemies.

Kaiser and Zoe slid into the last pew. Zoe whispered, "I've never seen this many people at a funeral." "You will," Kaiser murmured. "This city buries a lot of kings."

A string quartet began to play somber, trembling through the vaulted space.

Kaiser felt the tension in the room shift, as the whole cathedral inhaled as one. The doors closed. The service was about to begin. The choir began softly, carrying through the vaulted ceiling like a slow-moving tide. The cathedral filled with sound, but no one moved.

Moonpie and Zoe remained in the last pew, silent observers in a room where they did not belong but could not be absent. Up front, the Castenllo family occupied the first two rows. Black veils. Sophie Castenllo sat between her godfather on one side and a pair of heavyset family loyalists on the other. Her posture was perfect but her eyes trembled each time the choir rose in volume.

Vincent Castenllo Sr. stood beside the closed casket, shoulders hunched, head bowed low. His hands gripped the edges of the podium in front of him, knuckles white. Kaiser tilted his head slightly. "He looks smaller today." Zoe nodded, her voice barely above a whisper. "Grief does that."

But Kaiser saw something else under the grief: a quiet, controlled fury, buried deep but pulsing.

The Archbishop began the opening rite, voice deep, steady, accustomed to shepherding powerful families through their darkest hours. "Brothers and sisters… We gather today to honor the life of Vincent Castenllo Jr…" Heads bowed.

Kaiser scanned the pews, reading faces the way other men read books. There were three city council members, two state legislators, a known Castenllo rival from the North Shore, sitting conspicuously alone, and two federal agents Kaiser recognized instantly watching everything. Zoe leaned toward him. "They're here already?" "Yeah," Kaiser murmured. "Like vultures circling."

The Archbishop continued, speaking of family, legacy, and the fragility of life. Sophie's jaw tightened with each word. A woman near Kaiser sniffled softly. A man two rows ahead crossed himself slowly.

Then the quartet shifted. A violin carried a melancholy solo that seemed to pull the air thinner. As it played, the family rose as one for the reading of Scripture.

Kaiser watched Sophie. Something was changing in her, something that would matter later, something that had nothing to do with faith and everything to do with *resolve*. Zoe whispered,

"She's not grieving. She's transforming." Kaiser didn't answer. He was thinking the same thing.

The Archbishop closed the Bible gently. "In death, we are reminded of the sanctity of life… and the responsibility we bear to one another." Kaiser's jaw clenched. Responsibility. That word was going to mean something very different to the Castenllos after today.

Zoe glanced at him. "You alright?" Kaiser exhaled. "I hate funerals." Zoe frowned lightly. "Most people do." "No," Kaiser whispered. "Most people fear them. Detectives… remember them." She didn't ask what he meant. The choir rose again, filling the cathedral with a mournful harmony. Outside, the bells began their slow tolling once more. The service was not over, but something in the room had already shifted.

A quiet demand for answers that had nothing to do with spiritual closure. Kaiser felt it settle over him like a second coat. **The investigation had just inherited the weight of this room.**

The Archbishop stepped back from the podium. All eyes turned to **Vincent Castenllo Sr.** He didn't move at   first.
Just stood there, one hand resting on his son's casket, the other gripping the podium as if letting go would drop him through the floor. Sophie reached out and

touched his arm, a brief gesture, steadying, grounding. Vincent Sr. inhaled shakily, then stepped forward.

The cathedral fell completely silent. Even the air felt still. He looked down at his son's casket for a long moment before he lifted his gaze to the hundreds of faces staring back at him, family, rivals, politicians, cops, criminals, the curious, and the grieving.

"My son," he began, voice raw, "was not a perfect man." A murmur passed through the pews out of respect. Honesty carried weight in a room built on shadows.

"He made mistakes," Vincent Sr. continued. "Some big. Some small. Some that cost him friends, others that won him enemies. He was stubborn. He was proud. He was reckless at times." A faint, hollow chuckle escaped him. "But he was mine." His voice cracked, but it echoed like a gunshot. "He was my blood. My firstborn. My legacy. The one who was supposed to bury me… not the other way around."

Zoe swallowed hard. Kaiser stared at the floor. Vincent Sr. steadied himself on the podium.

"My son protected this family with everything he had. He stood for us, fought for us, and, God forgive me, died for us." The choir's quiet hum faded into the background as Vincent Sr. continued.

"Whoever did this…" His voice darkened. "…took more than a son. They took a part of this city. A part of our history. A part of our family that we can never get back." Sophie bowed her head, but her eyes shone with something sharp beneath the grief.

Vincent Sr. lifted a trembling hand and placed it flat on the casket lid. "This will not be forgotten," he said. "This will not be forgiven." A ripple passed through the crowd. It was a promise dressed in mourning clothes.

Kaiser felt Zoe glance at him. "That didn't sound like a eulogy," she whispered. "Wasn't supposed to be," Kaiser murmured. "That was a declaration."

The Archbishop moved forward gently, laying a hand on Vincent Sr.'s shoulder, guiding him back to his seat, but the damage was done. The cathedral was no longer just mourning, it was simmering. And at the center of it all, Sophie sat with her hands folded in her lap, her eyes fixed on the casket, her body motionless except for the faint rise and fall of breath. A young woman who had just inherited a man's war.

The quartet began a slow, aching musical interlude. Vincent Sr. covered his face with his hands. Sophie stared ahead with a look that was no longer just grief. It was resolve. And somewhere deep in the pews, unseen but unmistakable, the first spark of retaliation breathed into life.

The funeral procession wound slowly through the Garden District, black cars rolling like a river of shadows beneath the old oaks. Kaiser and Zoe followed behind in their unmarked sedan, keeping a respectful distance but staying close enough to observe.

The cemetery gates swung open. St. Roch Cemetery was quieter than the cathedral, more peaceful than the city, with its white tombs catching the late-afternoon sun like small, silent monuments to all the stories New Orleans refused to forget.

The Castenllo family gathered around the gravesite, a tight protective circle around Vincent Castenllo Jr.'s casket. The vault stood open.

Marie was not present; still sedated, still recovering. So Sophie stood in her place. She stepped forward alone. Her black dress fluttered slightly in the breeze as she looked down at the polished casket. Her face was calm. The kind of calm that comes after the storm breaks something inside.

Zoe whispered, "She looks like she's holding herself together with thread." "No," Kaiser murmured. "She looks like she's turning into something else."

The priest spoke briefly with simple words, softer than those spoken in the cathedral. The family repeated the responses automatically, voices low, heavy. Sophie did not cry. Not when the wood touched the lip of the vault, nor when the workers guided it inside.

Vincent Castenllo Sr. stood behind her, one hand on her shoulder. His face was carved from grief and stone, but he stayed upright, present, and anchored.

When the priest finished, the family approached one by one, each placing a white flower on the lid of the vault. Sophie waited until the very end. Then she stepped forward, knelt, and laid her flower gently on the center.

Kaiser watched her fingers linger for a beat longer than the others. Detectives always recognized the moment grief transforms into something sharper. Zoe felt it too. "She's changed, Moonpie." Kaiser nodded once. "This is where people choose what kind of life they're going to live after loss." "And what kind of war," Zoe added quietly.

Sophie rose slowly, lifting her chin, eyes clear. She glanced once toward the cluster of bodyguards and family lieutenants waiting respectfully in the background. Zoe whispered, "She's stepping into the vacuum." "No," Kaiser said. "She's filling it."

The burial workers began sealing the vault. Stone against stone. Mortar smoothing over edges. A finality that was supposed to offer closure. Instead, it lit a fuse. And when the vault was fully sealed, Sophie took her grandfather's arm and straightened him gently without a word. Kaiser studied her one last time before she turned away. "That girl," he murmured to no one in particular, "is going to change everything."

The family had begun to disperse from the gravesite, grief-heavy bodies moving slowly toward the line of waiting cars. Conversations were hushed, respectful, but beneath the surface, Kaiser could feel the tension tightening like strings being pulled at both ends. Moonpie and Babineaux approached cautiously, stopping just outside the Castenllo family's inner circle.

Sophie noticed them first. She squared her shoulders, wiped a stray strand of hair from her cheek, and stepped forward to meet them. Her grandfather moved with her, instinctively placing himself half a step in front, but Sophie touched his arm lightly. "It's alright," she said. He grudgingly stepped aside.

Kaiser nodded respectfully. "Miss Castenllo." She met his gaze with eyes that looked older than they had that morning. "Detectives." Zoe spoke gently. "We're sorry for your loss. Truly." Sophie acknowledged the sentiment with the smallest incline of her head, then cut straight to the point. "You have something for us." It wasn't a question.

Kaiser's expression tightened. "We do. And we wanted to tell you ourselves before federal agents start spinning their own version of events." Sophie's eyes sharpened. "Go on."

Kaiser kept his voice low. "We've identified a suspect. Not the killer inside your home, but one of the spotters. Someone involved in the surveillance that made the attack possible."

She simply asked, "Name?" "Miguel Ramos," Kaiser said. "Thirty-eight. Former Mexican Special Forces.." Her jaw tightened. "And you're certain?" Zoe stepped in. "We have multiple camera angles. Gait analysis. Movement patterns. It's him."

Sophie's eyes flicked briefly toward her grandfather. Vincent Castenllo Sr. was staring at the sealed vault, hands trembling slightly. He hadn't heard a word. Sophie returned her attention to the detectives. "Where is this Ramos now?" Kaiser hesitated. "We don't know. He's off-grid. Likely back in Mexico.."

Sophie's expression turned cold. "Then find him." "We're trying," Kaiser said carefully. "But you need to understand that this man is dangerous. Professional. He may be tied to a larger group." "A contract team," Zoe added. "Well-trained. Coordinated. They planned the entire operation down to the second."

Sophie's face remained unreadable, but her fingers curled slightly at her side. "What about warrants?" she asked. Kaiser exhaled. "We can issue a BOLO. We can seek a federal warrant for questioning. But without a confirmed current location, it's complicated." Zoe added gently, "He's not in our jurisdiction. The FBI is about to take over the case."

Sophie's gaze hardened like cooling metal. "So you're telling me you found the man who helped murder my father, and you can't touch him?" Kaiser didn't flinch. "Not yet. But this is a start." Sophie stepped closer so Kaiser could see the faint shimmer of tears she refused to let fall. "I don't want starts," she whispered. "I want ends."

Her grandfather placed a firm hand on her back, a subtle pull, a signal that she'd said enough. But Sophie wasn't finished.

She looked directly at Kaiser. "You keep looking," she said quietly. "You keep digging." "And if the law can't reach him…" She didn't finish the sentence. The unspoken hung between them heavy, unavoidable, and dangerous.

Zoe glanced nervously at Kaiser. Kaiser kept his voice steady. "We'll do our jobs, Miss Castenllo. All of them."

Sophie studied him for a moment… then nodded once. "Good." She turned away and rejoined Vinny Sr. Her shoulders were rigid, her spine perfectly straight like her grief now forged into weaponry.

Zoe exhaled shakily. "Moonpie… she scares me."

Kaiser watched Sophie walk toward the waiting crowd forming a second line, her silhouette sharp in the late-afternoon sun. "Yeah," he said quietly. "She scares me too."

The funeral crowd thinned as the second line led by the brass band marched away from the cemetery. Kaiser and Zoe lingered near the wrought-iron gate, the late-day sun dipping behind the mausoleums, shadows long and heavy across the stone paths. Their unmarked car sat idling a few yards away, engine humming softly. Zoe checked her phone. "FBI just sent over their formal request. They want everything on Miguel Ramos." Kaiser snorted. "Of course they do." Zoe scanned the email. "They're calling it an 'intersecting federal concern.'" Kaiser leaned against the car, lighting a cigarette. "Translation: they want ownership, but they have no idea what they're actually dealing with." Zoe looked up. "Moonpie… you know, once we hand this over, we lose control." "We're not losing anything," Kaiser said. "Not unless we stop working."

Zoe stepped closer, lowering her voice. "Let's be real. Ramos is gone. He left Louisiana before the murder was even reported. And if he's part of a contracted unit…" Kaiser finished the thought. "…then he knows how to disappear." Zoe nodded. "We can't extradite someone if we don't know where they are. And even if we *did*…"

Kaiser exhaled a slow stream of smoke. "Yeah. We'd need country cooperation, approved warrants, and federal court signatures. Which we won't get for a suspect who's only tied to surveillance."

Zoe crossed her arms. "So what do we actually have?" Kaiser tapped ash off the end of the cigarette and flattened his voice. "A name… A face…. A pattern." "And no jurisdiction," Zoe added bitterly. He nodded. "That's what makes this man dangerous. The system has no hold on him. No leash. Not even a file that isn't halfway redacted."

Zoe pulled out her notebook. "We identified him. We found where he staged. We know he's part of a team." "But we can't arrest him," Kaiser finished. "Not yet," Zoe said. "Not ever," he corrected quietly, "if he doesn't want to be found."

She looked away, angry at the reality closing around them. A soft breeze rustled the cemetery magnolias. Somewhere behind them, a grave worker hammered the final seal into the Castenllo vault.

Zoe's jaw tightened. "Sophie's not going to sit still." "No," Kaiser said. "Neither is Tony Russo. And neither will whoever killed Vinny Jr." Kaiser flicked the cigarette butt into the gutter and pushed off the car.

"The funeral just ended, Zoe." She looked at him, unsettled. "And?" "And now the real trouble starts."

Tony Russo waited beside his truck at the edge of the cemetery, arms crossed so tightly they trembled. His eyes were red from holding everything inside with brute force. When Kaiser and Zoe approached, Tony didn't look up at first. He just stared at the cemetery gates as if expecting Vinny Jr. to walk back out.

Finally, he spoke. "You got something?" Tony said quietly. Kaiser paused. "We found a name."

Tony turned sharp. "Say it." Kaiser lowered his voice. "Miguel Ramos. Former Mexican Special Forces. He was one of the spotters." Tony absorbed that in silence, jaw clenching hard enough to crack teeth.

Tony stepped closer, anger radiating off him. "I don't give a damn if he held the knife or the stopwatch. If he was part of it, he's part of it." Kaiser didn't argue.

Tony paced once, hands gripping the back of his neck. "I trusted Vinny. He trusted me. I let that family eat in my place, laugh, live a normal night, and those bastards were already watching them."

Zoe hesitated. "Tony…" "No." Tony's voice broke in two directions, rage and grief. "Don't tell me to calm down. I stood next to that kid when he was ten years old. I watched him grow into a man. And now he's in the ground because some ghost with a stopwatch decided it was his time."

Kaiser stepped closer, voice steady. "Tony. Listen." Tony stopped, breathing hard. "We are on this," Kaiser said. "We found Ramos. We're building the team. We're not backing off."

Tony stared at him, searching for the cracks where truth might be hiding. "Then why can't you arrest him?" Tony asked, voice shaking.

Zoe answered softly, reluctantly. "He's gone. Out of state. Maybe out of the country." Tony's hands curled into fists. "Then bring him back." "We can't," Zoe said. "Not yet."

Tony turned to Kaiser. "And what are you gonna do when the FBI takes the case away from you, huh? Sit behind a desk and file reports while the people who killed Vinny walk free?"

Kaiser didn't respond immediately. Because there wasn't a simple answer.

Tony stepped even closer, voice low and dangerous. "I swear to God, Moonpie… if the law can't handle this, the family will." Zoe stiffened. "Tony… don't…" "I'm not making threats," Tony said. "I'm telling the truth."

Kaiser met his eyes, unflinching. "If you move too soon, you'll get people killed. Including yourself." Tony swallowed hard, chest rising and falling like he was fighting to control the storm inside him.

He finally spoke, voice a hoarse whisper, "They killed my friend." Kaiser nodded once, solemn. "I know." "And they're still breathing." "I know."

Tony's eyes burned. "Don't make me bury anyone else." The words hung between them, edged with a promise Kaiser prayed wouldn't come due.

Zoe took a step forward. "Tony, let us work…" He shook his head. "Work fast." Then he turned, climbed into his truck, and slammed the door. The engine revved, growling with the same fury vibrating inside him. A moment later, he pulled away in a cloud of dust.

Zoe exhaled shakily. "Moonpie… he's not handling this well." Kaiser stared down the road where Tony disappeared. "No," he said quietly. "He's handling it exactly like a Martello would."

The sun had dipped low enough that the cemetery shadows stretched long across the gravel paths, turning the air cool and dim. Most mourners had drifted toward the second line forming and the gates of St. Roch. But **Sophie Castenllo** remained.

She stood alone near the sealed vault, her black dress brushing the stone edge, hands clasped in front of her. Her posture was still, like she'd anchored herself so deeply to the moment that nothing could move her.

Zoe and Kaiser watched from a respectful distance. "Should we…?" Zoe asked softly. "No," Kaiser said. "Let her be." But Sophie turned before they could step away.

"Detectives," she said quietly, beckoning them forward. She looked different now. Not older, but sharper. Her grief hadn't softened her. It had refined her.

When Kaiser and Zoe approached, she didn't acknowledge the lingering funeral staff, the bodyguards, or even her grandfather being supported down the walkway. Her full attention rested on them.

"My brother was not a saint," Sophie began calmly. Her voice was steady, almost eerily composed. "But he deserved to die old. Surrounded by his family. Not like he did. Now my father was even less of a Saint, but he deserved to outlive his father and meet any future grandchildren he might have, and now my family has been robbed of that." Zoe nodded gently. "We agree." Sophie studied them with eyes that held no tears now, only fire.

"The FBI wants the case now that the suspect has been identified as a foreign national," Moonpie said. "And he's out of reach." Sophie's voice did not waver. "I remember what you said." Zoe hesitated. "Sophie… we're doing everything we can." "I know you are." Sophie drew in a breath. "And I know the law has limits." That sentence carried the weight of a thousand unspoken decisions.

"Miss Castenllo," Kaiser said, "I need you to understand something. The people who did this, they're not regular killers. They're trained. Disciplined. Coordinated. Going after them without the right tools will get you hurt. Or worse."

Sophie stepped closer, lowering her voice to match his. "Detective Kaiser," she said, "I grew up in a world where men like this do not disappear without consequence." Zoe's heart skipped. "Sophie…"

"They killed my brother," she continued, "Now, they have killed my father in front of his wife. In his own home. They made a mockery of our security. Our name. Our strength." Kaiser saw it then, the shift he had sensed earlier becoming something undeniable. Sophie Castenllo wasn't grieving. She was awakening.

"Miss Castenllo," Kaiser said softly but firmly, "don't do anything you can't come back from." Sophie's expression didn't change. "I won't," she said. "But they will."

She glanced once more at the vault, then back at the detectives. "Find them," she said. "Before we do."

Then she turned and walked away toward her grandfather, who was being helped into the waiting limousine. As she reached the door, she paused, one hand resting on the frame.

Without looking back, she said, "I don't want war." A beat. "But I will answer one."

Zoe swallowed hard. "Moonpie… she means it." Kaiser watched Sophie disappear into the car, the black door closing like the lid on something dangerous. "She does," he said quietly. "And that scares me more than anything we've found so far."

The limousine pulled away, leaving the detectives standing alone in the settling dusk caught between justice, vengeance, and the knowledge that the line separating the two was already cracking.

As the last of the black cars rolled away from the cemetery, a sound began to rise from the far end of the block; soft at first, then louder.

A **brass band** started with a slow tempo, Low and heavy. The kind of dirge that wrapped itself around the bones of the city and squeezed until tears found their way out.

Outside the cemetery gates, residents had gathered. Some were dressed in funeral black. Others in jeans and T-shirts. Some carried umbrellas decorated in purple and gold. A few held candles.

The band swelled, trumpets leading a long, low lament while drums thumped slow and solemn. A banner lifted above the crowd: **IN MEMORY OF VINCENT CASTENLLO JR.**

Zoe watched as people began to sway, stepping into the rhythm, moving forward with a kind of reverence that belonged only to New Orleans. "It's beautiful," she whispered. "It's complicated," Kaiser replied.

The funeral staff closed the cemetery gates just as the band approached. Sophie's limousine had vanished down Esplanade Avenue, but many in the crowd lifted their hands or hats toward the sealed vault, paying their respects in their own way.

Despite the grief, despite the tension coiled into the air like a storm, the city refused to let anyone bury a man without a celebration of the life he'd lived and the legacy he'd left behind.

The trumpets lifted into a higher harmony. The drums shifted into a syncopated beat. A saxophone wailed with aching beauty.

Zoe stepped closer to Kaiser. "Do you think this is for the family… or for the city?" Kaiser watched the umbrella twirlers, the dancers, the slow stride of mourners moving to music older than grief itself. "Both," he said. "Maybe more."

The band pivoted, turning onto the next street with a crescendo rising, tempo quickening. The sorrowful dirge transformed into something livelier, defiant, almost joyful. A celebration of a life. A refusal to let death have the final word.

But beneath that celebration, beneath the color, sound, and movement, there lay something cold. Zoe felt it too. "This doesn't feel like healing." "No," Kaiser said quietly. "It feels like gathering."

The second line continued down the street, drawing more residents into the procession as it passed. A city marching together, but for different reasons.

Zoe laid a hand on the cemetery gate, staring past the stone vaults to the one that now belonged to Vinny Castenllo Jr. "This city's about to boil over," she murmured. Kaiser nodded once. "It already has."

A final trumpet wail echoed across the rooftops, lingering in the air even as the band moved out of sight. It was a mournful, triumphant, volatile sound that promised only one thing: **Nothing in New Orleans was going back to the way it was.**

The second line's last notes drifted away into the twilight, dissolving into the warm New Orleans air. The crowd began to thin, umbrellas lowering, brass instruments returning to cases, voices fading to murmurs as people slipped down side streets toward home, bars, or trouble.

Soon, the street outside St. Roch was almost quiet again. Detective Matthew "Moonpie" Kaiser remained standing at the cemetery gate long after Zoe had stepped aside to call in a follow-up request to the lab. Kaiser watched the final few stragglers of old men tapping their feet, women folding handkerchiefs, and teenagers recording the tail end of the procession on their phones. A city grieving in layers.

Above him, magnolia leaves rustled in the breeze, their shadows dancing across the stone like restless spirits. Zoe returned, slipping her phone into her jacket pocket. "Lab's going to prioritize the gear clip we found at the warehouse. They'll run material analysis tonight." "Good," Kaiser said quietly. Zoe studied him a moment. "You're thinking too hard." "Someone has to," he muttered.

Zoe stepped beside him at the gate, her shoulder almost touching his. "Talk to me, Moonpie." Kaiser exhaled, leaning on the metal bars. "This funeral… this crowd… Sophie… the family… the city… It's all moving. Not in one direction. In several. And none of them lead anywhere peaceful." Zoe nodded slowly. "You felt it too."

Kaiser looked down the road where the second line had disappeared. "Funerals don't start wars, Zoe. But the wrong death at the wrong time… absolutely does."

Zoe swallowed. "Vinny Jr. wasn't just some mob figure. He was a pillar in this world. A connector. A stabilizer." "And now he's gone," Kaiser said. "And people like Sophie don't grieve quietly. They reorganize." Zoe's voice softened. "You're worried she's going to move." "Oh, she's going to move," Kaiser said. "The question is when. And how many people she takes with her."

A pair of elderly women in black passed by them, whispering prayers. A man tucked a white handkerchief into his pocket and headed for Bourbon Street. A teenager hopped onto a bike and pedaled away. The world resumed.

Zoe wrapped her arms around herself. "Moonpie… the killers are gone. The FBI is circling. The Martellos are grieving and plotting. And we're stuck in the middle." "That's where we always are," Kaiser said. "Between the law and the fire." Zoe looked at him. "Feels hotter this time." "Because it is."

A funeral worker approached and locked the cemetery gates for the night. **CLANG.** The sound rang out a final punctuation mark on the day.

Zoe looked at Kaiser. "So… what now?" Kaiser pushed off the gate and headed toward the unmarked car. "Now we go back to the office." Zoe followed. "Tonight?" "Tonight," Kaiser said firmly. "Before the Bureau takes everything out of our hands."

They reached the car, the night thickening around them. Zoe hesitated before getting in. "Moonpie… one more thing." He turned. Zoe looked toward the cemetery once more. Toward the sealed vault. Toward the lingering scent of incense, brass, and grief. "This isn't just a homicide anymore," she said quietly. "This is a fuse. And someone just lit it." Kaiser nodded once. "Yeah."

He opened the driver's door. "And we're the ones standing closest to the fire." The doors shut. The unmarked sedan rolled away from the cemetery, its red taillights glowing like embers in the dark.

Behind them, the music was gone, the crowd dispersed, and the city's heart beat a little faster and a little more dangerous as night settled in.

Epilogue

Tony's Italian Restaurant was closed to the public, but the dining room was full. Men who had served the Castenllo family for decades leaned in clusters around linen-covered tables, speaking in low, wary tones.

The air was thick with cigar smoke and expectation. Everyone knew why they were here. At the head of the long table sat **Vincent Castenllo Sr.**, pale and exhausted, suit collar loosened, grief etched into every deep line on his face. He looked like a man held together with string and stubbornness.

At his right stood **Tony Russo**, arms folded, jaw tight and still smoldering from the funeral, still dangerous in his sorrow.

The room stirred when the back door opened. **Sophie Castenllo** stepped inside. Conversation died instantly.

Her heels clicked softly against the floor as she crossed the room. Her black dress was simple, elegant, and severe. Her hair was pulled back. Her expression was unreadable.

She stopped behind her grandfather's chair. Vincent Sr. looked up at her with eyes full of pain and something else, something resigned. "Sophie," he murmured. "Baby girl, you don't need to…" "Yes," she said softly, laying a hand on his shoulder. "I do."

Tony straightened, watching her with a mixture of surprise and recognition. Sophie scanned the room. These were men twice her age. Men who had grown up under her grandfather. Men who had learned the streets, paid their dues, collected their scars. Men who had once dismissed her as a young woman who smiled too easily and spoke too softly. None of them were dismissing her now.

She pulled out the empty chair beside Vinny Sr. But she did not sit.

Instead, she rested her hands lightly on the back of the seat, claiming its space without lowering herself to it. "I know why you're here," she said calmly, her voice carrying without effort. "I know what you're expecting." A few men exchanged glances.

"My brother and now my father is dead," she continued, "and my mother is fighting for her mind. My grandfather…" She glanced down, her voice tightening for the first time. "…is grieving more deeply than any man should ever have to." Vincent Sr. closed his eyes. Sophie lifted her chin. "And through all of that, the people responsible for destroying my family are still breathing."

A murmur rippled across the room. Sophie placed her palms flat on the table. "I'm not here to grieve," she said. "I'm here to lead." That landed like a weight dropped from the roof.

Tony's jaw clenched. Her grandfather opened his eyes again, this time with something like pride breaking through the sorrow. Sophie finally took her seat. Silence swallowed the room.

She looked at every man sitting before her. "Let's begin." The room reacted exactly as Sophie expected. With the unmistakable shifting of weight, the quiet recalibration of power inside men who had survived decades of Martello politics.

Tony Russo stayed standing, arms crossed, watching every face. Vincent Castenllo Sr. rested back against his chair, weary but unwavering. Whatever this moment was becoming, he had chosen to let it happen.

Sophie laced her fingers together on the table. "You all served my father," she said. "And my brother. You've protected this family for years. You've put your bodies between us and bullets. You've kept businesses running. You've kept alliances steady, but now things are different." That made every head rise.

Sophie continued, voice calm, precise, "My father's death wasn't random. It wasn't petty. It wasn't a street-level hit. It was organized. Planned. Executed by trained professionals." She let the words settle in.

"You saw the homicide detectives today. You heard what they found. You know what it means."

Tony's jaw flexed. "It means someone hired a kill team to gut this family." Sophie tilted her head slightly. "Yes. And whoever did it thinks we're weak now."

A soft, dangerous tension rippled across the room. Sophie leaned in. "They think we're broken." Her eyes hardened. "They think we'll fold."

Silence. Then she said, with a quiet authority that felt heavier than a shout, "They are wrong."

Several men straightened, but not all. At the far end of the table, **Marco Santori**, an old-school lieutenant with thirty years under the family's banner, cleared his throat. "It's not that we doubt you, Miss Castenllo," he said carefully. "But leadership… real leadership… requires more than bloodline. Your family built this city. Your father commanded loyalty. You…" Tony cut him off sharply. "Watch yourself."

But Sophie raised a hand, stopping him. "Marco," she said, "you may speak freely." He hesitated, then continued. "You're young. You've never led crews. Never sat across from men with guns pointed at you. Never negotiated territory or called hits. The men in this room… we've bled for this family." Sophie nodded. "I know you have. And I respect every one of you for it." "Respect is good," Marco said. "Experience is better."

Some men murmured in agreement. Tony bristled, but Sophie remained still. "Marco," she said evenly, "you're right." That silenced the murmurs.

"I don't have years in the streets. I don't have negotiations with rival crews under my belt. I haven't led soldiers." Her voice sharpened. "But I *have* something none of you have." Marco's brow furrowed. "And what's that?"

Sophie looked him dead in the eyes. "Nothing left to lose." A cold ripple passed through the room.

Marco opened his mouth, then shut it, but Sophie wasn't done. "You all built this family with your hands. I watched my father build it with their lives. Now I will build what comes next... with mine." A thick, loaded silence followed.

Then Tony stepped closer to her chair, placing one steadying hand on the back of it like a public declaration. "She's right," Tony said. "There is no one else. Not now."

A divide in the room was forming. Lines were being drawn. And everyone knew it.

Sophie's gaze swept across her father's loyalists, then the old guard, then the young soldiers. "You can stand with me," she said quietly. "Or you can stand aside."

Marco swallowed. "And if we stand against you?" Tony stepped forward, but Sophie gently reached out, touching his arm again. She answered Marco herself. A heavy silence settled over the restaurant, the kind that made every man suddenly aware of how loud his own heartbeat seemed.

Santori didn't answer right away. He studied Sophie with an expression equal parts caution and calculation.

He wasn't alone. Across the long table **Nico Gallo**, one of the younger captains, leaned forward with interest, it was the first time anyone had seen him look at Sophie with something approaching respect. **Ralph "Four-Fingers" Donati** kept his gaze low, avoiding choosing a side too soon. **Luca Vendetti**, old-school to the bone, stared at Sophie as if trying to see whether a girl in her twenties could really fit into the shape of a leader. And near the edge of the room, a cluster of newer soldiers watched the exchange like spectators at a boxing match, waiting to know where to throw their loyalty.

Marco finally spoke. "Your grandfather's not dead," he said. "He's sitting right there. We don't cast aside a Don without ceremony." Sophie didn't flinch. "I'm not casting him aside."

Marco gestured to Vincent Sr., who sat slumped in his chair, exhausted and hollow. "He's grieving. He shouldn't be making decisions, fine. I agree with that. But handing you power without a structure? Without counsel? Without a plan? That's not leadership. That's chaos." Tony snapped, "The only chaos came from the men who killed Vinny…" Sophie touched his arm again, halting him gently.

Her voice remained calm. "This is not a coronation," she said. "And it's not a takeover. I'm not replacing my father. I'm stepping in because no one else is strong enough right now." Tony nodded. Several younger men nodded with him.

Marco leaned back. "Strength is one thing. Strategy is another. And I don't know your strategy." Sophie took a breath. "When my father died," she said, "I expected justice to come from the police. From detectives. From the law." Her eyes hardened. "But the law can't reach the men who did this. And the people we trusted cannot protect us."

Tony lowered his gaze, understanding exactly what she meant. Sophie continued, "The killers were professionals. Coordinated. Trained. They didn't come to attack our family. They came to test it." A murmur rippled through the room. Sophie pressed on. "If we respond wild, we lose the city. If we respond slow, we lose our power. We must respond correctly."

Nico Gallo nodded. "Then what's the move?" The entire room waited. Sophie placed her hands flat on the table, leaning in slightly, commanding without raising her voice. "We rebuild. Tighter. Smarter. Quietly." Tony looked impressed and caught off guard.

Sophie continued: "We don't lash out. We don't spray bullets into the night hoping to hit the right ghost. We gather strength. Information. Allies." She scanned the faces of the old guard. "If you stand with me, you'll help rebuild this family into something stronger than before. If you don't… then you're making room for someone else to stand in your place." That landed like a fist made of velvet.

Gallo spoke first. "I'm with her." A few of the younger soldiers followed: "Me too." "Yeah." "We need direction."

Ralph Four-Fingers slowly raised his chin. "If Tony's with her, I'm with her." Tony didn't move, but his presence alone was a declaration.

Marco exhaled through his nose, weighing the shifting tide. He wasn't a fool. He could feel the room moving under him. But he wasn't ready to surrender either.

"I hear you," Marco said carefully. "But rebuilding requires planning. Structure. Meetings. Not just… speeches."

Sophie didn't blink. "That's why this isn't ending here," she said. "This is beginning here."

Marco hesitated. But he didn't challenge her again, bit the wedge had formed. Younger men gravitated toward Sophie. Tony's silent support solidified her claim. The old guard bristled but did not break. Fault lines ready to widen.

The heated undercurrent inside Tony's Restaurant had begun to settle, but only on the surface, like a pot that still boiled underneath its lid. Sophie sat tall, composed, absorbing every reaction in the room. Tony Russo stood silently at her back, a presence that made several uncertain lieutenants keep their mouths shut.

But outside this room, the world was not idle. A phone buzzed on the table. Nico glanced at the screen, hesitated, then cleared his throat. "Sophie… you should see this." He slid the phone toward her. She picked it up. A news headline glared across the screen: **FEDERAL PRESSURE IN CASTENLLO HOMICIDE: FBI AGENT CALLAHAN ASSERTS TEAM LEAD AS NOPD STEPS BACK** Zoe's warning from the cemetery hit Sophie like a spark in dry grass.

She read the subheading silently: **'Federal authorities believe the murder may have international ties.'** Tony muttered, "International?

They don't know a damn thing." But Sophie wasn't listening to him.

Her eyes had narrowed with a calculating and cold glare. Marco rubbed the side of his face. "This means we've got two eyes watching us now, the streets and the feds." Vendetti added, "And any wrong step gives Callahan an excuse to crack down on every one of our operations."

Sophie placed the phone back on the table. "For years," she said quietly, "the police left us alone as long as we kept boundaries. As long as we kept the peace." Marco nodded reluctantly. "Your father was very good at that." "Yes," Sophie said. "But the world does not treat us the way it treated him." Tony stepped forward. "Meaning what?" Sophie's eyes hardened. "Meaning the law won't protect us. Meaning our enemies won't fear us. Meaning every group that ever envied or resented this family now sees vulnerability."

She looked at each man in turn. She leaned back slightly. "Everything is shifting." A chill of understanding moved through the room.

Nico, always quicker than the others, asked, "Do we know which cartel connection the feds are talking about?" Tony grimaced. "Guillén Vásquez and the Gulf Cartel are unpredictable right now. His son's family's deaths lit fires down south that haven't burned out." Sophie nodded once. "Exactly. That instability won't stay contained. It never does." Marco interjected, cautious but attentive. "What's your point?"

Sophie looked at him, expression unwavering. "My point is that the Martello family cannot stay what it was. Not anymore. The city is changing. Our enemies are changing. So we change too." Tony reacted first. "I agree. We adapt or we die." Marco didn't disagree , but he didn't fully agree, either. "Change is dangerous without direction."

Sophie gave him a thin smile. "I'm giving you direction." Marco studied her, and for the first time… respect, not skepticism, crossed his face.

This wasn't Vincent Jr.'s daughter anymore. This was the next generation's pivot point. Around the room, men who had thought they were attending a post-funeral gathering realized they were witnessing **the start of a new regime.**

Tony broke the silence. "So what's the next step?" Sophie folded her hands, calm as an ocean before a hurricane. "We tighten the circle," she said. Only the loyal stay close. Everyone else keeps their distance." The room shifted again. "We reorganize. We watch every movement in this city. Every phone call. Every visit. Every business. Every rival. Every ally. There will be no leaks, no surprises, no weaknesses." A breath. "And when the time comes…

we will take back what was taken from us." No one argued this time.

Sophie had said what the room had needed someone strong enough to say, the old Castenllos were gone. The new Castenllo era had begun.

The atmosphere in Tony's dimly lit back room settled into a thick, contemplative silence shaped not by grief now, but by **calculation**. Sophie had taken the reins. Outside the walls of the restaurant, the world was already responding.

A rap on the door made several men reach for weapons. Luca stepped over and cracked it open. A breathless soldier leaned in. "My apologies, there is an urgent update." Tony bristled. "What kind of update?" The soldier swallowed. "Detectives Kaiser and Babineaux just left the precinct. FBI's moving in on the case. Agent Callahan's already setting up in their office." A low rumble of dissatisfaction rolled across the room.

Marco muttered, "That arrogant prick…" Sophie didn't flinch. "So the Bureau has control." "They always do," Tony growled. "But now they'll bury anything that threatens their narrative." Nico added, "Including suspects they can't reach."

Sophie rested her elbows on the table, fingers interlaced. "Good," she said. That drew several confused looks. "Miss Castenllo?" Luca asked carefully. "If the FBI takes the case," Sophie said calmly, "then the NOPD can't follow certain leads. Local law enforcement's leash gets shorter." Tony understood immediately. "Which leaves a lot of space for... unofficial channels." Sophie nodded.

Marco frowned. "Meaning what exactly?" "That the police will hit walls they aren't allowed to climb over," she explained. "Walls built by international law, federal oversight, political interest."

"And we?" Nico asked. "We don't have those walls," Sophie replied. Silence fell again, but this time it was thick with agreement, not doubt.

Sophie continued, "The feds tightening their grip doesn't weaken us. It frees us. Because the more pressure they apply to the police, the less scrutiny falls on us." Tony smirked, just a little. "Clever." Sophie looked at him. "We don't fight enemies head-on. We move while everyone else is pinned down."

Marco studied her for a long moment, then exhaled. "You really are your father's daughter." That line landed with a quiet force, the kind that rewrote the room's atmosphere again.

The soldier who brought the message cleared his throat nervously. "There's... another piece of news." Tony's eyes narrowed. "Well?" "The Gulf Cartel," the soldier said. "Word is, Guillén Vásquez is sending his men back from Texas. Rumor is... he's looking to make a play on the Louisiana drug trade." A ripple of tension cut through the room.

Sophie's jaw tightened. "Why?"

"Because," the soldier whispered, "someone told him the murders of Vinny III is what sparked the murder of his son and he wants to finish the job." Tony cursed under his breath.

Nico leaned back. "Great. Now the cartel's hunting more control in the area." Marco rubbed his face. "This city isn't ready for cartel blood spilled on U.S. soil again."

Sophie considered this, her expression unreadable. "The cartel moves for vengeance," she said. "We move for justice. Our paths may cross… but our goals are not the same."

Tony nodded. "And if they gain control first?" Sophie's voice dropped, cold and certain, "Then we take it from the cartel too."

The men who minutes earlier were split between skepticism and loyalty were now quietly gravitating toward a single gravitational center, **Sophie Castenllo.** Even those who weren't ready to admit it out loud felt the inevitability of it settling in their bones.

Sophie rested back in her chair, still calm, still composed, but sharper now, like the blade had fully revealed itself beneath the softness. She surveyed the room. "You all know," she said softly, "that this family has survived because my father kept the right people close. He trusted carefully. He listened more than he spoke." Vincent Sr., eyes distant and grief-stricken, lifted his head slightly. A flicker of pride crossed his face, brief but real.

Sophie continued. "But today taught me something important. Trust cannot be assumed. It must be proven. By action. Not history."

A couple of the older lieutenants shifted uncomfortably. Santori spoke first, cautious. "And who exactly needs to prove themselves?" Sophie didn't look at him. She didn't need to. "The Martello organization," she said, "will operate with a smaller inner circle from now on. Only those who show loyalty will remain in the decision room." Tony smirked at Marco from behind her. A quiet *told you.*

Marco forced a civil expression. "You're restructuring." Sophie nodded. "Yes." "How?" Nico asked, leaning forward, more eager than concerned. "By tightening everything," she said. "Meetings. Contacts. Money. Territory. No more loose ends. No more assumptions. No more trust based on decades-old favors." Ralph Four-Fingers scratched his jaw. "People aren't gonna like that."

Sophie didn't blink. "People don't have to like it. They only have to follow it." Tony let out a small, appreciative breath. "Spoken like a Don." The words lingered in the air. Not yet a title, but no longer unthinkable.

Sophie continued, "We will not act loudly. Not yet. The first strike will not come from us. Not until we know who is truly with us… and who stands in the way." Marco frowned. "So what happens now?" "Now?" Sophie repeated quietly. She looked around the table, her gaze cutting through every man one by one. "Now we watch."

Nico nodded. "And after that?" Sophie smiled, and there was no warmth in it. "After that… we decide who joins the circle." "And who falls out of it," Tony added. He didn't need her permission this time. They were aligned.

Marco leaned back, studying her more carefully than before, as if realizing he wasn't looking at a placeholder, but at the architect of a new order. "You're going to make enemies," he said. Sophie met his gaze without hesitation. "We already have enemies," she replied. "Now we'll know which ones are inside the room."

Around the table, men who had known Vincent Castenllo Jr. as their anchor were beginning to see Sophie as the axis around which the future of the organization would turn.

And Sophie? She seemed to know and embrace it. She rose slowly, placing both palms on the table. "This family," she said, "will not be defined by what was taken from us." The men straightened, instinctively. "We will be defined by what we build next."

Tony nodded once, a gesture like a seal being pressed into hot wax. Nico bowed his head in agreement. Even Marco's jaw tightened with reluctant respect.

Sophie stepped back from the table. "We begin tonight."

The chairs scraped back as the meeting dissolved into murmured conversations. **A shift had happened tonight.** A shift the city would feel before it understood.

Sophie remained standing at the end of the long table, fingers lightly resting on its polished surface, posture unyielding. Tony Russo stood a half step behind her, no longer simply family, now a lieutenant by choice.

Vincent Castenllo Sr. sat quietly, watching her through tired eyes. His grief was still heavy, still raw, but in that moment, pride cut through the fog. He whispered, only loud enough for her to hear, "Your father would be proud."

Sophie inhaled once then turned to the rest of the room. "Gentlemen," she said, her voice cool as steel, "we are done here for tonight. Tony will distribute new protocols in the morning. Be prepared."

The men filed out one by one. Nico offered a respectful nod before leaving. Ralph Four-Fingers clapped Tony on the back. Marco paused at the doorway, studying Sophie with a complicated mix of admiration and caution. "You've got the room," he said quietly. "Keep it." Sophie didn't break eye contact. "I will." He left without another word.

The restaurant fell silent. Tony exhaled, running a hand down his face. "Well… that could've gone a lot worse." Sophie turned to him. "That could not have gone any other way."

Vinny Sr. rose slowly, leaning on the back of his chair, "Soph… you don't have to do all of this alone." She walked to him and placed her hand over his. "I know," she said softly. "But I do have to do it."

Vincent Sr. looked at her long and hard, seeing her not as the granddaughter he watched grow up but as the leader she was choosing to become. Finally, he nodded. A passing of the torch without ceremony.

Tony opened the back door for Sophie. "You want a ride home?" "No," she said, stepping outside. "I want to walk."

The night air was cool, laced with the faint scent of the river and distant music drifting from Frenchmen

Street. Streetlamps cast long golden halos across the pavement.

Sophie walked down the sidewalk alone, the city breathing around her. Every step echoed with purpose. Every breath carried the weight of a name that had ruled New Orleans for generations.

She paused at the corner, looking out toward the lights of the Quarter, toward the pulse of the city her family helped build. A city she now intended to shape.

Her voice was a whisper, barely audible over the hum of traffic, "They took my brother, and now my father." Her hands curled into fists. "They won't take anything else."

A breeze swept through, stirring her hair. Somewhere in the distance, a brass trumpet let out a single, lonely note. Sophie Castenllo turned toward it, her silhouette framed in the lamplight like a coronation.

She was no longer a princess. Not merely a successor.

She was a Tigress.

ABOUT THE AUTHOR

David Preston is a lifelong student of history and an avid reader with a passion for storytelling. With a background in Political Science from the University of South Alabama, he has spent his career navigating the worlds of politics, journalism, and business. A former politician and reporter, he now channels his deep knowledge of history and human nature into writing compelling historical and crime fiction.

Born in Gurdon, Arkansas, David has lived in Plano, Texas, and Hernando, Mississippi, before settling in Mobile, Alabama, where he has called home for the past 30 years. His novels, including *Unknown Soldier: World War I, 1828*, and *The Killer Family: A Martello Family Thriller*, bring history to life and deliver gripping, suspenseful narratives that keep readers enthralled.

Through meticulous research and immersive storytelling, David crafts novels that explore the past while delving into the complexities of human nature, crime, and the pursuit of justice.

ALSO BY THE AUTHOR

Unknown Soldier Series:

Unknown Soldier: World War One

1828 Series

1828

The Martello Family Series

The Killer Family

The Afsar Ramos Series

Son of Afghanistan

If you enjoyed this book, please consider leaving a 5-star review at the link below. Every review truly does help. Thank you.

- David